TANGLED PLANET

KATE BLAIR

FROM THE AUTHOR OF *TRANSFERRAL*

DCB

First published in Canada in 2017
First published in the United States of America in 2018
This is a first edition.

Canada Council for the Arts | Conseil des Arts du Canada

Canadian Heritage | Patrimoine canadien

Canada

The publisher gratefully acknowledges the support of the Canada Council for the Arts and the Ontario Arts Council for its publishing program. We acknowledge the financial support of the Government of Canada through the Canada Book Fund (CBF) for our publishing activities, and the Government of Ontario through the Ontario Media Development Corporation, an agency of the Ontario Ministry of Culture, and the Ontario Book Publishing Tax Credit Program.

LIBRARY AND ARCHIVES CANADA CATALOGUING IN PUBLICATION

Blair, Kate, author
Tangled planet / Kate Blair.

Issued in print and electronic formats.
ISBN 978-1-77086-504-4 (softcover). — ISBN 978-1-77086-505-1 (HTML)

I. Title.

PS8603.L3153T36 2017 JC813'.6 C2017-904445-1
C2017-904446-X

United States Library of Congress Control Number: 2017945945

Cover design: Angel Guerra / Archetype
Interior text design: Tannice Goddard, bookstopress.com
Manufactured by Friesens in Altona, Manitoba, Canada, in August 2017

Printed and bound in Canada.

DANCING CAT BOOKS
an imprint of Cormorant Books Inc.
10 ST. MARY STREET, SUITE 615, TORONTO, ONTARIO, M4Y 1P9
www.dancingcatbooks.com
www.cormorantbooks.com

This book grew out of my often misplaced fears for my family,
and my desire to protect them from the world.
Matt, Amelia and Rowan, I love you so much.
Be safe, but be brave, and I will try to be brave too.

CHAPTER 1

We're never going to survive on this planet if we can't start a fire.

Astra stands in the center of the crowded circle holding a lit stick against a cluster of kindling at the bottom of the heap of wood. But it doesn't catch. The flame stays daintily perched on its twig. The wind tugs at it, and it quivers, almost disappears.

About two hundred crew members, almost half the ship, are gathered in a wide circle around the fire on log benches, huddled together, murmuring words that are snatched by the unpredictable breeze. All around us the world is dark. Dark mud. Dark figures. Dark bonfire. The only light is Astra's weak flame and the bioluminescence of the glowferns in the forest around us.

It looks magical in there. Glittering. Enticing. Like something out of a fairy tale. I shiver. Bad things happen to girls in fairy tales.

Come on, Astra. Stop trying to light the bonfire the pre-industrial way. Use your blowtorch. I get that she's going for atmosphere, but it's ridiculously ineffective. The tiny flame twists as if it's considering the jump to the twigs, but decides against it.

Almost all the planet-side crew are here. Most of them have been at bonfires before. This isn't new to them. They're not thinking about all the fire warnings on board the *Venture*. I realize I'm holding my breath, like I'm expecting an explosion.

Get over yourself, Ursa. It's wood, not chlorine trifluoride. Focus on the job.

I look down at my jacket, laid out on the mud in front of me, pieces of a broken landbike scattered over it. As soon as I've fixed it, I'll make an excuse. Head back to the shuttle, spend the night there. I'll sleep in a bucket seat or on the floor, I don't care. I'm craving the solidity of metal over the damp mush of mud.

I need to take baby steps on Beta. Get comfortable with it. I've done well for my first time back down here since Maia's death. I can get used to the planet. I'm sure I can.

I'm lucky to be here, I know. Lucky to be alive now. Lucky I'm part of the generation that gets to colonize Beta. Four hundred years of ancestors stretch out behind me. People who lived and died on the *Venture* so I could be here, on a new world.

It's great. It really is. It's just a lot to get used to. And that's okay. We still have the *Venture* to go home to. She's safely in orbit above us.

For now.

I concentrate on the pieces of the landbike in front of me, the comforting logic of engineering. The motherboard is fine. It's just a blown connector. I dig in the gear bag on my hip and grab a spare and some solder wire.

"Look!" My ex-boyfriend Sabik's voice comes from a nearby bench. He's still embarrassingly keen, I see. I follow his gaze back to Astra.

Her flame finally has a twin growing below the logs. There's a snap. We all jump, then laugh. But the scattered giggles soon fade, replaced by the sinister rustle of the trees, as if they object to their fellows being burned.

Astra tosses her stick into the kindling and dusts off her hands.

The fire licks over the log from underneath, disappearing and reappearing, curling around, seizing the wood in its grasp. The bark blackens. The flames slither to the next log and begin to consume that, too.

A gentle warmth grows with the fire, touching my face, lighting my hands as they work on the landbike. Under the ship's lights, my skin is a deep brown, like the earth here on the rare occasions that it's dry. But the flames bring out the undertones in my fingers, burnishing them bronze.

Astra coughs, and I look up. She runs a hand over her gray hair. It's nearly as curly as mine, but hers is long and she pulls it back into a tight bun. "It was traditional, on Alpha Earth, to tell stories around the campfire." The flames cast light on her chin, shadows stretching up to her eyes. Her face changes and flickers with the fire, sharpening her friendly features. "Ghost stories. Tales of the deep, dark woods."

Smoke blows in my face. I blink, eyes stinging. But the smell is warm and earthy. Not what I'd expect from the toxic by-products of combustion: carbon dioxide and monoxide, I know, and a chemical cocktail dependent on various elements in the wood.

I breathe it in. Try to relax. Try not to think about carcinogens.

Astra continues. "In the darkness, it's easy to imagine creatures stalking the forest." She creeps around the fire, the crooked fingers of her shadow leaping in the firelight, grasping at us. "Witches, vampires, and the big bad wolf."

A shiver tickles up my spine. I guess she thinks it's fun, but I wish she'd stop. We don't need fantasy to make Beta Earth frightening. There are a hundred ways to die down here: heatstroke, hypothermia, exposure, lightning. A construction accident, like Seginus. Slipping through the fragile ice, like Maia.

Astra smiles, warm as the fire. She straightens up. "But like our own tales of the hollow knocks on the outside of the airlock, they're nonsense, told to scare children. We're safe here." She addresses that last line to me.

Yeah, right. I glance around and realize I'm not the only one who's uncomfortable. A few others hug their arms around themselves, eyes darting to the sky, to the woods, to the flames.

I turn back to work on the landbike. Even with the bonfire, it's pretty dark, but I could solder a connector to a motherboard with my eyes closed. I position the wires. Place the bead of liquid metal. Hold it up to check the link in the unpredictable glimmer of the firelight.

Perfect.

There's whispering from the log bench behind me. My sister, Celeste, and her husband, Orion, fighting in hushed tones, again. I peer back at them. He's gesturing away from the fire, to the path through the woods to the shuttle camp. I guess that's where his other wife, Vega, is tonight. I swallow down the heat that rises in my stomach at the thought of Vega. It still hurts that she chose to marry him rather than stay friends with me.

I don't want Celeste and Orion to catch me staring, so I look at the sky. There, one star among many, is the sun of Alpha Earth, where our ancestors came from. I can't see the *Venture*. I'm not even sure when she'll be passing overhead next. I should be up there, working on the maintenance backlog.

Mealpacks are passed around. As they reach me, I take one and hand two to Celeste, but Orion stands. "I promised Vega I'd be there," he says.

My jaw clenches. He should stay with Celeste: she's the pregnant one. But that's Orion's way. He's never there when you need him. Like he wasn't for Maia on the day she died.

"It's dark," Celeste points out.

"I'll take a landbike."

"I don't think there are any spares," Celeste says.

"There's that one." Orion nods at mine. "Is it almost fixed?"

I keep working, lining up the pieces.

"Ursa? Is it nearly ready?" he asks.

I lift up a wire, check it by the firelight's glimmer.

"Ursa." Celeste's voice this time. "Is the landbike almost fixed?"

I look up at my sister and smile. "No, sorry," I lie.

"Then I guess I'll have to walk." Orion strides off, passing Astra by the fire. She's obviously heard the whole thing, so she tries to stop him with a gentle hand on his shoulder. But Orion shrugs her off and strides into the forest.

I turn back to Celeste. She's staring after Orion. I stand, move back, and sit down on the bench next to her. She's still holding the two mealpacks.

"More for us, eh?" I say.

Celeste laughs. A laugh too close to a sob. "I could use the extra."

I give an exaggerated sigh. "You're going to use that old 'eating for two' excuse?"

Celeste places a hand on her landsuit, stretched over her bump. It's funny how easy she is to cheer up, sometimes. Her pregnancy calms her. But then she's always been excited about our feminine duty to squeeze out as many bawling babies as possible to populate this planet.

Can't say I feel the same.

"Why do you put up with him, Celeste?"

She shakes her head.

"He's such an —"

"Leave it, Ursa."

A lone tenor begins on the other side of the fire. It's Yuri, Head of Agricology, his voice rising and falling with a familiar melody that wraps over us all like a blanket. More voices join in. But it's not the song I know. It's an old tune with new words.

The wide-open skies, the fast-running streams,
The light in the air, the land of our dreams.

Celeste starts singing too. She nudges me, obviously wanting me to join in. But I'm in no mood for it, and I don't know the words, so I shrug and lift the lid from my mealpack. I peer in at the sandwich. Limp lettuce and kelp spread. I don't think I'll be fighting Celeste for the extra meal after all. Still, food is food.

I lean back as I eat. There's real warmth from the fire now. Smiles in the half-light, the song rising and falling with the flames. I try to focus on the melody, try to let its familiarity soothe me. Relax, Ursa. Shoulders down. Hands unclenched. You can't fall through ice at a bonfire. And winter is over. Be rational.

Two children run between the log benches, giggling. The youngest of Captain Cassius's brood, their faces lit by the flames and their own laughter. A spark flies out from the bonfire, propelled by an updraft, twisting, shining. A temporary star that fades into the night sky.

Then the song is done, the crew lapses into silence, and the wind reasserts itself. I wait for someone else to start singing, but I guess they're too busy eating. I lean a hand on the log bench, and the rough bark digs into my palm.

"I've an idea." Sabik's voice, from the other side of the circle. He jumps to his feet, his messy hair bouncing with him. He jabs a slice of bread on his fork and squats by the fire, holding it out and grinning.

To think I used to love his over-the-top enthusiasm. Beta is still the promised land to people like him. Perhaps it's because he's never been one to over-think things. Perhaps I'd love it too, if I could turn part of my brain off.

Sabik peers at his bread. It dangles on the end of his fork. I guess he's toasting it. But it's such an inefficient way to cook. He can't get close to the fire because of the heat. He needs a longer fork, or a metal cage on a stick that could warm both sides at once. We really need some kind of structure around the bonfire to harness the full thermal output of the combustion within a contained system. All that heat energy, billowing out into the night, wasted.

Eventually, Sabik lifts his bread up triumphantly. One side is slightly browned. Wow. How exciting.

"My back is aching. I'm going to bed," Celeste says.

I turn to her. "Do you want me to come with you?"

"I'd like to be alone, if that's okay, Ursa."

I nod at the bump. "Not possible for a few weeks. But Astra can babysit once she's out."

Celeste smiles, then stands and waddles toward the huts.

The loneliness presses in on me.

I was never alone before we came to Beta. Maia volunteered for the same shifts I did. If she were here now, she'd have been helping with the landbike. Passing me the soldering iron or digging in her own gear bag for screws. And of course, there was Sabik.

"Ursa!" Sabik's voice. He's looking over, pushing his messy hair from his face. For a moment, I wonder if I spoke my thoughts out loud. I've gotten in the habit of talking to myself. Well, to Maia, but it's the same thing.

"Why don't you join us?" His fellow agricologists are clustered around the flames, goofing around. From the shrieks and laughter you'd think toasting bread was the most thrilling activity in the world.

But they're too close to the fire, especially Sabik. My throat is tight. He's paying attention to me, not to the flames looming behind him. Doesn't he see the sparks? Doesn't he know it's dangerous?

"No, thanks," I say, hiding the fear in my voice. "I'm heading to the shuttle camp in a bit."

"Why?"

Other people glance over, putting me on the spot. Captain Cassius. Astra. I'm not about to tell the truth: that I'd be more comfortable sleeping in the metal bulk of the shuttle than in the flimsy wooden huts of the forest camp. So words tumble out before I've thought them through.

"There are some improvements to the boosters I've been thinking about."

Astra hurries over, wiping her hands on a cloth. Great. As if this wasn't awkward enough.

"Aren't you going to stay at the forest camp with us?" I wrinkle my nose as she comes close. I guess it's sweat from the fire's heat, or maybe it's because the showers aren't working here yet. "Your mother and I would like that. It's not often we're all together anymore."

She's right. And I'm still not used to it being just the three of us. I grew up in a full cabin with my dad, his two wives — Astra, his prima; my mother, his secunda — and my sister, Celeste, Astra's daughter. But Dad got frail and faced the Exit, then Celeste got married, leaving two empty bunks.

I glance at Mom, on the other side of the campfire, sitting in the middle of the tight clique of medics. She looks up, smiles. She can't hear us. Just as well; I don't want her coming to argue with me.

"I have work to do," I say.

Astra shakes her head. "You're just like your dad. Can't it wait? It's dark."

"I'll take a landbike."

"That?" Astra asks, pointing at the broken one.

"Yup." I flip open the casing, shove in the motherboard, and link up the new wire to the engine. I slam the casing closed and screw it shut. The display screen lights as it hums into life. The battery display is low, but I do a quick mental calculation. There's enough zap to get me to the shuttle camp if I drive slowly. I pick up my red jacket and shrug it on.

Astra frowns. "Ping me when you get to the camp. Please."

"I can ping you the whole way, if you like."

She looks at me, face long and sad in the firelight.

"I love you, Little Bear. So much. Are you sure you're okay?"

"I love you too." I feel bad enough to give her a quick hug before I grab my gear bag, throw my leg over the landbike, gun the engine, and speed away toward the forest path.

It's important to make an exit, Maia used to say. The hum of the machine reverberates through my body. My hood blows back, off my cropped hair. Once I'm out of sight I slow to a walking pace to save the battery.

I have to save enough power to zoom past Orion without offering him a ride.

The forest presses in on either side of me. The glowferns glitter between the tangled trees. The swing of my light casts movement at the edge of my vision, but when I peer into the darkness there's nothing there. Obviously. It's the wind blowing the branches. These woods are uninhabited apart from the bugs and bacteria sent ahead by the seeding ships.

I pull my hood back up for warmth, and I check behind the bike before I start talking. I don't want to look crazy.

"You wouldn't be afraid," I say to my memory of Maia. It's reassuring, hearing my own voice. "You'd think this was an adventure."

The noises here are strange, so it's good to talk over them. The howl of the wind, and a sharp single note that echoes through the woods, like the twist of metal under pressure or a human scream. It sends shivers down my back.

"It's the breeze," I tell Maia. "I'm being silly."

My words fade into the darkness. Maia isn't here to laugh at me anymore, so things aren't funny. The landbike hums as it bumps its way over the path.

A flash of movement up ahead. A black shape in front of the glowing plants. The shine of teeth.

My breath stops. But something is breathing.

The pant of in and out. Just for a moment, then it fades into the hiss of the trees. I can't see the shape anymore. Maybe it's deeper in the trees. Maybe it was never really there. It shouldn't be there. It's impossible.

The landbike's headlight hits the nearest branches. Makes them stand out clear as knives, but deepens the darkness beyond. Trees. Branches. Ground. Caught in the shaking light, a patch at a time. My heart is hammering against my rib cage.

I make myself breathe. Force the air in and out. I'm imagining things. Astra and her stories have gotten to me. Big bad wolves creeping through the deep, dark woods.

Everything is fine. In and out. Deep breaths.

I want to put my foot down, speed toward the shuttle camp. But the battery won't get me far at speed. I keep the landbike steady. Bumping over the path. There's nothing there. I know there's nothing there.

"This planet is making me irrational," I whisper to Maia.

I'm checking either side, trying to see into the darkness clutched between the branches.

That's why I almost hit the body.

CHAPTER 2

His legs are bent at the knees, and I swerve to avoid his boots. The rest of him sprawls across the path, head almost in the undergrowth at the side of the track.

My hand flies to my mouth. I stop the landbike, twisting the handlebars to let the headlight fall on him. I don't want to see. I can't look away, but I don't want to see. The landsuit is ripped open at the shoulder. There's flesh underneath. Torn and red, like the clothes. A splash of curly light brown hair, messy with mud.

It's Orion.

I slide off the landbike and drop to my knees. Fingers searching for a pulse. My shadow stretching over his body, blocking my headlight. There's too much mud on his neck. I try to find his skin under the wet dirt, mentally running through my emergency training, but it's wet and soft, and my fingers sink further in.

The mud is warm. That's when I realize: it's not mud.

His neck is open.

I yank my hand out, clutch it to me. Oh Beta. My fingers were in his neck.

There's nothing I can do for him.

There's blood on my hand, I think. I can't tell for sure. Dark liquid on dark skin, a gleam in the night. I rub my forefinger against my thumb to check. It doesn't feel like mud, but if it's blood, it isn't congealed at all.

I stop moving, apart from the trembles that shake my body. I'm listening. Whatever happened to Orion, it was minutes ago. And I saw what did it. A shape in the forest. A shape with teeth.

No. That makes no sense. The animal releases aren't scheduled for days. The woods are uninhabited.

But something killed Orion.

I hold my breath. Just the rustle of the trees. Logic comes back slowly. I can't stay here. I'm alone in the deep, dark woods with a body. I need help.

If I were on the ship, this would be easy. I could hit an alarm. I could yell and someone would probably hear. Here, we're so far from each other. So far from help.

I need my linkcom. I reach into my pocket. Pull it out with a shaking hand. It slips from my wet fingers, falls out of the headlight's circle, and bounces into the darkness, into the churned-up mud at the edge of the path. I scrabble for it, fingers sliding through the sludge. I can't find it. I grope and scrape at the cold ground, crawling forward, desperate. Cold mud under my fingernails, soaking through the knees of my landsuit.

Then my hands are sliding from under me and I'm falling sideways, onto Orion's body. His blood, the staring eyes, the wounds in his shoulder. I gag at the smell: sweat, piss, and the metallic scent of blood. Too much blood.

I push myself off, crawl backwards. Breathe. I try to wipe my hands on my landsuit, but that's bloody too. I stand up and stumble back, feeling sick.

Worse: helpless.

The trees sway in the wind. Long shadows cast by the headlight of the landbike leap around me. The glowferns' eerie light glimmers on Orion's open eyes, his olive skin.

I have to get help.

My linkcom can stay in the mud. It can lead them to the body. I'm going. Now.

I grab the landbike and pull myself up on it. My hands, slick with blood and mud, slip on the handlebars. But I get on, hit the starter. The wide wheels start to turn, thick tracks gripping in the mud. It makes a splattering sound as it spits out behind me, over Orion's body.

I speed into the dark. My hands shake on the steering bars. I twist the accelerator as far as it can go. The display is red now. The battery won't last long.

Orion's body was slashed. Raked across by something sharp. Throat opened.

Something in this forest, something on this planet did this to him.

I finally allow myself to mutter the thought that is practically heresy.

"I hate it here. I hate it here. I hate it here."

IT STARTS TO RAIN. I forgot about rain. Forgot how annoying it can be, this excess water. Spiteful droplets spit in my face, making me blink, making me take a hand away from steering to wipe at my eyes. The display beeps as the battery gives up, and the landbike slows to a halt.

But I can't be far from the shuttle camp now.

I throw myself off the bike and run, stumbling and slipping through the mud. This stupid uneven path. Breathless. Each step desperate. Hoping there's nothing in the trees. The glowferns don't illuminate the path enough to avoid the pits and holes, and I tumble into the mud. Then real lights finally appear through the branches ahead. Bright, man-made lamps. I'm there. At the camp.

I start shouting.

There's no one in sight as I burst out of the forest, but a light comes on in the duty protector's hut. I wipe the rain from my eyes. The door opens and there's Vega. Her face is crinkled in a sleepy frown, and for a second I'm pleased to see her. Until I realize she's waiting for her husband.

That stops me like a punch.

Oh no. I can't be the one to tell her. We've barely spoken in the months since she chose him over me, but I've seen the way she looks at me. I know she hates me as much as I hated Orion. It would hurt too much coming from me. But everyone else is at the bonfire.

Vega rubs at her eyes. "Ursa?" She stays under the shelter of the hut's overhang. "You woke me up."

"I … I …" Words won't come. I'm not even sure how to say what I saw. I don't know *what* I saw. I can't do this. I need to send for help. Someone who can break the news to her properly. "Could I borrow your linkcom?"

"What's wrong with yours?"

I just shake my head.

She lets out a huff of air. "Who are you going to call? Why were you shouting?"

I try to swallow down my panic. Blink through the rain. There's a world between what I saw in the woods and Vega here, her usual grumpy self. I can't make them fit.

"You should … should go back to sleep. Please, just lend me your linkcom."

"Where's Orion? He was meant to be coming here."

The panic tightens to a knot in my chest.

A light comes on inside the next hut. A head peers out, silhouetted against the beam from inside. Guion, one of Mom's medical team. He steps out, and the rain pastes his thin gray hair against his scalp. "I heard the shouting. What's going on?"

Thank Beta. "I need a linkcom," I say, trying to keep my voice steady.

He doesn't hesitate, holds his out. I grab it and take a few steps away from Vega. Once I'm out of earshot, I wipe the droplets of water off the screen, then ping Astra.

"Guion?" Astra's voice is unnaturally high when she answers. "Is everything okay?"

"It's me."

"Ursa? Why are you using Guion's linkcom?"

It's hard to hear her over the hiss of the rain. "I need you to get the protector on duty."

"It's busy here. Sabik burned his hand."

Of course he did. "This is important. There's been an incident in the forest."

"What incident? You're meant to tell me if there's an incident." Vega's voice from behind makes me jump. The mud muffles footsteps here. "Is that blood?"

I look at my hands. I've smeared Orion's blood over the white of the linkcom. Droplets of water are turning it pink, washing it away. My landsuit is covered with it, but it's just a dark stain against the red.

"Blood?" Astra says in my ear. "Did she say blood? Are you okay?"

I try to reply quietly. "Call the protector on duty at the forest camp. Tell them to head for my linkcom signal. Make sure they're armed."

"I'm coming," Astra says.

"No!" I don't want her coming through the forest. Not if there's something still there. "Get the protector on duty. Keep close to Celeste. She's going to need you."

Vega grabs me, spins me around so fast Guion's linkcom drops from my hand. I turn to pick it up, but she grabs my wrists, makes me look at her. "What's happened to Orion?"

My hands are slippery with the rain, the mud, the blood, so I pull them away easily. But Vega's eyes are wide. She doesn't look angry now. Her face is open, like it used to be, back when we were friends.

I'm not going to lie to Vega. I owe her that much.

"I'm so sorry. It's Orion. He's in the forest."

"What do you mean?" Her voice is too calm.

"He's dead."

Behind her, Guion puts a hand to his mouth.

"No. There's been a mistake. You made a mistake." Vega is almost pleading with me. And I wish I could take it back.

"I'm sorry, Vega. I really am. I'll call Astra again. Ask them to send someone to take care of you. Get your dad, maybe."

Vega looks around, as if for help, eyes filling.

"Are you sure he's dead?" Guion says, taking a few steps toward the woods. "I could go. I could see if ..."

"I'm sure, Guion."

"But ... how?" Vega's voice is a croak. She swallows, hard.

"I don't know. I'm so sorry, Vega. Look, let's go to your hut. You need to sit down."

"No, I have to see him. I have to check."

"You shouldn't see him like that," I say. "Please, Vega. Trust me."

"Come with me, Vega," Guion says.

But her gaze slides off us, and she shakes her head. "He could need help." Then, faster than I can react, she turns and runs for the woods.

"No! Vega!"

I grab at her sleeve, but she's too strong. She wrenches out of my grip, and I fall to my knees. She's fast, sure-footed in the mud. She passes Guion.

"It's not safe!" I yell.

Guion runs after her. "Wait, Vega!"

I push myself to my feet, stumble after them both. Vega keeps running, Guion behind her, both sprinting for the forest path. I take a few more running steps, to the edge of the trees.

But Vega's sobs and Guion's shouts have already faded, their figures disappearing into the dark. I slow to a walk, fighting with the panic in my gut. I feel the trees pressing in either side of me, the darkness and the eerie glowferns between them. My legs shake so much they barely hold me.

I can't catch up to them, and I can't be alone in the forest again.

I stop, take a few unsteady steps back to the lights of the shuttle camp, the rain pouring down on me. Guion will catch up with Vega. He'll make sure she's okay.

I hope.

CHAPTER 3

It's a somber trip back up on the shuttle the next day. The joy I used to feel at the boosters firing is smothered by the sorrow around me. By the weight of Orion's body in the hold.

Just like Maia's, three months ago.

I always imagined her as a pale and perfect snow princess when her brother, Jovan, found her. Drifting among the shattered ice, eyes closed as if she were asleep, just caught in a fairy tale. Red locks floating in the icy water around her.

But now I see her like Orion. Beta's omnipresent dirt in her hair. Eyes open and staring.

I blink to clear my tears. Glance around at the shuttle. Our acceleration is smooth and even, all within normal parameters, gravitational force around that on the *Venture* or Beta. The shuttle banks as we climb. I'm in a bucket seat by the window, Celeste next to me, Astra on the other side of her. Mom is in the row behind us. Vega is slumped in her seat at the back of the shuttle, sedated up to the eyeballs.

Celeste clutches her hands together on her bump. I catch glimpses of her wet cheeks through the veil of her thick, wavy hair. A loose red thread on her landsuit brushes against the golden-brown skin of her thumb, moving in the circulated air of the shuttle. I wonder if it tickles. But she doesn't seem to notice.

I haven't told her about what I thought I saw, only about finding Orion. She's already in shock. She's under so much stress, and I don't want to make things worse for the baby. I'll tell her back on the ship. When we're safe. When the time is right.

The woods play tricks on you. If it were someone else, I'd be sure they'd imagined it. It's not rational. But my memories are as clear as the glint of teeth in the beam of the headlight.

Perhaps I should try to warn people. But they'll think I'm mad. Perhaps crazy enough to have slashed Orion's throat myself.

And maybe I am losing it. It makes more sense than the alternative. After all, I'm talking to my dead best friend when no one else is around.

I stare out of the tiny window at Beta shrinking below me. There's our entire colony: the runway and the shuttle camp, the narrow path through the trees to our little town square, surrounded by habitation huts, fields, and the clearing with the charred remains of last night's bonfire.

There's a small bald patch in the woods to one side of the runway. Our graveyard, with two bodies in it already: Maia's and Seginus's. I guess we have another to feed to the dirt of the planet, once the investigation into Orion's death is done.

The muddy gap of the graveyard is one of a small number of cleared spaces in the woods that appear as we climb higher. Twenty other patches form a rough circle around the settlement. One for each of the *Venture*'s carriages to land when she's pulled apart and drops down through the atmosphere to Beta. The ship was never meant to stay in orbit. She was designed to separate from her spokes, descend to the planet, and form the core of our colony.

I shudder. I don't want to think about Betafall right now.

As we ascend, it's clear our new home is only a scratch on the surface, hemmed in by endless forests, seas, and rivers. And even that scratch is swallowed up by the wilderness as the shuttle climbs toward orbital height, up into the blackness of space.

It puts it all into perspective. Our colony is a microscopic blip, a tiny flame in endless darkness, vulnerable and quivering. It could be snuffed out so easily, like Maia's life. Like Seginus's or Orion's.

It was meant to be easier than this.

Beta didn't get the chance to develop past single-celled organisms. It had similar gravity to Alpha, the building blocks of life, and an almost-breathable atmosphere before humanity started work on it. The planet was bioengineered for us. Waves of unmanned seeding ships terraformed it with bacteria, genetically engineered plants, and bugs, all ready for our arrival, while mechanical landclearers sent on the last seeding ships prepared open fields, ready for the carriages to land. Ready to build and grow.

But we were delayed. Only by eighty years, which is good, really. There were always going to be unexpected maintenance issues in a flight as long as ours, and we were able to eke out our supplies just enough to reach the planet. Mostly thanks to my father, the ship's captain in the last two decades of our flight and an expert engineer.

The seeding ships sent ahead could fly faster. They didn't have to worry about the force of acceleration damaging fragile human bodies. But that speed and our delay meant the landclearers broke down, one by one, in the decades before we arrived. The forest took over. In the end, there was barely enough clear space to land the shuttle.

The planet's a mess.

Now there's the curve of Beta's horizon, and the reassuring darkness of space beyond, dotted with the fairy lights of far-off suns. I float up in my seat, the straps holding me in place. We're back in the world I know, the world of my childhood. The sound of the engine changes as the acceleration builds from a hum to a growl as we speed up enough to match the *Venture*'s orbital velocity.

And there she is.

It's still strange, seeing our ship from outside. The wheel that is my home. She's an icosagon: twenty carriages around the hub, half of them for growing food, the other half for everything else — the genelab, the medcarriage, storage, habitation carriages 1 to 5, and the generator carriage. Kilometer-long spokes lead to her engine room in the middle. One full rotation a minute to create the illusion of a gravitational force that matches Beta's.

There are scars on her hull where the ship's main thrusters used to be. We've started nibbling at the *Venture*, cannibalizing her metal to print new parts. The secondary boosters and our generators are enough to keep us in orbit. But there's no going back to Alpha.

The shuttle stabilizes. We're now matched to the *Venture*'s speed, steering in to her rotation. I'll go to the engine room as soon as I can. I'll be alone there, and it'll be easier to think, in the weightlessness.

Docking is quiet. The usual chatter and laughter have been drained from the shuttle by our collective shock, leaving an unnatural silence. We latch onto the side of the *Venture* and begin to spin with her. My weight returns, and I settle back down in my seat. There's a hiss as the airlocks open. I take a deep breath and taste the familiar air of the ship.

There's clacking as everyone unstraps, and the rustle of fabric and grunts as we stand and file off. Celeste waits until almost everyone else has left, so I do too.

Stepping through the airlocks and into the clanging echo of the *Venture*'s loading bay, Celeste pauses, watches them unload Orion's coffin from the hold. They'll take him to the medcarriage and conduct an autopsy, just like with Maia and Seginus, then return him to the planet for burial. A session of the council has been convened to investigate. Perhaps we'll get answers then. People squeeze past us respectfully as they move the other cargo into the ship.

Astra puts her arm around her daughter and leads her away, which is almost a relief. Astra's better with people than I am. But she looks more stooped than ever. It's lucky that we abolished the Exit when we landed, or she wouldn't have long left.

Mom's silent next to me, standing tall, back straight and long arms hanging at her sides like someone forgot to wind her up. "This must be hard for you, after Maia," she says, eventually. "Are you coming back to the cabin?"

I can't think of anything worse. Sitting in silence with Mom in that tiny space. And anyway, I need to clear all this nonsense of forest monsters from my head before I speak to the council.

"I'm going to head up to the engine room. Check in on the air circulation data. See how the new rotors are working."

Mom sighs, like I've said the wrong thing. "I suppose it is best to keep working. If you're sure you don't need me, I'll get back to the medcarriage."

I nod, turn away, and head along the corridors, turning my body toward the wall as I pass other people in the narrow passageways. It must be break time for basic training, as the children run up and down the corridors, bouncing off each other and giggling.

Several of them clutch new colorful objects — balls, spinning tops, and dolls, freshly printed — and they squabble over them. There were no toys when I was growing up, nothing to spare. Dad was mad at me for a week after he caught me twisting a short length of wire into a makeshift bracelet. And I'd only meant to wear it for a minute.

Even with the resources of the planet to reshape in our printers, the toys seem like a waste when there's so much that needs to be done around the ship. Lights burned out, casting the corridor in pools of darkness. Doors stuck permanently open. Creaking fans in the vents above me, old rotors we haven't been able to fix yet. We need more power. We're wasting most of the generator's output ionizing fuel into plasma to send the shuttle to and from the surface. Captain Cassius gives too many resources to the agricologists and builders. Squanders resources on toys for his children and their friends.

But it's good to be back. It smells right, here. Not like the empty scent of Beta.

It's the smell of hundreds of years of skin cells, waste reclamation pipes, and generations of people stuffed in a cramped space. I never noticed it until we went to the planet, where the air is so cold and clear I choked on my first breath. Here it's rich and musky. The smell of home. The *Venture* is cozy, human-sized, lived-in, unlike the muddy mess of the planet below.

The walls around me are decorated with engravings, memorial panels and stories of those who lived and died on the *Venture*. To my right is the tale of the Clearsighters. They didn't believe in the reality of the ship. They thought it was a trick, a social experiment, and that we'd never left Alpha. The scene on the wall is the twelve of them crammed into an airlock, smiling and laughing, moments before they opened it into the emptiness of space and proved themselves wrong.

We're surrounded by our ancestors up here. Cradled by the journey we all took, welded into the walls around me. I can walk the *Venture*'s passages with my eyes closed, reading my route by the grooves and ridges of the engravings at my fingertips. It was a game Maia and I played when we were younger, giggling as we roamed the vents and passageways. We didn't need toys. We had the *Venture*.

I run my hand along the cool metal. Let my fingers tell me the story of our launch, of the crowds who gathered to watch my ancestors blasting off into the skies. Then I'm at the elevator.

I hit the call button, it takes a moment to come, and the doors slide open. I step inside, hold on to the strap, and stare at the padded walls as the doors close. The stuffing is coming out in a few places. I'll have to check that's on the maintenance lists. My spirits rise with the elevator, weight decreasing as I move closer to the ship's axis. The centrifugal force that creates the *Venture*'s artificial gravity grows weaker toward the center of the ship. It's one of my favorite feelings. As if my cares are lifting from me along with my weight.

By the time I reach the heart of the *Venture*, there's no gravity at all. It's only the strap that's stopping me from bobbing freely around the elevator. The doors open. Aldrin is on duty in the chair.

"Want a break?" I ask.

He stretches. "I wouldn't say no. Nessus was awake half the night; he's teething. And Mira kept having to get up to use the wash cubicle."

"She must be due soon," I say.

His smile makes the bags under his eyes disappear for a moment. "Two months left," he says. Then he unbuckles and pushes himself toward me. "Ping me when you need me back. Thanks, Ursa."

I swing out of the elevator to make room for him, then wait until the doors close. I should be glad Antares lets us get away with anything. When Dad was Head of Engineering, he'd never have allowed an unapproved break for the engineer on duty.

But things were different then. The urgency of repairs was a panicked rhythm throughout my childhood, the stress etched into my father's forehead as he tried to eke out the supplies through force of will. I joined in the bustle as soon as I was old enough, rushing from one repair to the next as we tried to hold on long enough to make it to the planet and the resources that saved us.

Now the corridors are quiet. Sometimes it feels like I'm the only one who sees that the ship is slowly falling apart. The bustle has moved to the planet: building, planting, and fixing the endless injuries.

The moment Aldrin is gone I kick off the wall and float into the engine room. I do a clumsy somersault in midair and spread my arms and legs out, stretching properly, drifting across until my hands touch the opposite wall. I push against it gently and drift backward to the operator chair, mounted on a bar that extends out from the curve of the wall.

My aim is nearly perfect, and I twist my legs up in front of me, knees bent, to land butt-first in the bucket chair. I slide my arms through the straps and buckle them at my waist.

"Did you see that, Maia? Bull's eye."

I should keep this visit short, try to catch the start of the hearing. Also, Aldrin's comments reminded me I didn't use the wash cubicle before I came up here, and you don't know when your bladder is full in zero-G. I've made the mistake of waiting too long before.

But it's so good to be home. The engine room sparkles with thousands of lights on the curved walls around me. Control panels blink opposite me, display screens glow above me. Tickers below me scroll the temperature, speed, rotation, all updating constantly. Three hundred and sixty degrees of activity, of reassurance that the *Venture* is operating as it should. I try to ignore the niggling doubts. The radiation shielding coil in ecocarriage 6 seems a little weak, but since we're within Beta's magnetic field, it's not an issue. A water discrepancy in habitation carriage 2 suggests a leak. That would have been an emergency once, but now we've got plenty on the planet. It literally falls from the sky. So I'll get to those later.

I close my eyes, savoring the weightlessness.

The repairs are never-ending. Our tech is basic, compared to what they had on Alpha Earth. It has to be. No AI. No nanobots. Nothing so complicated that we couldn't fix it ourselves with the printers and supplies onboard. We're on our own out here. Just one tiny flame in the dark.

The main engines are offline now that we're at our destination, so every other sound is clearer. The clicks and whirrs as the *Venture* adjusts her orbit, her rotation. If you listen carefully, you can tell whether the shuttle is docked or not by the tiny countermeasures her boosters take to even out the extra weight on the hub. You can tell the time of day by the water reclaimer use. It's all there in the sound of the *Venture*. The sound of home.

Dad taught me to diagnose faults from the sounds the ship makes. The *Venture* talks to me, tells me what she needs. Unlike the planet. Down there the wind and the trees speak a foreign and sinister language.

I'm going to lose all this. When the *Venture* breaks herself apart and falls to her final resting place on Beta, the engine room, her golden heart, will be wrenched out. We won't need it down there, and the main propulsion system is too radioactive to risk on the planet. So while the carriages will land on Beta, the engine room boosters will fire one last time to propel this perfect place into the void.

Gone forever. I shiver at the thought. There are too many memories here.

Dad's baritone used to fill the engine room. He knew all the songs. I can almost hear him now. When I'm here, I feel as if he's just out of sight. I close my eyes tight, hoping that when I open them again, he'll be here and everything will be the way it was four years ago. Before my small world fractured. Before Dad's Exit, Celeste's marriage, Maia's death. Before we arrived at this stupid planet.

The whoosh of the elevator doors makes me turn.

Astra is there, holding on to the strap. She always looks dignified in weightlessness. I look like a toddler bobbing around. But Astra soars when she's moving and floats like a ghost when she's still.

"I thought I'd find you here," she says. "Your father came here to think, too. Want to float in the middle?"

She always understands me. "Yeah. Thanks."

You can't float in the middle of the engine room on your own, as you need someone to position you, then to push you back to the side when you're done, or you get trapped in the weightlessness because you can't reach the walls.

I used to do it all the time with Dad. It was my favorite game when I was a little girl. Although Maia thought it was funny to leave me here, stuck in the middle, pathetically flailing. She could be a jerk sometimes.

Astra pushes herself gently from the elevator wall and allows the inertia to bring her across the space toward the operator chair. I unbuckle myself, and she gives me a big hug, her copper-brown cheek squishing against mine.

"I love you, Little Bear. So much."

"Love you too," I say.

She holds on to the operator chair with one hand and guides me out to the middle of the engine room with the other, steadying me when I get there. I float, suspended in the weightlessness, then curl into a ball, hugging my own legs. It feels good to hide my head in my knees, to close my eyes and feel nothing.

"How's Celeste?" I ask. My voice is muffled in my clothes.

Astra pauses. "Heartbroken. Scared about the baby. She wanted a moment alone before the hearing starts, so I came to see you."

"Poor Celeste," I say, staring into the darkness of my arms. "I mean, I didn't like Orion, but he didn't deserve ..."

"It's a terrible thing." I hear Astra buckle herself into the seat. "How do you feel about the council meeting?"

"I don't know. Do you think Captain Cassius will be fair?"

"He'll pretend to be impartial, but I'm sure he'll value what his daughter has to say."

And Vega doesn't like me. Great.

Astra continues. "They'll find the DNA of whoever did this."

That's not reassuring. My DNA will be all over Orion, for starters. But what if they find other DNA? What if I didn't imagine the thing in the woods?

"Do you want to talk about what happened?"

Astra's good at listening. It's her job. She's too old for the more physical aspects of protector duties, so she specializes in questioning. I have to tell her the truth. She can always tell when people are lying.

I peek out from behind my knees. I let my eyes wander over the ecocarriages' fogponics feeds, the tank readings, air composition stats, the output rating of our generator. I can barely see any of them, but I'd notice if any were outside normal parameters.

I clutch my legs tighter. "I thought I saw a creature."

The pause before she speaks feels very long. "Describe it."

I exhale. I knew I could talk to her. Knew she'd take me seriously.

"It had teeth. It was just an impression in the flash of the headlight. It was almost as large as the landbike." It seems dumb now, in the safety of the engine room.

"Fur or scales?"

"Fur. Like a wolf. But bigger, I think, from what I've seen on the Alpha vidstreams. I guess it was my subconscious, after you mentioned the big bad wolf. I probably saw a tree moving or something."

"That doesn't sound like a tree."

"But the forest is uninhabited. They haven't started releasing animals yet."

"We know something killed Orion," Astra says. "And obviously it wasn't you."

"Of course not!"

She's silent for a moment. "Are you going to tell the council?"

"No one will believe me. They'll think I'm insane."

"If you have worries about the safety of the planet, it's your duty to share them."

I open my mouth to speak, then close it again. I hide my face in my knees.

"What is it, Ursa?"

"It doesn't matter," I say into the darkness of my knees. "Even if it isn't safe, we'll still have to live there, won't we?"

"That's the intention, yes."

I want to kick at something, like a child. "But what's the hurry? Why don't we patch up the ship and wait a bit? At least until the landclearers are fixed and have done their job?"

"Most of the crew want to live on Beta now. We have to stick together. Remember *Venture 2*? We don't want our own civil war, and Cassius would never agree to delay the colonization."

"But maybe he would if they realized how dangerous it is! Look at what happened to Maia! Or Seginus and Orion!"

"So the more we know about the dangers, the better."

There's a beeping on the comm screen. I keep my eyes closed, arms wrapped tight around my knees. I can't see Astra, but I hear the rustle of movement as she checks it.

Maybe she's right. Maybe people would consider delaying full settlement if they knew what I saw. Or maybe they'd think I was a traitor, trying to start a war like the Returners who destroyed our sister ship. Or they'd think I'm crazy, like the Clearsighters.

Crazy enough to have killed my brother-in-law.

Another rustle and the clank of Astra's seatbelt. Her fingers grip my shoulder, and I open my eyes and uncurl as she pulls me out of my floating position at the center of the *Venture*. I straighten up. She brings me within reach of the control chair, and I grab it.

"It's time, Ursa," Astra says. "You're being summoned to the hearing."

CHAPTER 4

Astra hurries off, taking the elevator down to her daughter, while I ping Aldrin and wait for him to return to work. Then I descend in the elevator, down the spoke that'll take me closest to the council room. The centrifugal force of the spinning *Venture* grows the further I get from the axis of the ship, increasing the gravity and pushing me slightly to the side on the way down. Soon my feet are stuck to the floor once again, and I release the strap.

The elevator slows, and the doors swish open to reveal my mom. I was expecting her to be inside already, with the other heads of sectors. But it makes sense that she's waiting for me, since I'm not of age yet. I'm seventeen in Alpha Earth years. Or I was, until we got here. This planet makes me younger: thirteen in Beta years, because of its stupid overlong rotation around Sol 2.

"Don't worry," Mom says. "They're not accusing you of anything. This is purely a fact-finding meeting."

But her words make my stomach clench. People love to jump to conclusions.

She takes my hand, our fingers entwining. She's taller than me, her skin a warmer tone of brown. She's wearing her hair loose today, and it stands out around her head like a dark cloud. Together we stride down the patched and dim corridor. We pass the carving of Eve, the first baby born on board; I turn toward the carving as we squeeze past other people. Her face is angelic, eyes too wide to be real, and she's not screaming like babies usually do.

We pause at the engraving of my father. The light panel above it is out, so his familiar face is shadowed, the thin carved lines that make up his features almost invisible, fading him into a ghost in the wall. But still, I run a hand over the grooves, press my palm against the cold alloy that is his face, younger than I remember it. But his eyes stare into the distance, over my shoulder.

"I'll fix the light," I say.

Mom nods.

I pull strength from Dad. I am the old captain's daughter. I am an engineer. This is my ship. I square my shoulders, and we start walking again. When we reach the double doors at the end, I don't pause. I hit the opening panel, the doors slide apart, and I stride in.

The council is already in session, the dining tables folded away in storage and the benches rearranged into rows facing the front. But the space still smells of chickpea stew, and I realize I'm hungry. Captain Cassius is standing at the front, beneath the giant steel orb of Beta. He's shorter than my father was. Too small behind the podium. Trying to make up for his lack of gravitas with insincere smiles as we come in.

Protector Sirius is at the witness stand, but he's fallen silent, looking at me. He only became a full protector a month ago. He's a year older than me, and he looks too small in his uniform, sitting as straight-backed as he can.

The place is about half full, people lined up on the narrow rows of benches. They look around, to watch me enter. It's probably the first time in my life that I've turned heads, and it's for all the wrong reasons.

Celeste is on the front bench, next to the wall; Astra's next to her, arm around her shoulder, holding her close. Mom and I head up the aisle and sit on the cold metal next to them. There's an air circulation vent above Celeste. Her hair trembles in the breeze, but the rest of her is completely still.

"You're certain about the tracks?" Cassius's reedy voice echoes off the patched metal walls. "The weather monitors indicate it was raining at the time."

"I ... yes, only one set of landbike tracks." Sirius pauses. "But there were signs of a struggle."

"A struggle?"

"Slip marks in the mud. And couple of handprints, too small to be Orion's. You can see them in the images we took of the scene."

Ah, yes. Those will be my handprints.

The door at the back of the room opens, and in walks Vega. She half sits, half collapses into a chair at the back. The hiss of whispers fills the air.

"Quiet, please!" Cassius turns back to Sirius. "Is there anything we should know about the condition of the body that isn't clear from the images?"

He looks pale. "It was still warm. Time of death was likely only minutes before we reached him."

When he says it like that, it doesn't sound good.

"Thank you, Protector Sirius. Your service is appreciated at this difficult time." He gives Sirius a thin smile. "Please feel free to return to your seat."

Sirius avoids my eyes as he stands up and marches past.

Cassius consults his display screen. "Protector Vega."

They usually call the protectors first. But I can't help but wonder if Cassius is giving his daughter preferential treatment.

Vega stumbles down the aisle, eyes unfocused. Her hair is coming out of her normally neat ponytail. I'm not sure she even sees me.

Cassius reaches a hand toward her. "Are you able to testify? Do you need more time?"

"I want to do this."

He takes a deep breath. "Okay, but let me know if it gets too difficult."

She nods.

"Can you tell me what happened on the night of the thirty-second of fifth month, year one?" He could have said "last night," but that's Cassius for you. More concerned about the historical record than being understood.

Vega sways in her seat, but when she speaks her voice is clear and sharp.

"I was the protector on duty in the shuttle camp. Due to the recreational campfire, we were on a skeleton rotation. Just myself and Medic Guion." She's being official, I see. She gets that from her father. Unlike him, she used to know when to switch it off.

"I was waiting for my husband, who had indicated that he was looking forward to joining me that evening."

Next to me, Astra takes Celeste's hand.

"Suddenly, I heard a strange noise. I left my hut and encountered Junior Engineer Ursa, who was shouting and covered in blood."

My mouth falls open. More whispers around us.

"She demanded my linkcom and would not explain herself, even though I offered assistance."

She makes me sound like I was unhinged. I want to argue, but it's true, technically.

"Her shouting attracted the attention of Medic Guion, who came over and undermined me by offering his own linkcom before I could ascertain what the situation was."

Cassius is making notes on his display screen.

"Ursa then pinged Astra and asked her to summon a different

protector, in spite of the fact that I was available and ready to help. I knew she was trying to hide something."

"That's not fair!"

"Sit down, Junior Engineer Ursa." Cassius puts the emphasis on "junior."

I hadn't noticed that I'd stood up. I thud back onto the bench.

There are mutterings in the audience.

"Your turn to testify will come, Ursa," Cassius says. "Vega, please continue."

She's staring at me now. "I finally got Ursa to confess that Orion was dead in the forest."

Confess? I open my mouth to interrupt again, but Mom puts a hand on my shoulder, and I get the message.

"It's no secret that Ursa hated Orion. She should be treated as a suspect."

"Vega," Captain Cassius says, gently, "that is for the investigation to determine, but we will be open to all possibilities." He glances at me, an appraising look on his face. "For now, we need an overview of the facts. What happened after Ursa told you that Orion was dead?"

Vega closes her eyes, swallows. "I ran to the forest, hoping that Ursa was wrong, hoping that he could be saved. But Protector Sirius was already there, and he confirmed that my husband had been murdered."

Tears streak her cheeks, but she holds herself steady in her chair.

Captain Cassius sighs. "I think that is enough for now. You are excused, Protector Vega."

Vega heads along the aisle back to her chair. I look down in my lap, but I can feel her staring at me as she passes.

Cassius consults the display screen in front of him. "I think it would be most helpful to question Junior Engineer Ursa next, if she is ready." He peers at me from beneath his bushy gray eyebrows.

I lick my lips and lie. "I'm ready."

The gaze of the audience is itchy on my back as I walk toward the witness stand, boots loud on the metal floor. So many eyes are on me. Shouldn't they be busy? There's plenty of work to go around. I scan the crowd. It's a mixture of those who knew Orion well and the ship's biggest gossips. I trip over a badly patched section of flooring. Vega's words spin through my head. Treated as a suspect? She can't seriously think I'd slash Orion open.

The metal seat is uncomfortably warm. Cassius sucks in his cheeks and begins.

"Junior Engineer Ursa, do you swear, on Beta Earth, to tell the truth?"

I pause for a second. Vega wasn't made to swear. Then I realize the implication. By getting me to take the oath, he's ensuring anything I say can be used in a later trial against me. I swallow and raise one hand, palm up, toward the steel globe above us both.

"On Beta Earth," I intone.

"Then we shall begin. Can you explain why you followed Senior Protector Orion into the woods on the evening of the thirty-second of fifth month, year one?"

Ah. It's going to be like that, is it?

"I wasn't following him. I was returning to the shuttle camp."

"Why didn't you wait for the morning?"

I shift in the metal seat. Cassius is a protector. He's trained in telling whether or not someone is lying. "I decided I'd spend the night in the shuttle."

"Not at the forest camp?"

"I'm still not comfortable there. Not after ... Maia."

Cassius nods. If it were anyone else, I'd think he looked sympathetic for second. But it was probably just a facial tic. He continues. "Perhaps you would have been better off waiting for the sunrise?"

"In retrospect, yes."

"So, you were traveling through the forest. Tell us what happened then."

I wrap my arms around my stomach. "I saw his legs first, then the rest of him. He had been cut open by something and —"

Cassius interrupts. "Something? Don't you mean someone?"

I bite the inside of my lip. I shouldn't have let that slip. "I guess. I don't know what happened to him."

Cassius types on his display screen. I glance out over the audience. Celeste's eyes are wide, glistening.

Cassius continues. "There is no need to go over the injuries again, especially as it would cause upset." He glances at his daughter as he says this. "Did you disturb the body in any way?"

"I checked his neck for a pulse. Then I … panicked." That's hard to admit.

"Panicked? In what way?"

"I dropped my linkcom. I tried to find it in the mud, but I slipped and fell onto Orion's body."

Cassius taps on his display screen again, as if I've made a confession. I suppose I have kind of backed up Vega's version of events, of me being unhinged. Damn.

"Then what did you do?"

"I couldn't find my linkcom, so I decided to head back to the shuttle camp. To get help."

"Did you stop or see anyone on the way? Any sign of other landbikes or people?"

I pause. But he's asking about people. Not strange creatures. And Vega's testimony has already made me sound crazy.

"No."

"About how long did it take you to get back to the camp after discovering the body?"

"Maybe ten minutes."

This doesn't look good. He must have died right before I got there. My DNA will be all over him. People are going to think I'm a killer anyway. Does it matter if they think I'm crazy too?

"You saw and heard nothing?"

I meet Astra's kind eyes in the front row, and there's strength in them. Time to make up my mind.

I am under oath.

"I didn't see any signs of landbikes or other people."

Cassius's bushy brow furrows. "So, what did you see?"

I knew I couldn't get that past him. I take a breath. Celeste is staring at me. I should have talked to her first. Should have told her in private. She deserved that.

"I thought I saw something with teeth."

In the front row, Mom's mouth falls open.

Cassius leans back. "An animal in the forest?"

"Yes. Something big."

"You are aware the releases haven't begun yet?"

"Of course."

"So, you know what you are claiming is ridiculous?"

"I ... well, how well do we know the planet? It's covered in trees. Perseus nearly died because the trees meant he couldn't see a cliff right in front of him. Who knows what the forest could be hiding?"

Cassius stiffens at the mention of his son. "That's impossible."

"I would have thought so too, but —"

"So, you thought you saw a creature in the forest. You then headed back to the shuttle camp on the landbike. But according to the records, you abandoned it some distance away. Why?"

"The battery was dead."

"Then you entered the shuttle camp, screaming and shouting?"

"I called for help."

"But when Protector Vega offered help, you refused."

"I didn't want her to find out her husband was dead from me. She should have heard it from a friend."

There's a murmur from the audience. It sounds like agreement. I feel it echo from the metal ceiling. I pull myself up in my seat.

Cassius exhales. "You know procedure. You were to report it to the protector on duty."

"I did. Just not right away."

"And then what happened?"

"Vega ran into the forest. Guion went after her. I stayed in the camp until other people arrived."

"So, you were alone again. For how long?"

"Maybe half an hour, until Vega came back with Sirius and Guion."

Cassius nods. "And from then, we have their testimony."

"You do." I stand up, ready to head back to my seat.

"A couple more questions, Junior Engineer Ursa, if you will."

I sink back down.

He taps on his display screen. I wonder if he's really checking something or just enjoying making me wait, hoping I'll squirm under the gaze of our audience. It's working. My blood pulses through my head. The ceiling feels too low, the room too hot.

"I notice from your service record that you've hardly been on the planet, even though your sister lives there and your mother spends a lot of her time there."

I glance at them both in the front row. Mom's biting her lip.

"I went down a lot at first. At the start of the winter. Before Maia died."

"But until the day of the bonfire you hadn't been planet-side for three months."

"There's so much to do on the *Venture*."

"And there's plenty for an engineer to do on the planet. Fixing landclearers. Preparation for the hydroelectric plant. Yet you have not volunteered for a planet-side task for a long time."

"I guess not."

He leans forward, puts on one of his fake concerned faces.

"Junior Engineer Ursa, do you like the planet?"

I stare at him. He doesn't break eye contact. I'm under oath. I don't want to lie. And why should I?

"I think it's dangerous."

"Dangerous?"

"Three people are dead. Mom's been rushed off her feet, dealing with injuries. I'd call that dangerous, wouldn't you?"

"What would you have us do? Return to Alpha Earth?"

There's a buzz in my ears. "Of course not! I just think we should slow down the settlement. We're so vulnerable there."

I see some quiet nods in the audience. Recognize a few people who have been on the *Venture* almost as much as I have these past few months. Interesting. I'm not alone.

Cassius puts his hands together. "It sounds to me as if you are letting your fears get the better of you. Clearly, I need to question you further, and you need the privacy to speak freely."

I hold my breath, dreading what is coming.

"You will take the next shuttle down to Beta, and we will schedule private interviews. I am reassigning you to planet-side duties, pending the outcome of this investigation, at which point we will decide whether there is any evidence that warrants charges against you."

He might as well have punched me in the stomach. I think I'm going to be sick.

"But I …"

"That is my final word, Ursa. You may return to your seat."

CHAPTER 5

I want to stay for the rest of the hearing, but the next shuttle leaves in just over an hour. So I head back to our cabin, head reeling, and start packing, pulling clothes down from the overhead storage, swearing as I do so. It's the only way to keep the tears away.

I used to calm down by staring out the window. I'd watch the stars turning through our little porthole until my breathing slowed. But that won't work now. It hasn't since we arrived. I can't stand the way Beta lurches in and out of view as we rotate.

"Down to the planet," I complain to Maia. "Interrogation by Cassius! He's going to try to pin Orion's death on me."

I punch the metal wall and split the skin on my knuckles.

"Yeah. That was smart." I imagine Maia laughing.

I turn to my engraving of her, propped up in the corner. Everyone else has stopped carving memory panels to use in ship repairs. And I know there's no point, since we're going to pull the *Venture* apart. But I hurt less when I'm bent over the metal, burin in my hand, recreating her familiar face.

It's a portrait of her the last time I saw her. It's hard to capture the mischief in her eyes, her red hair in wisps across her features, the snowflakes in her eyelashes, but I'm trying. I like to think of her as she was on that day.

It was two months after our arrival. I'd lost count of the number of times I'd been down to the planet by that point — enough for most of the initial shock to wear off. I was no longer astonished by the vastness of the sky, the green of the trees, the strength of the wind, and the endless space. But I couldn't get used to it.

I don't think I ever will.

We were working on the shuttle. It still needed tuning up, since we'd assembled it from the pieces in storage while in orbit. It was easier to do the fixes on the planet, where we didn't need to worry about EVA suits. Maia crouched on the wing next to me, handing me tools, her landsuit lurid red against the white metal. Our onboard overalls were gray long before I was born, from washing and constant patching. The landsuits were among the supplies waiting for us on Beta. New, bright, and stiff.

I had to take off my gloves in order to get a proper grip on my wrench, and my fingers ached with the cold, barely feeling like a part of me. When I was done, I pulled my gloves back on.

"Done." I stood up. Maia rose next to me, and we looked out over Beta.

"Beautiful, isn't it?" she said.

Snow coated the trees then, stretching in all directions, covering the planet as far as I could see. The sun gleamed on it, making it sparkle. White, clean, new. It was strange to see so far. We'd all had to have our eyes adjusted to be able to focus at a distance, after the close quarters of the ship.

I pulled in a lungful of air. The cold tingled on my teeth, as if I'd bitten metal.

"It's better than autumn, at least," I said.

Maia laughed. "Remember how you wanted to fix the trees?"

"You have to admit, it's weird that things kept dropping off them."

"Leaves, Ursa. They're called leaves. You prefer winter?"

I blew through the thick fabric of my gloves. My hands prickled as warmth returned. "It's freezing."

"I guess it is pretty cold." Wisps of red hair whipped around her face, escaping from her hood. Her skin was light pink, almost as pale as the snow. She blended in there. Part of the landscape.

"Yeah, let's get down from here before I freeze up completely."

We slid down the slope of the wing toward the ladder, holding on to each other for balance on the slippery surface and giggling. I went down the ladder first, hand under hand, jumping the last few rungs, my boots kicking up the snow as I landed. It was loose that day, as light as the dust from the air filters.

"We should move down here," Maia said as she landed next to me. "As soon as possible."

She was always in a rush.

"Winter's only just begun. It's going to get colder," I said. "Maybe in spring."

"Yeah, that'll be something to witness. Images of spring on Alpha Earth look gorgeous."

"But will it be the same here? No one knows what a Beta spring is like."

Maia turned to me, grinning widely. "We'll be the first people to see it. Isn't that amazing?"

I nodded. I didn't know then it would be mostly mud.

"Do you want to go see the lake again?" Maia said. "I hear it's completely frozen now. We could grab some spare landclearer blades, tie them to our boots, and try skating, like in the old vidstreams."

"Sorry. Sabik wants to show me the progress on the forest camp. He's coming here to pick me up."

She raised an eyebrow. "Choosing your boyfriend over your best friend?"

"We've been working together all day. You should be sick of me."

"Why? Are you sick of me?"

I fought the urge to roll my eyes.

"No, Maia. That's not what I meant."

"Come on, just have a look down the path to the river, at least. Pick some glowferns."

I glanced toward the tree line. I could see the sparkle of the plants among the black trunks, and the lights tugged at me. So beautiful. Bioengineered just for us.

Maia followed my gaze, saw my resolve weakening. "Sabik isn't here yet."

"I guess some glowferns would look lovely in the cabin."

"Race you to the tree line," Maia said.

She leapt forward, across the runway toward the woods. I followed. But it was harder going than I'd thought. As soon as we left the runway, we were calf-deep in snow. We hopped from one foot to another, sinking into the white, listening to the muted crunch of each step.

We must have looked daft. Two red figures bounding across the frozen field, giggling like Clearsighters, leaving monster-sized footprints behind us.

I tried to catch up with Maia, laughing and breathless. But I slowed down as we approached the forest. The lights glowing between the trees were too strange. The alien glow of them, so unlike our simple, bright panels on board. They emphasized the tangle of trees rather than illuminating them.

I should have trusted my instincts.

Maia lunged forward and slapped her gloved hand against the loaded branch of the nearest tree, knocking off the snow and uncovering the dark green of the needles beneath.

"Beat you!" But her smile faded as she saw me, lagging behind. "What's up?"

"Nothing."

She waited. She knew me too well.

"What if we get lost?" I shut my mouth. It sounded stupid when I said it out loud. But what were the right words? The ones that would have stopped her going?

"We could leave a trail of breadcrumbs behind us," Maia said.

I put my hand on my hip.

"There's just one path to the river. And we have our linkcoms." She held hers up.

Then there was the hum of a landbike approaching. I turned back, saw a figure riding up the forest path toward the shuttle. Floppy black hair sticking out from a red hood. Sabik.

I was pleased at the time, relieved to have a reason to stay out of the woods. Sabik spotted us, turned the bike, and headed across the field, the wide wheels leaving a thick furrow in the snow behind him. He stopped carefully, got off, trudged over.

He addressed me, like he always did. Ignoring her as if she were already gone.

"Hey, Ursa. How's things?"

Maia answered. "Want to come exploring with us?"

I turned to Maia. "Sorry. I did promise I'd see the camp."

"Fine." She kicked up some snow. "I guess I'm on my own today."

"Just for a bit. The launch is at 1700," I said. "I'll meet you half an hour before, at the shuttle. We'll sit together, okay?"

"I guess." Maia peered at me, blue eyes wide under her hood.

"Okay, then," I said. "See you at the shuttle." I headed toward the landbike.

I'd only gotten a few steps away before I heard the tramp of feet behind me, and cold hit the back of my neck. I yelped as a snowball slid down into my landsuit, a wet chill shivering down my spine.

I turned, and that was my last sight of Maia. Grinning. Cheeks flushed with mischief, snowflakes in her red eyelashes, powdery traces of the snowball in her red glove.

That's the image I'm trying to capture, to save. That's where I wish I could be. If I were there, I could stop her going into the forest, or I could go with her.

But at the time, I bent down to scoop up a fistful of snow instead. When I straightened up Maia was already disappearing, dashing into the woods, laughing.

I tried to aim at the red shape moving down the path among the black trunks, but I was hurrying and didn't squeeze it into a proper ball. When I threw it, it turned into a spray of snow that blew back into my own face.

I blinked to clear my stinging eyes, and Maia was gone.

She didn't meet me back at the shuttle at 1630. I reported her missing to Orion. But he wouldn't take me seriously. He insisted that she was probably just messing about and that it was nothing to worry about. He didn't start the search until the shuttle was due to take off.

There might have been time to save her, if Orion had listened to me.

It was Jovan who found her. He went into the woods with the protectors, when the search finally started. They found her in the lake, floating amid the broken ice that hadn't held her weight.

I should have forced Orion to start the search. I should have gone with her into the forest when she asked. But I was with Sabik.

He never liked Maia. He tried to be sympathetic afterwards, but he didn't feel the loss of her in his core like I did. He carried on going down to the planet, not caring that it had killed her. And he didn't understand my worry, the way my stomach snarled up each time he was on Beta. I couldn't focus until he came back safely to the *Venture*. Even after Seginus died in a building accident and Perseus was injured, Sabik didn't get it. He just told me he'd be fine and that I should relax. But I couldn't, and he wouldn't stop going down to Beta.

So we broke up.

I stayed on board. Things are okay up here, if I don't think too much about them. It's been nice to have Astra all to myself. The *Venture* is safe and warm. Her metal walls are strong and covered with happy memories. It's like I could step sideways into the past and Dad would still be captain. We'd still be en route, full of anticipation. And Maia would be at my side, instead of staring out at me from a memorial panel.

But now I have to leave all this. Have to go down to Beta.

"Stupid Cassius," I mutter, throwing clothes into my bag, harder than necessary.

There's a knock on the door. Mom, Celeste, and Astra wouldn't knock, so I have no idea who it could be.

The door's automatic release hasn't worked in my lifetime. It's on the list of repairs, and I give an unattractive grunt when I heave it open. That wouldn't normally bother me, but standing on the other side is Jovan. Gorgeous Jovan. Super-talented geneticist Jovan.

Maia's brother Jovan.

I hope he didn't hear me talking to myself.

"Hi, Ursa. How're you holding up?" he says, like we chat all the time. Which we do, of course, but normally just in my imagination. Not in actual life.

"Um. Yeah. Hi," I manage. Smooth.

He grins, one side of his mouth higher than the other. I stare, remembering when my brain would have been short-circuited by his gorgeously uneven smile. But it's sad now, broken by Maia's death. It doesn't hold the energy and hope it used to.

"Could I come in for a moment?" he says.

"Um. Yeah. Sure." I step to one side. Apparently, I can only talk in monosyllables.

He shuffles in, and it's only then I remember the patched underwear strewn over my bed. He pauses, taking in the tiny cabin. I'm glad I haven't used the wash cubicle recently. That always stinks up the place.

But then I see his face properly. See the dark circles under his eyes. He takes another step into the room, then freezes. I follow his gaze.

To my engraving of Maia.

"Oh," I say. "I ... that's just something I was working on. I ..."

"It's her," he says, finally, in a voice barely above a whisper.

"Yeah." I say.

"No, I mean, it's really her. That's ... you've captured her. Her face. Her spirit." He swallows.

"I'm sorry. I didn't know you were coming. I should have put it away."

"I'm glad you didn't. I'm glad to see it." He stares at it for a long moment, then turns back to me and smiles properly. "You're planning to put it in one of the corridors?"

"There's a damaged panel in the second habitation carriage. I was going to replace that with this. If that's okay with you."

"Of course. It's wonderful."

"It's kind of pointless, what with the ship coming down to the planet. But maybe we can save the engravings when we dismantle it."

He runs a hand over his hair. It's curly and short, like mine. "What happened to your knuckles?"

"Oh." I peer at them. They're throbbing and bleeding a little from when I punched the wall, but somehow I didn't notice it in Jovan's presence. "It's nothing."

"You should get that looked at."

"Yeah."

He looks at the floor. There's barely room for both of us to stand here. He's so close I can smell the musk of his skin and the scent of soap. So familiar, it's like breathing in the past. Breathing in the times when I would talk Maia into hanging out in her cabin, just so I might run into him.

"I owe you an apology," he says.

"What?"

"I should have come to you sooner. It's just, Maia's death hit me hard. And I kind of closed down. But I wanted you to know, I appreciate your being Maia's friend."

It's etched into his stance. The loss. The loneliness. A mirror to my own. The words come out before I can think.

"I … I should have been at the lake that day," I say. "I'm so sorry. I didn't know she'd go on the ice alone and I …"

He takes my hand in his. His skin is soft, and almost the same deep brown as mine.

"No. It's my fault," he says quietly. "I was responsible for Maia. Our parents are dead. I should have been looking after her."

I can't hold back a laugh. "You remember Maia, right? Can you imagine her letting you watch over her all the time?"

And he gives a small snort too. "Yeah. I guess she'd have hated me for that."

I let my head drop forward, to hide the tears that fall. I look back up at Jovan, and he holds my gaze with his wide, kind eyes. I could get lost in them. Dark as space, and just as vast. And there it is, the recognition. Someone carrying the same burden.

"I heard what you said at the hearing," he says after a long time.

Oh no. He must think I'm crazy. "You were there?"

He nods.

"That must have been hard, listening to that. After you found …"

He takes a long breath in. "Yeah. It did bring some stuff back."

"I'm sorry."

"But that's not why I'm here." He lets go of my hand but moves closer, leans toward my ear. My pulse increases. He looks around, as if afraid we'll be overheard in this metal cube, then takes a breath. "It was what you said. About the planet." But then there's the scrape of the door opening.

Jovan steps away from me quickly. I want to snatch him back, pull him near again. But there's Mom, in the doorway.

Great timing, as always.

"Oh. Hi, Jovan," Mom says. To her credit, she manages not to act surprised to see a gorgeous man in our cabin.

"Hi, Nashira," he says to Mom.

He turns back to me. "Um, I should go. Perhaps we could meet up on the planet? Maybe go visit Maia's grave together? We've got a lot of catching up to do."

"Okay. Sure," I say. My cheeks burn.

Then he steps out of the cabin, squeezes past my mother, and he's gone, giving me a smile as he disappears. Mom raises an eyebrow.

"Don't," I say. "Don't say anything."

"I just … it's good to see you with other people."

"I said 'don't.'"

Mom presses her lips together, hiding a grin. Then she glances at my clothes, still strewn over the bed.

"Let me give you a hand. We need to leave as soon as possible. Boarding is in twenty minutes."

CHAPTER 6

I don't sleep well that night, in Mom's hut. It doesn't rain, but that's almost worse. It's too quiet. There's no hum of fans or gentle purr of boosters correcting our spin. There's just the random hiss of the breeze and the creaking of insects outside. My bed is wide open on both sides, and I'm afraid of rolling out. The ceiling is too high above us. After a while, there's a strange, monotonous buzz like a broken circulator, but when I get up to find the cause, Mom turns over in her bed.

"It's just a fly," she says, voice muffled by her blankets. "Ignore it. It's engineered not to bite, and it'll find its own way out."

But I can't ignore it. There's another creature in here with us. The thought makes my skin prickle. And although the noise grows and fades, it never disappears. It drills itself into my head, keeping me awake.

The next morning, we get up before it's light. We wash in a bowl of cold water Mom gets from a pump in the village. It's freezing, which helps wake me up, but I still feel grubby when we're done.

They're going to get some showers running soon, apparently.

Mom is excited about that. "The ones on the ship are barely a trickle," she says. "Down here, they'll be like a waterfall."

"That sounds painful."

Mom laughs, as if I'm joking.

I grab my gear bag, and we head out of the hut and away from the habitation huts toward the center of the forest camp. Although now that I'm seeing it in the gray dawn light, I guess it's probably not fair to call it a "camp" anymore. Foundations have been dug, and permanent walls are going up among the huts and tents. It's still a muddy mess of holes and half-filled trenches, but the skeleton of a town square is appearing through the chaos. The buildings are almost all wooden. It's taking longer than they thought to make enough bricks.

A few landbikes wait to take the agricologists to the further-off postings, but for now, they cluster around Yuri, Head of Agricology. The builders and architects huddle around Capella, Head of Construction, ready to be brought up to speed.

Construction is the newest specialization. They haven't figured out who they are compared to everyone else. The other sections have clear identities. Protection has bossy and self-important sewn up. Engineering has the monopoly on loner nerds. Medics already took earnest and hardworking, and education are the pushovers. So, what does that leave construction? They can't go arrogant, because that's genetics' territory, and agricology has the overenthusiastic goofballs.

"I'd better check in," Mom says. She kisses me on the cheek. "I've got a morning shift, then a sleep break before my night shift, so I probably won't see you until tomorrow. Okay?"

"Sure," I say, like I have a choice in the matter. And she's gone, ducking into the half-finished hospital.

There are new huts everywhere. Mom had to remind me where hers was yesterday. My feet don't know how to take me where I want to go. I'm lost, even amid faces I've known all my life. I find a patch of mud that's drier than most, lean against a wall, and watch everyone else scurry around.

I'm not going to volunteer for anything. Antares, Head of Engineering, should assign my work, but it would be just like him to forget I'm even down here.

Beta's sun comes up slowly, dimmed by clouds, gray as light through a blanket. There's an exposed pipe above me, and the wind blowing over it produces warped, whistling notes. They rise and fall with the breeze, like a song without the structure of melody. I should probably move away from the wall. It was a half-finished building that fell on Seginus. It turns out it's harder than you would think to follow instructions when you have no real experience of construction. Perhaps that can be their specialization's thing — incompetence.

A small child jumps in a muddy puddle, feet together, eyes wide. I think it's Aquila, Phoebe and Yuri's daughter, but it's hard to recognize her with her landsuit hood up.

"Aquila!" An outraged shout confirms my suspicion, and Phoebe appears, grabbing the sleeve of her daughter's landsuit, dragging her away too late, the bright red of her legs already splattered by dirt.

"Ready for our forest adventure?" a voice says beside me.

I spin around. Sabik has snuck up on me, his right hand bandaged.

"What?"

His hair still looks a mess. It's a shame. It's beautifully silky when he brushes it. It never used to get so tangled on the ship, without a breeze to mess it up. His light skin is a shade darker than I remember, probably due to the ultraviolet radiation from Beta's sun.

This planet changes everything.

"I'll be working with you today," he says.

"But ... I should be supervised by an engineer."

He shakes his head. "Cassius spoke to Antares. The captain will be assigning your work."

I roll my eyes. But I shouldn't be surprised. Antares is old, and as weak as a hydrogen bond. He'll do whatever Cassius says.

Sabik continues. "We need you to fix a landclearer we found in the forest. I'm not able to do much else with this." He holds up his bandaged arm. "So I volunteered to take you."

"You're my supervisor?"

"We're not as hung up on hierarchy down here. I won't be filling in a report on your work. Plus, I think Cassius wanted you to feel at home. You do have friends down here, you know. Come on."

Then he's walking away from the town square toward the habitation huts at the edge of the camp. There are cracks in the clouds now. Shafts of light beam down randomly on the planet. I exhale and follow him. I guess I'm lucky. Cassius could easily have stuck me with a worse assignment.

We're soon through the village and hiking across the fields. Tiny shoots stick out from the mud, transplanted from the ecocarriages back on board. I'm careful to follow the paths, so as not to tread on them as I pick my way through. It's weird, food coming out of dirt. Yet another thing to get used to.

A dark mass of trees glowers at the edge of the field. We're heading straight for it.

"Are you okay?" Sabik asks.

"I'll be fine."

He raises an eyebrow. "I heard about your testimony. Everyone's talking about it."

Great. I guess I shouldn't be surprised.

"You really think you saw a creature?"

I nod.

"I've been working in the forest for four months, Ursa. I haven't seen any animals."

"So you think I'm making it up?"

"I didn't say that. But wouldn't we be able to find something down here? Do a scan of the planet or something?"

I laugh. "You're kidding, right?" The ship was only set up to enable us to check the weather at the landing site and allow basic communication by linkcom. We weren't meant to stay in orbit long.

Sabik sighs. "Give it a chance and it might even be a fun day. The clouds are going to clear in an hour or two, and there's the first bird release scheduled later. They say they fill the air with song."

I don't smile.

"C'mon, Ursa. You used to be up for anything. Where's your old sense of adventure?"

"It drowned with Maia."

Sabik looks away.

We trudge on across the fields in silence. I let him walk ahead for a while, wondering if he'll check to see if I'm following. I soon realize he won't, and I'll get in trouble if I don't complete my assignment.

Sabik stops as he reaches the trees. "The landclearer left a rough track behind it before it broke down twenty or so years ago. It's a path of sorts, but quite overgrown."

There's a gap between the trees about the width of a corridor on the *Venture*. But glowferns have reclaimed the ground, and saplings are pushing up here and there. Branches reach out from high up on the trees on either side and meet in the middle, forming a kind of tunnel.

"You're going to have to stay a lot closer if you don't want to get lost in the woods." He takes his machete out of his bag and steps onto the path.

I pause, feeling vulnerable. I rummage in my gear bag and pull out my wrench before following him. I hold it up as the woods swallow me whole.

This is worse than the path through the forest to the shuttle camp. Roots and undergrowth trip me. Thin branches reach down to try to scratch me. Glowferns swish against my ankles.

The forest either side is much deeper, more tangled. But I can see how this was a decent path once. If the landclearers had done their job, we'd have been striding down clear roads and looking out over fields ready for sowing. It would all have been so easy.

It wouldn't have saved Maia, but it would have made life down here bearable.

Maybe.

The tunnel path ahead is clear, but I can barely see a few meters to each side through the confusion of branches and trunks. There could be a creature right by us and I wouldn't see it until it was too late. Sabik glances back at me every so often as he strides along, but he looks strange as the shadows of the trees move over his face. There's an odd noise over the rustle of branches and snap of twigs underfoot. It takes me a while to work out what it is.

"Are you humming?"

"Yup."

I concentrate, and after a while the melody clicks. It's the one from the campfire. The one where they changed the words to make it all about how ridiculously fantastic the planet is.

"You still like it here?" I'm breathless as I say it.

Sabik turns around. "Am I going too fast for you?"

I want to say no, but instead I rest my hands on my knees and breathe deeply.

"I'm sorry," he says, stopping. "I should have realized. You've been on the ship this whole time. You're unfit."

I pull myself up. "I do my exercises."

He shakes his head. "Not the same as working on the planet all day. Look. You take a break. I'll tap this tree."

I lower my head, watch the glowferns around my ankles sway. "Don't you find it spooky?"

He gives a little laugh. "No. You just aren't used to it. It's a big change, but it's a good one. I love it here."

"Why?"

Sabik has his machete out. He hacks at the tree's trunk, and red liquid flows out of the black bark. I know it's just an organic polymer, bioengineered for use in the printers, but I still shudder as it trickles out like blood.

"I've always been waiting for this." He waves his bandaged hand to encompass the strangling branches of the woods. The dirt. "To be free, to have space to run."

"But it's a mess. It's all too hard and unpredictable."

"Much like life," Sabik says.

I fight the urge to slap him.

"You used to love to explore," he continues. "Back on the ship. I miss the old you."

I straighten up. "I'm still the old me on the *Venture*."

The planet turns me into someone else. Someone weak, fragile.

Sabik puts away his machete, gets out a metal bucket, and clips it onto the tree, positioning it so the red sap seeps into it. "Life is better down here. And there are more resources."

"And we could put them to good use if Cassius wasn't in so much of a hurry to settle."

Sabik shrugs. "It's not sustainable to keep running the shuttle back and forth to the *Venture*. It's a huge power drain, and we should be using that energy to build our future. We need to bring the ship down as soon as possible."

"We need time — to get used to Beta and to get the planet into better shape. We're not ready."

"Lots of us are ready. Not stuck to the old ways."

My body tenses. "The old ways worked for our ancestors for hundreds of years. Kept us going. Brought us here."

"They worked on the ship, yeah. But it's time for change. For example, on Beta we won't need to select for gender at conception anymore, so no more primas and secundas, unless that's what people actually want."

Sabik always said he only wanted one wife. That he was raised by two men who loved only each other and that monogamy was best.

Not practical, though, on a ship with two women to every man.

"And there will be flowers, soon," he says.

I stare at the ground. Sabik tried to grow me some on the ship once, hidden in the air ducts. But they never bloomed.

"Done," Sabik says, finishing fixing the bucket. "That should be full by the time we come back this way."

We start hiking again.

"So, you don't want to settle here?" He slashes at the forest.

"I do. Of course I do. But why can't we take our time?"

"Because of the axial tilt. This planet has seasons, Ursa. If we don't plant now, we won't be able to colonize for another year."

"I'm not an idiot. What's wrong with waiting a year?"

"You want to wait a whole year? Just orbiting the planet? Doing nothing?"

Fury rises in my gut. "You agricologists may have been doing nothing, but some of us have been working hard keeping the *Venture* running against all the odds, and for what? So she can be torn apart and dragged to the ground for her parts?"

Sabik stomps faster through the forest.

"Oh, we've been doing plenty," he says. "Do you know how hard it was to feed all of us? To keep the ecocarriages producing enough food as we ran low on supplies? While your father gave the engineers all the resources?"

My hands curl into fists. "He got us here. There was no other way."

Sabik pauses. When he speaks again, his tone is softer. "What I meant is not doing anything to move forward. Just waiting for our lives to start."

I'm stung. "I thought my life had started. At one point I thought I was in love."

His mouth is a straight line. "At one point."

I shake my head. "What I mean is, we had lives on the ship. Generations of us did."

"And they did it all to get us here."

"So we shouldn't throw that away by rushing the colonization and endangering people."

"Hiding from the planet isn't the answer."

"It's not hiding!"

I kick at a root that tries to trip me. I want to keep arguing, but what is there to say? He's made up his mind. Plus, I'm totally out of breath again. Instead I follow Sabik, trying to step where he steps. He's not humming anymore. There's just the rustle of wind through the trees, the pant of our breath, and the occasional thwack of the machete against a branch, eliciting a trickle of red from each severed stump. The sky slowly clears above us, and the forest feels warmer, muggier.

"Come on," Sabik says after a long time. He's going faster. I try to speed up, stumbling on tree roots. I try to follow him more closely, step in his footsteps.

"Look ahead," he adds. "It's easier that way."

I can't see anything up ahead, so I go back to focusing on the mud, and Sabik's footprints in it. It's clear other people have been this way before, probably when they were looking for the land-clearer, so there's more than one set of prints to follow. That makes it a little easier.

Or at least it does until one set breaks off from the others and heads through a gap in the foliage to my right. I stop.

Most of the footsteps remain on the path Sabik walks ahead of me, but there are marks in the mud heading through the wood to my right. Left by someone with big feet.

"Where does that path go?" I ask.

Sabik keeps walking. "There's no path there."

"Yes, there is." I peer down it. It's even narrower than the path we're on. "And someone has been down there." I point at the marks in the mud.

Sabik pauses, turns back. "Sometimes the forest does that. It's not a real path, but it can trick people. You follow them for a little while, then they peter out. It's a good way to get lost. The footsteps just mean someone has already checked it out. Come on. We're not far."

But we keep hiking through the forest for what feels like ages. Sweat trickles down my back. I'm gasping. Everything down here is a major workout. But it's dumb to be afraid of the forest now. The sun has climbed above us, and the thick branches above cast roving patches of light on the ground. It's almost pretty.

Finally, we step out into a larger space between the trees. In front of us, in the sunlit clearing, half-swallowed by vines, is the yellow bulk of a landclearer.

I don't think I've ever been so happy to see machinery before. Coming across a landclearer in the depths of the forest is like finding an oxygen tank in the vacuum of space.

I drop my gear bag and rotate my shoulders to get some of the soreness out, still gazing at the machine. It looks so bright, so solid. Nearly the size of my whole cabin back on the *Venture*.

Sabik takes in the way I'm looking at the landclearer. "Should I leave you two alone?"

"Sorry. It just looks more real than the trees. Don't you think?"

"That's because it's neon yellow. You don't get neon colors in the forest."

"I knew that," I say, even though I didn't.

Sabik hands me a water bottle. I take a long, deep drink, then I head for the landclearer and pace around it. The solar panels are covered in mud and needles. The wiper is gone. Snapped off. I'll have to order another from the printers. But for now, I pull a cloth out of my kit bag and wet it with the water bottle. I stick a foot onto the front ledge of the machine, pull myself up on a metal arm, and start scrubbing at the mud, humming a working song as I do it.

"Is that all that needs to be done? Just clean off the solar panel? I could have done that."

"I don't know." I'm slightly out of breath as I speak, chest pushed against the outer casing as I scrape off the dirt. "We'll find out once the battery has had time to charge."

The mud comes off easily, already damp from the recent rain. It only takes a few sweeps until the panel is clear enough to collect the light.

"Now," I say, as I step back down, "we wait."

Sabik nods. But then there's an odd sound from above us. Tuneless high notes.

We both look up. For a second, I'm terrified. I take a step closer to Sabik. Is it the *Venture*? What could have happened to her? But it's too quiet, too close.

Then they dart out above us, above the trees, in a V shape. I duck, covering my head, peering up from under my crossed arms. Dozens and dozens of miniature brown shuttles flying over us. It takes me a moment to clue in.

Birds.

The first release. Of course. It's just small birds now, ones that feed on the bugs and plants sent by the seeding ships.

Good. Maybe they can eat the fly that was bothering me last night.

I straighten up, let my shoulders relax, and watch properly. The birds zoom over us, as if delighting in their new freedom. Hundreds of them, spreading out, colonizing the woods. And there are new sounds now: tweets, rustles in the trees. My mouth falls open.

"Wow," I say.

"Yeah. That sums it up." Sabik is grinning like an idiot. But for once, it feels appropriate.

"Try to imagine what it's going to be like, Ursa. We'll have chickens in a couple of days. Fresh eggs! You haven't begun to see how this planet will look." He waves a hand at the forest. "Rabbits, squirrels, and wild boar in the woods. Fish shimmering in the water. Cows and chickens in the farms. Full food chains, everywhere."

I shudder a little. They're experimenting with eggs, as chickens are sustainable with all this space, but they're not planning to reintroduce meat into our generation's diet. I know they ate it on Alpha, but it's an inefficient energy source, so we never had it on the ship. And I'm fine with that. Who wants to eat corpses?

Reminded of my hunger, I pull the mealpack from my bag.

"Is it okay if I stick with this for now?"

Sabik laughs. "Sure. Let's have a picnic. I know a better place than this, and if we're lucky, we can grab some more food on the way. Follow me."

He's back in the trees before I can stop him or ask where we're meant to get food. So I shove my mealpack back into my bag and scramble after him. Fortunately, he's going slower now — partly because there's no path here, and partly because he stops every few steps and checks at his feet. A couple of times he bends over, pulls up a patch of the undergrowth with his good hand, and shoves it in his bag.

We have to push our way through branches as the forest grows darker around us. Climb over raised roots. I can see why they engineered the glowferns. It makes it easier to see where you're going, but it casts a sinister light on my legs, and I can't help checking around me for any glimpse of teeth among the branches.

I'm just about to ask Sabik if we can go back when there's a strange hiss. At first, I barely catch it over my own breath. I think it's the wind picking up, but there's no change in the breeze on my skin, and it's getting louder, clearer, changing into a splashing, bubbling noise. There's more light ahead as the trees thin, and then we step out of the forest, and there, a few paces ahead of us, is a river.

It's shallow — about knee deep — and large rocks peek out. The gurgling, rushing noise sounds as if the water is talking to us. Laughing at us.

Sabik spreads his arms wide, proudly.

"Is it safe?"

"We're not going swimming. We're fine."

"What about flash floods? They told us to stay away from the rivers in case of flash floods."

"Those only happen after heavy rain or a sudden thaw."

I stare at the water. The sunlight skims over the surface, glittering like knives. There's no ice now. It's warmed up a lot since Maia died. But still, I take a step back.

"Can't we go somewhere else?"

"You used to like visiting the water."

"Not since they found her body."

Sabik's eyes go wide. "Sorry. I should have thought."

"You know it's not safe. Are you trying to kill me?"

"Ursa, it's okay. We'll stay back from the water."

But words are pouring out of me. "What were you thinking? The whole planet is unsafe. Look at your hand. And what about

Seginus or Perseus? What about Orion? We're not ready for this. It's too dangerous."

"Of course there's danger. But that's true of everywhere, even the *Venture*. I love this planet."

"So did Maia. And it killed her."

"I really am sorry, Ursa. This isn't the lake where Maia died. That's why I didn't think. But I shouldn't have brought you here."

Sabik does look sorry. I might have gotten a bit worked up. And for a moment I feel the distance between us like an ache. I didn't realize how much I missed him.

"We can go back to the landclearer," Sabik says, "if you'd rather eat there."

I pause. Sabik's right. I used to be brave. I can barely remember those days. Is this who I want to be? What would Maia think of me now? In, out. I focus on slowing my breathing. Feel the sun on my skin. Watch the rush and ripple of the water over the stones. There's no ice. We're safe here.

"Maia would have liked the river," I say, finally.

"Yes. I think she would have."

"Okay. Let's stay."

Sabik points out a couple of large rocks, a good distance from the water's edge. "Those will be comfortable."

I swallow my fear and follow him. He takes the smaller of the two rocks, and I sit on the larger. The gray stone is warm from the sun. I keep taking deep breaths. In, out. After a while, my heart slows down to its normal rhythm.

I'm hungry, so it's good we don't have to hike back to the landclearer before I can eat. I open my mealpack and am about to take out my sandwich when Sabik holds up his bandaged hand.

"Wait," he says, reaching into his bag with his good hand. He pulls out some of the undergrowth he grabbed on the way here. He slides off his rock and heads for a little patch of green at the water's edge.

I hold my breath when he moves close to the rushing river, but his footing is sure. He takes a handful of the plants, then plunges them into the water and shakes the droplets from them.

"Cold!" He shivers as he walks back. "Chuck me your meal-pack."

"Why?"

"Trust me."

I put the lid back on and am about to toss it to Sabik. I automatically check if I'm facing toward or against the rotation of the ship, to compensate for the Coriolis effect. Then I remember I'm on the planet, and we have real gravity here.

I will never get used to all these differences.

I pass the pack to Sabik's good hand. He balances it on his knees, produces a knife, chops up half the greenery, and sprinkles it on my salad. He shoves some of the water plant into my sandwich and puts a brown-gray lump next to it.

"There you go." He holds the pack back out to me. I stare at it.

"Is that stuff okay to eat?"

"It's better than the stuff grown on board. It's all been genetically engineered for us. This is just what we can find in early spring. Wait until summer and autumn, when these trees will be filled with fruit."

I take the pack from him. Lift up my sandwich and peer at the leaves sticking out on top of the beige tofu patty.

"Why is it green?"

"It gets the full spectrum of light here, not like the UV in the ecocarriages. With the sun, we don't need to worry about saving energy."

It's not natural. Salad is meant to be purple. But I watch Sabik take his own food, add his plants, and start eating. I try a bite.

It tastes clean. Slightly bitter, almost spicy. It offsets the bland sliminess of the tofu patty. I devour my sandwich and turn to the salad. There are little green bits on top of the usual limp purple lettuce and soy sprinkles.

"What's this?" I point at it.

"Green onions and parsley," he mumbles through a mouthful of sandwich.

I place a pinch on my tongue. There's a bite to the salad now. A flavor that fills my mouth. I close my eyes, taste the tang of the onions, the crunch of the parsley. Fresh and cold. Like the water here, like the air.

"And that?" I point my fork at the brown-gray lump in the mealpack.

"It's a Beta morel," he says. "A type of mushroom."

It doesn't look like the mushrooms we grow on the *Venture*. It's wrinkly. I cut a piece off, place it on my tongue, and chew. It's slimy and tastes like dirt. I spit it out.

"They're better cooked," Sabik says.

"I certainly hope so."

Sabik laughs, and I find myself smiling at him. I take another bite of my salad.

"It's astonishing, Ursa. Just being here. Humanity, stretching out into the stars. We're the dream Alpha Earth had so many hundreds of years ago."

My mouth is full, so I just nod.

"Look," Sabik says, pointing to a patch near the stream.

There's movement. I tense, but it's a tiny bird. Its wings are pressed by its sides. It's hopping around, exploring its new world. It moves with an odd twitching, bouncing motion. Bursts of fast movement between stillness.

"Watch this." Sabik lifts up a piece of his bread, crumbles it in his fingers, and throws it on the ground to the side of us.

"I could have eaten that, if you didn't want it."

The bird tilts its head with little jerks to look at us and the bread. Then it begins to hop forward. It pauses, uncertain, then pecks at the bread again and again.

"With practice, we can get them to eat from our hands," Sabik says.

That doesn't sound smart. The bird's beak looks sharp.

Once it's eaten Sabik's food, its wings flutter and it takes off, hurling itself into the air. I watch as it becomes just a dot in the vast blue above us.

I don't think I'll ever get used to the clear blue sky. It's too blank. Unbelievably huge. I feel like I could be sucked up into its depths. Gravity is only a matter of perspective, after all. Being born and raised on a starship teaches you that.

"I guess we should get back to work," Sabik says.

I turn away from the bright sky. It takes my eyes a moment to adjust. He stands and brushes his good hand off against his leg. To my surprise, I find I'm a little disappointed to leave the river. Sabik refills our water bottles and we set off.

Once we get back to the landclearer, I clamber onto the machine and swipe away as many of the vines as I can until I can get to the reset switch. I hit it, but it doesn't react, although it's had enough time to recharge. I open the side hatch and lean in. I unscrew the main engine cover. A vine has grown up from the ground, found its way in through a gap in the bottom of the casing, and wrapped itself around the motherboard, corroding it. I'll need to get another printed and recycle this one. The main casing will need some mending too, like most of the landclearers. But that's best done on the *Venture*, and the easiest way to get it to the shuttle is a temporary fix, enough for it to cut its own way out of the forest.

The blades will need sharpening first, so I unscrew them. I pull out some rope from my gear bag and bind them into a bundle. I make a loop at the top. They're light, like most of the stuff sent by the seeding ships, and will be easy to carry.

I slap the side of the landclearer as I jump back off it.

"I'll print the parts and get the blades sharpened tomorrow, and we can get this up and running the next day and get it back to the *Venture* for a proper fix."

Sabik grins. "A good day's work, then. We can head back to the camp."

"I'm in no hurry. I have my first interview session with Cassius this evening."

"It probably won't be as bad as you think." He heads toward the trees.

"Not so fast, please."

"Do you want me to carry the blades?"

"Don't be ridiculous." I point at his bandaged hand. "You're more in need of help than I am. I just want you to go a bit slower."

And he does go slower. Slow enough for me to look around more. There's the occasional bird. A flutter in the branches making me jump. The buzz of insects. No teeth, thank Beta. No large bulk pushing through the trees. But it's such a huge planet. It could be anywhere in this tangled mess. Or it could all have been my imagination.

We've been walking for an hour when Sabik speeds up. I find myself panting as I match his pace. I trip on a root and have to focus on the ground again. Step in Sabik's footsteps.

"What's the sudden hurry?"

"I don't want you to be late and get into trouble with Cassius," he says. "Look! Another bird."

He gestures at a tree in front and to the right, and I squint at it. He's right. It's a tiny brown bird that darts away through the forest as we approach. But we've seen several in the last hour, and this one is the same as all the others.

I peer back over my shoulder, looking closely at the mud. Yes. One set of large footprints leads away from us, between a gap in the trees. It's the path I noticed earlier. Was that deliberate? Did Sabik point out the bird as a distraction?

I turn to face forward and stare at his back. He's slowed down again, no longer speeding through the forest. And then I'm sure. He raced me through that area, and he distracted me. He didn't want me to see that path again.

Sabik is lying to me.

My stomach is tight. We used to be totally honest with each other. Even though we broke up, I thought I could trust him. What's he hiding? And why?

There were never any secrets on the *Venture*. There was no space for them. I feel the distance then, stretching between Sabik and I. Stretching between all of the crew. The cracks between us are widening. But I know what I have to do.

I have to come back here and investigate. Alone.

CHAPTER 7

The shadows are lengthening when we step out of the forest, and the gentle luminescence of the glowferns is more noticeable as Beta's sun sinks. I exhale as we leave the trees behind. There are lights on in the little village, guiding us back across the fields. I'm glad for that. The trees all look the same. The fields all look the same. I'm not sure if I could find my way back without those lights.

As we reach the camp, the breeze brings a familiar smell. Vegetable stew, although it's just a bit different. A little sharper, warmer. It must be the air itself that's changing the smell. The scent of the pines mingling with the mundane and making it strange. There are lights on in the canteen hut, and the murmur of voices and staccato sound of laughter beckon from inside.

"Do you want to join me and the agricologists at dinner?" Sabik asks.

There's the hot gnawing of hunger in my stomach, but I check my linkcom.

"Nope. It's time for me to see He Who Must Be Obeyed."

Sabik makes a clicking noise with his tongue. "Give Cassius a chance."

I just turn away. Sabik's lying to me about that path. So why should I listen to his advice? Plus, I need to mentally prepare. The captain and Vega think I'm involved in Orion's death. I'm not giving Cassius ammunition to use against me in a trial. I know my rights. I only have to answer his questions honestly. I don't have to spill my guts to him.

I head away from the main square and the comfort of the canteen hut and trudge through the shadows to the captain's hut. That one's easy to identify, at least. It's finished, unlike everyone else's. There are solar panels on top. As I get close, the door swings open. Warmth comes from inside.

Must be nice to have a heated hut.

"Right on time. Come on in, Ursa," Cassius says. He's smiling that fake smile of his. I take a deep breath and slouch past him into the hut.

It's not that different from my family's cabin, although there's no bed. A wooden storage chest is in use as a table, with a small lamp from the *Venture* that casts a warm light. There are two wooden seats, one either side of the chest. It smells of vegetable stew in here too. Great. I'm going to spend the whole meeting being taunted by my stomach.

Then I notice the two mealpacks, one next to each seat. Generous servings, too.

Cassius gestures to the chair furthest from the door. "I thought you'd be hungry," he says.

I slump down into the seat. It's more comfortable than it looks. Not cold, like the metal benches of the *Venture*. I reach for the food. Cassius takes the seat opposite and runs a hand through his salt-and-pepper hair, making it stand up in all directions. He picks up his own stew and shovels some into his mouth.

"What do you think?" he says, once he's swallowed.

I wonder what he's talking about. Vegetable stew has been part of the meal rotation for hundreds of years before I was born. It's fine. It's fuel.

But then I put a forkful in my mouth, and I understand.

It wasn't the air of Beta making the food smell different. It is different. Like the changes Sabik made to my lunch, the taste is more complex. There's a new warmth to it. Something that brings out the individual flavor of each of the components — the carrots, the potatoes, the beans — makes them sharper, stronger.

I can't help myself. "Mmmm," I say. "What is it?"

"A few things, actually. More salt, some early herbs that are starting to come up, wild garlic, and green onions. Now that we don't have to worry about space to grow, we can plan meals around flavor, not just nutrition."

I continue eating. It is good. But I know what Cassius is trying to do here. And if he thinks all this will get me to drop my guard, he's wrong.

"Ready to talk?" he asks.

I swallow a mouthful. "I'm here, aren't I?"

He pauses, fork partway to his mouth. "Ursa, I'm not your enemy."

I shrug. "You're investigating Orion's death, and your daughter all but accused me of it."

"I have to investigate everyone."

I dig my fork into the stew. "Even Vega?"

"Of course, even Vega." He takes a bite of his food, chews it, then swallows. "I will be impartial in this."

I can't contain a snort.

Cassius tilts his head. "Perhaps we should talk about Vega, then. That may be a good place to start. You used to be friends, didn't you?"

"Is this anything to do with Orion's death?"

"Please answer the question."

I shovel more stew into my mouth, to delay.

"You fell out because you didn't like Orion, correct?" He picks up his fork again. Digs into his stew. "You blamed him for Maia's death."

"He waited half an hour before he started the search. He was negligent. He should have been disciplined."

Cassius sighs. "We went through this months ago. She probably died right away. Cold shock response."

"You don't know that for sure."

"So you felt betrayed when Vega married Orion."

I stare at the stew, not wanting to eat, not wanting to talk. I was hoping Vega would be there for me after Maia died. I needed friends. I needed her.

But she announced her engagement instead.

"I told her to choose between being friends with me and marrying him. She chose him."

Cassius tilts his head again. "Can I tell you a bit about my daughter?"

I examine his face, but it's hard to read, so I shrug.

"Vega has always been so proud, but she's not comfortable, socially. She doesn't make friends easily." He pauses as if he's thinking. "Do you know how she felt about children?"

I give a dry laugh. "She'd go crazy over babies. Wouldn't stop going on about how they were going to lift the breeding restrictions on Beta."

Cassius shifts in his seat. "And ... how can I put this? What was your impression of how the male crew members viewed her?"

I look at Cassius for a minute to see if he's serious. He meets my gaze, eyebrows slightly raised, waiting for my answer.

"It's like you said. She doesn't make friends easily."

"That's not what I meant. How would you describe her attractiveness? How she looks?"

I just stare. I've never thought about it. "I ... I ... she's Vega. She looks like Vega."

Cassius leans back in his chair. "My daughter has many good qualities, Ursa. But she is not conventionally attractive. And young men find it hard to look past appearance."

I open my mouth and close it again. I've never thought of her as beautiful, that's true. Her left eye is bit smaller than her right, and I know she hates the bump in her nose. But she's strong, and since she's been down on the planet, freckles have broken out over her tawny cheeks. They suit her.

"What do you think her choices were when Orion asked her?"

Now I think about it, he's right: the boys weren't lining up for her. I remember her saying she envied me, because Sabik and I were happy together, back then.

I see what he's getting at, although I note he's been careful not to come out and say it. Perhaps she didn't think she had any other options when Orion asked her.

The vegetable stew churns in my stomach.

"She could have had children on her own," I point out. But even I know the answer to that. She wanted a family. Not just a child.

"You should talk to her," Cassius says. "I think she'd still like to be your friend. She's been through a lot. First her brother was injured and now she's lost her husband. And she's more fragile than she looks."

"How ... how is Perseus?"

"It's not good. It's unlikely he'll walk again. My son will need all the resources we can give him for a long while." He exhales, heavily, then looks at me. "Don't think I don't know how dangerous this planet can be."

His eyes are fierce. I can't hold his gaze, so I look down to the chest between us.

"But if we weren't on Beta, he'd have faced the Exit," Cassius says.

That's true. The *Venture* can only support a limited number of crew, and all adults have to work. For four hundred years those who were injured or too old were euthanized.

"But if we weren't on Beta, he wouldn't have been injured," I say.

"We didn't value people on the *Venture,*" Cassius says, ignoring my comment. "We threw away lives, people like my son. But here, on the planet, we have the freedom to recognize them for more than their physical ability. We can recognize their value as people."

We sit in silence for a few long moments, until Cassius runs a hand over his forehead, pushing his messy hair back. "I'll be frank. I arranged these interviews because I need your help. We have a fear problem."

"What do you mean?"

"It's a huge adjustment, coming down to the planet. Deeply stressful for the crew. But we have to get used to it."

I slump back in my chair. Here comes the lecture.

"Most of the colonists are enthusiastic." He sighs. "But a few were scared of the sky, of the space. A large group moved back to the *Venture* after the first thunderstorm, and it took weeks to bring them back. People don't deal with change well. They're afraid."

"How many people?"

Cassius gives an odd laugh. "Pretty much all of them, to a greater or lesser extent. Me included."

"You?"

He meets my gaze again, his expression soft. "Of course. I have to keep them alive. That's terrifying."

"But in the hearing ..."

"I can't stoke that fear. For better or worse, this is our home. I haven't wanted to push people to come down here, but since you spoke, people have started canceling their shifts on Beta. Making excuses to stay on the *Venture*."

"I just told the truth. Isn't that the right thing to do? Shouldn't we take our time?"

"Dragging out the colonization is making things worse. The sooner we initiate Betafall, the better. The ship wasn't designed for long-term orbit."

"She's stronger than you think. She's got multiple redundancies in her systems. Look at the shuttle — it was meant for a few recon trips, but they built it to last anyway."

"The power drain of the shuttle trips is unsustainable. We can't keep up this many flights. And the delay is tearing the crew apart. We don't want to end up like the *Venture 2*."

I swallow. Our sister ship launched almost a hundred years after we did. But it was faster, closing the gap so it would arrive just twenty years after us. Like the first generations on the *Venture*, they found it hard to adjust to the small spaces, limited resources, and shorter lifespans on board. But unlike on our ship, thirty years into the *Venture 2*'s flight, some of their crew rebelled, built weapons out of engineering equipment, and tried to hijack the ship. They wanted to turn around, to return to the comforts of Alpha. The rest of the ship disagreed and fought back.

The last communication we received from the *Venture 2* was cut off by an explosion and short-lived screams.

A tiny flame of humanity, snuffed out in seconds.

Things changed after that. The launch of the *Venture 3* was cancelled, and communication with Alpha was minimized in case it might cause an uprising on our ship too. There wasn't much point anyway. By the end of our journey it took over thirty years for a message to reach them, and the same time for a reply. A conversation is a decade longer than an average *Venture* lifespan. According to the latest news they have, my father isn't even captain yet and supplies are so scarce we're not sure if we'll reach Beta. It'll be thirty years before Alpha knows we made it.

"It's my fault," Cassius says. "Some delay was inevitable, since we had to clear space for the carriages. But I decided to stay in orbit for a while, give people time to adjust." He shakes his head and drops his gaze. "It caused a deeper schism. Made people feel there was another option." He exhales. "Now they're scared of this 'creature,' too. I need you to help me calm them down."

I fold my arms. "I'm not lying for you."

"I'm not asking you to lie. I'm asking you to help me get to the bottom of this. I want the full details. But away from the rest of the colonists. Let's talk about this without causing more of a panic."

"You want the truth? Really?"

"Yes. Start at the beginning," he says. "At the campfire. How were you feeling?"

"I was giving it a try. I really was. The fire was nice."

He picks up on my unspoken word. "But ...?"

I shake my head, and then the words tumble out.

"It's just ... the glowferns reminded me of the day Maia died. And the songs have changed. And it was dark, and not like home, the noises were weird and ..."

I stop. It sounds idiotic when I say it all out loud.

"None of this is anything to be ashamed of, Ursa. The changes you have faced in the last few months are huge. I think you were brave."

A little laugh slips out. "Brave?"

"You took a landbike through the woods alone, in spite of your discomfort. That is brave."

"I didn't feel brave."

But he smiles. "Tell me what you saw in the forest."

"I heard something first." It seems so clear now. That noise I didn't recognize. "It sounded like the twist of metal, but it must have been a scream. Orion's scream."

Cassius's lips are pressed together.

"It wasn't long after that I thought I saw it. Just a flash in the dark. Sharp teeth and dark fur. Big. Maybe chest height on me."

"Be as specific as you can. How many teeth? Was the mouth open or closed?"

I try to concentrate. But I can't grasp the image, can't make it solid. It slips from my memory like smoke from the bonfire.

"It was only a second. And it was dark. I did hear breathing for a little longer, though."

"Even over the wind?"

"Yes."

Cassius leans back. "You're an engineer, Ursa. What do you think about what you saw? What would you think if anyone else had seen it?"

"I'd think they imagined it. I'd think they had the big bad wolf on the brain after the bonfire."

"But what do you really think?"

I rub my forehead. "I'm not sure. I could have imagined it. I ... it just seemed real."

Cassius nods. "You obviously saw something, but it's possible your brain changed it into the horror that was already on your mind. Or the killer wore a disguise."

A disguise is possible. Something could be made by the printers. It would make more sense than a creature on an uninhabited planet. But that would also make the killer one of the crew. Someone I've known my whole life. That doesn't feel right.

Cassius leans forward. "It's obvious to me that you didn't kill Orion. You're too smart to try to cover it up with an impossible story."

A weight lifts from me. I lean back in the chair. Exhale.

"But something happened to Orion. And there will be clues in what you saw. The truth is buried in your memory. We need to go into this further." Cassius checks his watch. "But it's late now. We'll meet again, same time tomorrow."

"Okay," I manage. I am tired. And wrung out, too. I have a lot to process.

"Tomorrow, then. Together we can work out what — or more likely, who — was really in the forest that night."

CHAPTER 8

I head back to the hut in darkness, dizzy with new information, mind spinning from one thing to another. It takes me a little while to get to the cabin as I get turned around and head in the wrong direction. I curse under my breath. If I can't even find my way around the village, how am I going to navigate a whole planet?

I wish I had someone to talk to, but I know Mom won't be home until the morning.

The hut is too big and empty. So much wasted space, enough for several sets of bunks. There's a warm, sweet smell from the cut wood, but I don't like the way the planks creak when I walk. It's creepy, like someone following me around the room. It's a relief to climb into bed and have the hut fall silent.

I can't hear anything from the other huts. On the ship, you could catch snatches of conversation through the vents, and it travelled fast as light through the corridors in the form of gossip. There were no secrets on the *Venture*.

I used to think that was a bad thing. I didn't realize how much that kept us safe. We knew what everyone else was doing. Problems were caught early. On the planet, anyone could be doing anything.

Anyone could be a killer. Spaces are opening between us; our society is fracturing. Maybe the bonds among the crew aren't strong enough to hold over the new distance.

I lie awake for a while, trying to hear the familiar murmur of voices. But there's only the unintelligible whisper of the breeze. Eventually I close my eyes and slip into confused dreams of Vega, Orion, and someone familiar dressed as a big bad wolf.

I WAKE DISORIENTED. JOLT up straight in bed, mentally fumbling for something familiar. There's only a vague gray light from the crack around the edge of the window, and I struggle to visualize the room, force the dark lumps of furniture to make sense, as my heart pounds. Then it clicks, and I'm in the hut, down on Beta.

I breathe deeply. Swallow down the fear. I'm wide awake now.

I reach for my linkcom and check the time. It'll be dawn soon, so I push off the blanket and shiver as the cold air hits my skin. I turn on the linkcom's light, use it to find some clean clothes in my chest, and pull them on. What now?

I swing open the hinged wooden panel that serves as a window and see the sky.

It's lighter now and turning pink and purple. I stare for a long few seconds. It's unlike anything I've seen. Colors smeared across the world. I head to the hut door and push it open. I've never seen the sunrise before. Not properly. Every other morning I've been here, it's been too cloudy. It just went from dark gray to light gray. This is something else.

It's in layers, brighter nearer the horizon, and it edges the gray clouds with copper.

The mud is dry today. Easier to walk on. I step away from my cabin, until the sky is clearer, stretching out all above me. It still feels too wide. The first time I stepped out under the huge dome of atmosphere, I felt it might crush me. If Maia hadn't been holding my hand, I'd have run straight back into the shuttle. It was beautiful, yes, but beauty on an inhuman scale, oppressive in its limitless.

Today, it feels almost weightless. Just above the trees glows the vivid orange of molten metal, so I can tell where the sun will rise. The sky itself is lilac. So many colors, merging into each other. The colors from the bonfire cast in the air.

I'm staring so much, I don't notice Mom approach until she's almost reached me, trudging over the ground from our makeshift hospital, shoulders rounded with fatigue.

"Ursa," she says. "What are you doing up so early? How did the interview go?"

I just shake my head and point at the sky behind her. She peers back, over her shoulder, then turns to me.

"Yes," she says. "Gorgeous, isn't it?"

But I can tell by her glance, the way she took it in so quickly, that she's already used to it, both the size and the richness of the spectacle. That she's seen dawns like this many times in the three months I've been hiding on board the *Venture*. What else have I missed?

Mom turns back to me. I see her weariness lift a little at my expression. She smiles, comes over, puts her arm around my shoulder, and watches the sunrise with me.

"It is amazing, isn't it?" she says. "Thank you for reminding me."

It feels better with her next to me. Her touch grounds me against the celestial display. We stand that way until the star crests the horizon and it's too bright to watch anymore. It's nice to have a moment together. But it's clear she's exhausted, leaning her weight on me.

"You should get to bed," I say.

"But let's make some mother-daughter time. I've got an afternoon shift, so maybe this evening?"

"I'm meeting with Cassius again."

"After your meeting, then?"

"I'd like that."

"Me too." Mom gives me a hug, then tramps back toward our cabin.

I head to the printing hut to start the day's work. I program the printers for the parts to fix the motherboard and wipers. There's a backlog on the machines, probably because they've been wasting time making toys, so I move on to sharpening the landclearer blades and a couple of quick fixes to landbikes and construction equipment. The morning speeds by, and it's soon midday. I take my break, timing it so I can meet the shuttle as it arrives from the *Venture*.

I climb on a landbike, gun the engine, and steer toward the shuttle camp.

I accelerate along the forest path, wind in my short hair. There's plenty of zap in this bike, so I speed up as fast as I dare, braking on the corners, leaning into the turns. The speed is fantastic. Even I have to admit there's nothing like this on the *Venture*. The black trees are a blur as I speed past. And the light of the glowferns is too dim to be seen in the bright sun. It seems ridiculous to imagine a creature in the woods today.

"Maybe I am going crazy," I mutter to Maia. "Oh man, you'd find this so funny." I pause. "But if I imagined the creature, who killed Orion?"

I'm still wondering when I pull up at the runway. But the spectacle of the shuttle's landing clears it from my mind. It's just a speck, at first, in the distance. It could be mistaken for one of the birds Sabik and I saw. But it gets closer, bigger, more real every moment, finally touching down and braking gently, until its white bulk is safely still on the runway.

It's good to have the shuttle back on Beta. There's a way back now, until the next launch. A link to my home in the stars.

Even better, Astra and Celeste are on board.

They're among the first to disembark, and they head right for me. I run to meet them. Celeste's face is tearstained, and as I reach her, she wraps her arms around me. I hold her tight, until her stomach lurches against me. We pull apart, and both look down at her bump.

"You felt that, didn't you?" Celeste asks. And she's smiling.

I just nod, baffled at the sensation. There's a creature inside her. A new human. It's weird.

Then Astra leans in, and she hugs me too.

"I'm so glad to see you," she says. "It's not right, you not being on the *Venture*. How have you been?"

"Okay." I turn back to Celeste. "How are you doing?"

"I'm ... well, I think it'll be best if I get back to work. As soon as possible."

Astra bites her lip. It's clear she disagrees.

Celeste stares at me for a moment, clearly wanting to say something.

"Celeste? What is it?"

"Did you really see something in the woods?" she asks in a rush.

Deep breath. "I'm not so sure now. There could be another explanation."

Astra tilts her head. "But you seemed certain, in the engine room."

"I know. I'm sorry."

Astra puts a gentle hand on my arm. "Don't be too quick to give up your truths, Ursa. I know this planet can be confusing. Be honest with yourself, and let everything come from there."

"Ursa!" Another voice, and we all turn to look. Jovan comes out of the shuttle and bounds down the steps. "I was hoping you'd be here. Are you on break?"

I just nod, tongue-tied. He looks good in his red landsuit. On everyone else it's puffy, making them look weirdly lumpy. But on him, it emphasizes his chest, his strong shoulders. His face is solemn, though, so I pull myself together.

"I was going to visit Maia's grave. You said you'd like to come, right?"

"Um … I …" I look at Celeste.

"I'm fine. I've got Mom."

"Great," Jovan says. "Give me a second. I'll let the geneticists know I'm taking a break." He starts striding away, back toward the shuttle.

"Jovan," Astra calls out. "How are you holding up?" She shakes her head. "I don't think he heard. Back in a minute."

I nod, and Astra hurries after Jovan.

"So, it went well with Cassius?" Celeste asks, rubbing her belly.

"Yeah. He's okay. Maybe I was wrong about a few things."

"Like?"

"Perhaps I've been unfair to Vega."

Celeste's hair blows in her eyes. She pushes it behind her ears with both hands, making her face look wide, puffy from the tears. "Vega?"

"I hadn't thought about things from her point of view. How much she wanted to have children …" I trail off. Celeste is staring at me. Breathing in and out as if she's gearing herself up to something.

"What is it?" I ask.

"It's about … about Orion." She's almost whispering. She pushes her hair behind her ears again, even though it was already in place. "I … you'd tell me, wouldn't you? I mean, I know you wouldn't have done anything deliberately. But if there was an accident, the landbike or something …"

My eyes widen. "Wait. You think I did something to Orion?"

"No! I just … I love you, Ursa. I mean, I know you didn't like him, and you're still heartbroken over Maia. You're my sister, no matter what."

"Celeste. I did not hurt your husband. I swear."

She drops her eyes to the smooth ground of the runway. Exhales. My immediate instinct is to be mad at her, but tears are already slipping out between her dark eyelashes.

"Sorry, Ursa. People say things. I've not been sleeping. I had to ask."

"People? What people?"

She rubs her eyes on her sleeve. "I shouldn't have let them get to me. It's just been tough."

I sigh.

She takes my hands. "Please don't be mad at me. It's good to have you down here. I've missed you."

"Yeah. I missed you too, sis." I glance at Jovan, now deep in conversation with Astra next to the shuttle. "I could come with you now if you need me. I don't have to go with Jovan."

A sniff. "You should visit the graveyard. Choose a good spot for ... for ..."

"Oh, Celeste." I move in again and hug her. She quivers for a moment with silent sobs. Then she pulls away and wipes her face on her sleeve again, adding to the trails of tears and snot on the wrist of her landsuit.

Astra approaches with Jovan. "I'll take care of her," she says, and puts an arm around her daughter's shoulders, leading her away from the runway.

Jovan joins me, and we watch them go. "It's awful," he says. "I mean, she's got the baby coming soon. It's so terrible this happened to her. But this planet ..."

His words hang in the air for a moment. Then he takes a deep breath.

"Come on. Let's go see my sister."

"Okay." I steel myself. "Which way?"

Jovan gestures toward a small path at the side of the runway leading off into the woods.

"Not too far. Just through the trees."

He starts walking, and I scurry to keep up until he reaches the tree line. He pauses at the start of the path, staring between the branches, wary.

"Are you okay?" I ask.

Jovan straightens up. "Just getting used to the woods, you know."

"Yeah. I know."

He nods. "Let's go."

Jovan walks slower than Sabik. He's less sure of his step, even though this path is clearer, more recently made. That's good, because I don't have to rush to keep up. The forest gets thicker around us. Branches to either side of us, glowferns beneath them. But the path is clear, and wide enough that there's blue sky above us.

Jovan jerks his gaze around at every sound. At the chirp of the birds and the rustle of branches in the breeze. But soon light appears between the dark trunks ahead, and we step out into a cleared area of land.

The ground is muddy and flat, scarred with soil in heaps where tree trunks have been ripped out. There are two mounds, right in the middle, one slightly smaller than the other.

A whole graveyard with only two occupants.

"It's bigger than I thought it would be," I say, staring at the bald mud around us.

"Room to expand," Jovan says. "What does that tell you?"

"That we're all going to die eventually?"

"Then why did they make it a priority to clear the space now? Ready for many bodies. Soon. Cassius knew Maia's and Seginus's deaths were only the beginning." Jovan starts pacing, up and down.

"Cassius knows the planet is dangerous."

Jovan's jaw clenches and releases. "And he's just accepted that? Unavoidable fatalities?"

"It sounds bad when you say it like that."

"It is bad. Cassius is sentencing many of us to death." Jovan kicks at a lump of dried mud. "He's convinced half the ship that there's no other way. That we just have to accept more deaths like Maia's."

I stare at the space around us, trying not to think of how many people would need to die to fill it. How many people I care about will end up under this cold earth.

Jovan moves toward the smaller of the two mounds. I follow, swallowing hard. Somewhere below that wet mud is Maia. It's wrong. She shouldn't be here, trapped under dirt. She should have been broken down, fed back into the system, used by the ecocarriages to keep us all going. The energy stored in her cells, Maia's irrepressible energy, should have been recycled back through the ship, through us, enriching the whole system.

Instead, she's here. Wasted. Swallowed whole by the earth, and with nothing to show for it. Not even a plant in the bare ground.

A leaf blows across my feet. This isn't the right way to think of her.

"She never stopped talking about you," Jovan says, then he gives a little laugh. "Used to drive me up the wall, sometimes. But now I'm glad. Having you here is like having a piece of Maia still around."

We stand together at Maia's graveside. He reaches a hand out to me. I take it. His skin is warm, and I clutch his fingers tightly. He squeezes back, almost too hard, then he glances around, as if afraid of being overheard, and leans in close.

"And ... look. There's something important. But I'm not supposed to talk about it. Section confidentiality and all that."

His eyes dart around again. I don't blame him for hesitating.

You don't betray section confidentiality. And the genetics section has lots of confidential information about the crew.

"We did the DNA analysis. On Orion's body."

"You found my DNA on him."

"And something else."

"Some*thing*?"

Another furtive look. "Yes. The sample size was small. We were only able to sequence fragments. But it's not human. And it doesn't match anything in the databases."

His closeness and the shock of his words mute me. After a few long seconds, I get control of myself. "Alien? But that's not possible."

"You're right, it shouldn't be."

Maybe I didn't imagine it, then. Dizziness sweeps through me. "Does Cassius know?"

"Yes, but he wants us to run the tests again. He thinks it was a mistake with the DNA amplification process."

"Could he be right?"

Jovan shrugs. "It's possible. Cassius says it's obviously an error, and that releasing the information would panic people and distract from the search for a human killer."

My voice is rising. "But if there is something —"

"Shh." Jovan looks around, although we're all on our own. "This is supposed to be confidential. I'd get in so much trouble if anyone found out I told you."

"We have to warn people."

"I wish we could, but I told you. It comes under section confidentiality."

I squeeze my eyes shut. This is so frustrating. Knowing this and not being able to do anything about it.

"We're settling this planet too fast. More people are going to die. We must do everything in our power to slow this down. Keep people safe," Jovan says.

"Maybe you could say something," I say. "Pretend you saw the creature in the forest. Section confidentiality wouldn't cover that."

He shakes his head quickly. "Everyone knows I'm no fan of the planet. Of the rush Cassius is in to settle it. They wouldn't believe me."

I must be out of the loop. I didn't know any of that. "Then what do we do?"

Jovan puts a hand on my shoulder. "You trust yourself. Don't let anyone mislead you. Someone else will see it soon."

I feel like my stomach is in a vise. "But other people could get hurt before then."

He moves away, stares at his sister's grave. "People are already getting hurt. Look at Zaniah."

Zaniah got frostbite after she got lost in the woods. She needed new fingers.

Jovan continues. "She could have frozen to death. Just being outside can be deadly."

"But the creature's different. It's not meant to be here. Maybe Cassius will be reasonable if the second tests confirm it."

"I wish I could believe it."

"I'll talk to Mom. She's on the executive. To Astra. To anyone who'll listen. Tell them I am sure, now. That I did see a creature."

Jovan nods, sighs. "Thank you, Ursa. Thank you so much."

I stare at the bare mound of Maia's grave.

"I should get back to the shuttle," Jovan says, after a while. "We're launching in an hour."

I wish I could go with him. Head home tonight, instead of sleeping down here.

"But it's been nice talking to you, Ursa. You get it, don't you?"

I do get it. I get the fear. The loss. The desire to protect the crew. I glance back at the trees. "Is it safe? Going through the woods, I mean?"

Jovan breathes in through his nose. "Orion was killed at night. I think it's nocturnal, or I'd never have brought you here."

Still, I reach into my gear bag and pull out my wrench again. "Well, let's move quickly."

"Agreed," Jovan says.

As we head back through the trees, I keep the wrench raised, keep checking around me, looking for any odd movements among the black trunks and glowferns. I'm not looking at the ground itself, so it's Jovan who spots it. He grabs my wrist, points.

It's a bird, on the forest floor. Or what's left of a bird.

Its head is missing. There's just feathers and a mess of blood and internal organs. I swallow down bile, trying not to think of Orion's corpse.

The trees are still, apart from the faint breeze. Nothing moving between them. Was the dead bird here on the way out? It could have been. It's easy to miss. But we can't take chances.

"Let's get out of here," I say.

We both run then, tripping and stumbling through the forest. We burst out from between the trees and into the muddy space around the runway. I stop, put my hands on my knees, and gasp for breath.

"It's eating birds," Jovan says.

I wait for the nausea to subside and try to focus. It's still impossible. How could there be a creature here? Nothing could have survived our bioengineering.

"That bird could have gotten caught in a landclearer," I say. "Or maybe a bigger bird ate it."

Jovan looks rattled. "We haven't released the birds of prey yet."

"Well. At least that's something that isn't covered by section confidentiality. I'm going to tell Cassius about the bird at our meeting tonight. Then we'll find out if he's reasonable or not."

I say goodbye to Jovan and take the landbike back to the forest camp at full speed. Not for fun, this time. I don't dare go any slower. I try not to look into the forest as I drive.

Back at the village, I finish my shift, putting together woodcutting machinery that came in the seeding ships, but I'm not my usual efficient self. My mind slides off my tasks, and more than once I have to start a checklist from the beginning, as I can't remember where I've gotten to.

Pressure is building in my head. Fear. Suspicion. People are lying to me. Sabik. Cassius. How can I trust anyone down here? They could be hiding anything.

When my shift is done, I hurry out of the equipment hut and cut through the village toward the captain's cabin. I won't let Cassius derail me this time.

I'm almost there when I see a familiar figure coming in the other direction. Vega. The moment she sees it's me, her face hardens. She walks past without saying a word.

Then it hits me. Cassius said she still wanted to be my friend. He told me to talk to her. This is my chance to see if his word is worth anything. I'm going to take his advice.

"Vega!" I call out. She keeps walking.

I hurry over. "Wait." I catch up with her, match my pace to hers. It's hard. She's walking too fast. She folds her arms. Doesn't look at me. This isn't going to be easy.

"I ... hey," I say. But I'm already getting breathless. "I know this is a hard time." I pause to try to catch a breath. "Maybe we could find time to talk ... if you want."

Her voice is hard as steel. "Get away from me."

I stop walking. There's heat in my chest. Humiliation. Anger. She keeps going.

Vega doesn't turn back. Her long, powerful legs carry her away quickly.

And that's when it occurs to me. She's big. Strong. Trained in combat. She was the one who lured Orion into the woods that night by making him come to see her in the shuttle camp. She could have waited in the dark, killed him, and been back to her hut before I arrived.

I shake my head. That doesn't explain the DNA, the dead bird. And why would she kill him when she wanted children? This thing is making me crazy. Making me suspect everyone.

I need some answers. I need to work out what's going on. I check my linkcom. I'm still early, but I don't care. I'm going to see Cassius now.

And I am going to give him hell.

CHAPTER 9

I don't knock. Just slam open the door to the captain's cabin.

Yuri, Head of Agricology, is there. Cassius is leaning across the chest toward him, gesticulating with one hand as he talks.

"... sounds like a snack or a picnic. He's been visiting a lot. It's only natural and —" Cassius stops. He stands, his chair scraping back on the wood. "Ursa, you're early."

"Well, you've got a lot to explain. I thought I'd give you extra time." My hands are in fists at my sides.

Cassius looks me up and down. "Well, perhaps we should start our session, then." He glances at Yuri. "We can finish this conversation tomorrow."

Yuri fixes me with his usual cold glare as he stands, filled with years of hatred for my family, stored up like the supplies his father stole from the *Venture*. He seems bigger than usual in the small hut. His black hair sticks up, matching his scruffy black beard.

"Are you sure it's wise to be alone with this one, Cassius?" he says.

My eyebrows rise. *This one*. Like I'm the threat on this planet.

But Cassius smiles. "It's fine. You are too suspicious, my friend."

"And you are too trusting," Yuri replies. He heads for the door, not taking his eyes off me the whole way.

"Please, sit," Cassius says. He pulls his own chair back into position and settles into it, wiping imaginary dust from his knees.

"I'd rather not."

He leans back. "Whatever makes you comfortable."

He looks very comfortable himself. Relaxed. That makes it worse.

I start to pace. My anger is bubbling over. I can feel it, like an out of control thermal reaction, spreading through me, heating my face, speeding my heartbeat as the horror of it all washes over me.

"What's the problem, Ursa?"

"The problem? It's obvious, isn't it? People are getting hurt. Killed! And you're here, kicking back and relaxing."

"Please, Ursa. Calm down. Take a seat."

I stay standing. "How many accidents have there been since we arrived?"

Cassius looks away. "I don't have the exact ..."

I slam a hand down on the table. "How many?"

He sighs. "Yes, it's a lot. But it's well within projections."

I want to hit him. "Jovan was right. You've just accepted that some of the crew will die."

Cassius winces. "This is a group of people who have never been outside, trying to survive in the wilderness. Throughout Alpha's history, colonists had high fatality rates. Look at Easter Island or Svalbard. We're doing very well in comparison."

"We shouldn't have fatalities at all. We have much better technology!"

"Yes, and we're using that to minimize risk. But we have no experience of farming, building, or even being outside. We can't stop all accidents."

"So, you expected this?"

"Problems have been anticipated since the planning stages of the *Venture* missions."

I stare for a moment. "Our ancestors expected us to die?"

"This isn't a secret, Ursa. But they paid their own price. Giving up sunlight, space, and the luxuries of Alpha. Shorter lifespans and premature aging."

I start pacing again. *Thump, thump, thump* on the wooden floor.

Cassius leans back in his chair. It creaks. "There's no point in being angry at people who've been dead for hundreds of years, Ursa. We just have to make the best of our lives."

"Yes. We have to retreat to the ship until we're ready."

"We'll never be ready if we stay on the ship. There's only so much we can learn from manuals and vidstreams. We need practical experience."

I keep quiet. Keep pacing.

Cassius watches me for a moment before speaking. "What's behind all this? What's changed since yesterday?"

"You lied to me."

"What makes you think that?"

"Dead birds. The ..." I'm about to say "the DNA," but I realize I'm not supposed to know about that. "Vega. She hates me."

The squeaking of the wooden boards beneath my feet is irritating me now. But I'm not stopping.

Cassius blows out a puff of air. "I spoke to her too. You know what she's like when she's made her mind up about something. But she'll come around."

I stare at my boots as they thud on the floor. The mud sticking to them looks like the stuff we scrape out of the wastewater pipes.

"You mentioned dead birds," he says.

"Yes, in the forest. A dead bird. Its head had been bitten off."

"Bitten off? How do you know it was bitten off?"

I stop. Put my hands on my hips. "It didn't fall off, did it?"

"Where was it? What were you doing in the forest?"

"On the path from the shuttle to the graveyard. Jovan and I were visiting Maia's grave."

Cassius's gaze is thoughtful. "That's not far from where Orion was found." He closes his eyes, rubs at his eyelids. "There could be a simple explanation for the bird's death. The bird populations are grown in the lab. Their behavior could be different from on Alpha, but I'd expect lab-raised animals to be less violent."

I throw my hands up. "We don't even know how the animals are going to behave, and we're still settling the planet as fast as we can? This is madness."

"We're burning through our energy reserves faster than the *Venture*'s generators can replenish them. We have to initiate Beta-fall and bring the *Venture* down or cut back on shuttle flights. The clock is ticking."

"Then cut back on flights!"

Cassius looks up at me. I was wrong. He's not relaxed. He's exhausted. "The flights are important, psychologically speaking. A link to the ship. They're keeping the colony from splitting in two."

He's drumming his fingers on the table. I don't think he even realizes he's doing it. The noise cuts through me.

"I'll need to investigate the area near the gravesite. Urgently," Cassius says. "Perhaps Yuri's right about some things."

My gaze snaps back to Cassius. "Yuri? What do you mean?"

"He's dreaming up conspiracies." Cassius waves a hand. "Don't worry. I told him you had nothing to do with Orion's death. But you know how he is."

I certainly do. He hates my family. All because my dad sentenced his father to the Exit for stealing rationed food supplies twenty years ago, when the crew was in danger of starving.

Cassius continues. "I'll have to see the area before word gets out. There's other information too. I don't suppose I can keep any of it under wraps for long. And perhaps it's better if I don't." He looks up at me. "Strange DNA that came back from Orion's body. It might be a replication mistake. They're checking now. I'm hoping it is."

I don't say anything.

"It's ... well, it doesn't match any identifiable species. Some similarities to wolves and tigers and a few other Alpha species. Not what I would expect from alien life. That's why it might be a mistake. Contamination of the sample in the genelab."

"And you won't delay settlement."

"We might be better off hurrying things along. If there are creatures, we could use all the *Venture*'s tech down here. We'll have to build a stronger village. Arm people."

"But ... that's worse. We need to wait things out on the *Venture* until we know what's happening."

Cassius shakes his head. "There are people — Yuri is one of them — who won't leave the surface. We can't let the colony pull apart, like the *Venture 2*. And I can't leave any of my people unprotected if there's something in the woods."

"So, you'd put us all in danger because of idiots like Yuri."

"This is why we're here, Ursa. We're the dream of humanity. We can do this. We can do so much more than this."

If that's meant to be inspirational, he's way off base. "We're so vulnerable. We're like a flame that can be snuffed out at any point."

Cassius nods. "We are like a flame. That's a good metaphor. We need room to spread. Room to grow. Then we'll be unstoppable."

"We have to take our time."

"We have to plant now so there's a harvest later. We can't leave the half-finished buildings to collapse or we won't have a home to settle at all."

"But what about the dead bird and the DNA? We need to know more."

"Yes. We do." He rubs his stubble. "Do you think Jovan will tell people about the dead bird?"

"It's not a secret, is it?"

Cassius exhales. "I guess it can't be. I really should look into this urgently. Before rumors spread. Can we cut our meeting short?"

"I … okay."

He stands. Grabs his jacket. "We'll talk tomorrow. Okay?"

I just nod.

Then he's gone, out of the cabin and into the dying light of the day.

I stand there for a moment in the empty hut, gripping the back of my chair, wood rough under my hands. Cassius's exit has left me off balance, drained the rage from me.

I take deep breaths in the quiet room. The wind hums tunelessly outside. The fragments of mud from my boots are scattered across the floor. Cassius's chair is empty. Then I notice two mealpacks on the table. The smell of kelp soup turns my stomach.

I need to talk to someone. I need some perspective. Mom's at work, and she's terrible at listening anyway. I need Astra. She's probably still at Celeste's. After a while, I lift my hands off the chair back and head out into the bustle of the breeze.

When I get to Celeste's hut, I knock on the door. It produces a satisfying echo. Astra opens it. She puts a finger to her lips and slips outside with a gentle creak of the hinges, closing the door behind her.

"She's sleeping," Astra says once we've gotten a few paces away. People pass by, wrapped up in their own worlds, wrapped up in their landsuits. It's strange how the wind puts distance between us. Snatches away the murmurs of conversation that would echo down the *Venture*'s corridors. It isolates us.

"I wanted to speak to you," I say.

"And I wanted to speak to you."

I turn to face her. The breeze steals strands of Astra's gray hair from her bun and dances them around her face. She smiles knowingly.

"What about?"

"Do you like Jovan?"

I wasn't expecting that. "I ..."

"It's nice to see you spending time with someone again. You've been on your own too much, talking to yourself."

I look at the ground, at the dark brown earth. I didn't think anyone had noticed me talking to Maia. Which is dumb. Of course people noticed. There's no such thing as secrets on the *Venture*. Not like down here, where they're as plentiful as water.

The sun is sinking behind Astra, casting her face in shadow. "I've been talking to him a lot since Maia's death. Making sure he's okay. He's a smart guy. He'll probably be captain one day. Or you will."

Is this why she wanted to speak to me? To give me advice on my social life? I don't have time for this.

"I think there really is a creature," I say.

She nods. "What changed your mind?"

"Weird DNA evidence. A headless bird in the wood."

Her eyes widen. "How do you know this?"

"Cassius told me about the DNA. Jovan and I saw the dead bird on the way back from Maia's grave. Cassius has gone to investigate."

"Perhaps we'll get some answers, then. And maybe Cassius will delay settlement."

I shake my head. "Cassius is talking about accelerating the colonization."

"What?"

"He thinks we'll need the *Venture*'s resources on the surface to defend ourselves."

Astra's mouth is open. I don't blame her.

"We have to do something, Astra ..."

She pinches the bridge of her nose. "Maybe I can talk to him tomorrow. I don't know."

We both stand there in silence. The wind is light on my face.

Astra sighs. "You should go and meet your mother. She's looking forward to spending time with you." She gives me a hug. "Don't worry, Little Bear. It'll be okay."

But that's hard to believe as I step in and out of the long shadows of the huts, heading toward the hospital. People are milling around, waiting for dinner, wandering between their huts and the central buildings. Children dash around, chasing each other, laughing and screaming, the colorful flash of new toys clutched tight in their fists. I'm walking toward the sun, squinting. It's too bright, too low. The people I pass are silhouettes against its glare. Familiar figures turned into faceless strangers.

I reach the main square and orient myself, blinking as I try to identify the buildings in the dazzling evening light. There's the hospital. I head for the entrance and pause at the doors for a moment. They're not automatic, and they don't slide back. They swing back and forth, like the hut doors, only heavier. I push at them, putting my weight into it, and they open into the echoing space of the hospital.

The hospital is about five times the size of the largest hut, as it'll house the Beta genelab as well as the sick and injured. The shutters are open despite the cold. They haven't gotten around to making glass yet, but the makeshift windows let the warm sunset light in, where it shines on the rough planks of the floor. The roof beams arch up high above me.

Only the far corner is in use so far, just four beds against a wall. I stride over, enjoying the smooth solidity of the clean white floor under my boots.

My mother looks up from the display screen, and a grin spreads over her face.

"You're early," she says. "Give me a second to ping for a replacement and finish my notes, and I'll be right with you."

I nod and lean against the wall.

They've brought some portable medtech down from the ship, and it stands next to the beds. The only lit screen is linked by wires to a sleeping figure at the far end. Perseus. Cassius's son, still recovering from his fall, his monitors a mix of green and orange lights.

He's a living reminder of how dangerous the planet is, and I'm glad we don't have the Exit anymore. Cassius is right about that, at least.

It's only a couple of minutes before Guion arrives. Mom has barely started to brief him when there's a sound from outside. It gets louder before I recognize it. The breathless keen of a child's scream. Then the doors swing open and Phoebe runs in, her daughter Aquila in her arms, face red, mouth open. Her shrieking echoes off the walls.

Mom rushes over. "Bring her to a bed. What happened?"

"She was climbing a tree. She fell."

Mom has the scanner in her hand even before Aquila is on the stretcher. She starts at Aquila's head and works her way down. Guion stands back and lets Mom work.

"Skull fracture. She'll need a calcium and collagen injection. But I don't want to seal the bone before I know if there will be any swelling. Tear in her shoulder muscle. Her leg is broken in two places, a complicated break. It'll need careful setting."

"Will you do it, Nashira?" Phoebe asks. I don't blame her. Mom is the best.

Mom glances at me. I'm about to nod when the doors swing open and Yuri, Phoebe's husband, storms in.

"How is she?"

Mom shouts over Aquila's cries. "Skull fracture, torn muscle, broken leg. I'm applying a PainFree patch now. She'll be okay, but she needs a lot of care."

"Guion can do it," Yuri says.

Everyone pauses except Aquila, who keeps wailing.

"Nashira's the expert. She'll do it," Phoebe says.

I can see Yuri's chest move. He's breathing in and out. He shouldn't even have to think about this. Mom is the best. Aquila's cries start to quiet as the PainFree takes effect.

Phoebe speaks quietly. "Yuri, I will not let your nonsense come between our daughter and the care she needs."

Yuri stares at his prima for a long few seconds. Her face is set. Yuri glances at Aquila, whimpering on the bed. There's a softening in his expression, and his eyes glisten. Then he turns and storms out.

The bustle around Aquila's form resumes. Mom is checking carefully. Taking readings, making notes. Phoebe is stroking her daughter's hand. Mom glances up at me with an apologetic look, so I think it's safe to assume that our mother-daughter evening together is cancelled. I'm exhausted anyway. I give her a weak smile and head back to the hut on my own.

I get washed and changed, and climb into bed. I'm almost asleep when a noise comes from outside, then the door swings open. Astra comes in. She smiles and washes her hands in the bowl of water, then heads for the bed, perching on the edge by my pillow.

"How are you doing, Ursa?"

I shrug, and move over to make room for her. She shuffles further onto my pillow and puts her legs up on my bed. "Come here."

I move over and rest my head on her soft lap. She smells of a little of something like urine, so I shift away slightly and try to ignore it. She is getting older, I know. Another reason to be glad they cancelled the Exit.

"Are you going to talk to Cassius?" I ask, looking up at her.

Astra strokes my hair, stares into space. "Tomorrow."

"I don't think he'll listen."

"It'll be okay, Ursa." She sighs, looks down at me, and smiles. "I promise."

"I should have listened to you," I say. "I shouldn't have doubted what I saw."

Astra kisses the top of my head. "You won't doubt yourself again, will you?"

"No."

I know it's silly. And I'm almost afraid to ask. "Will you sing to me?"

"Of course, Little Bear." She eases my head from her lap, stands, and gets a chair. She settles down in it, and I shuffle back under the covers. Then she starts singing, her familiar lilting voice taking me back.

"Our ship, our home, our one true place ..."

Dad loved this song. So do I. I close my eyes and imagine I'm still a child.

"Our scrap of safety in outer space ..."

I try to pretend Dad and Maia are still alive, pretend we're all together on the *Venture*.

"Our cradle, our grave, our spinning wheel ..."

But Astra's singing can't block out the silence of the hut. The lack of other voices, murmuring in the background, in other cabins. It can't hide the distances between us.

"Our ark, our dock, our even keel."

I slip into sleep feeling more alone than ever.

SHOUTS SEEP INTO MY dreams. They're distant and faint, but they churn up the weird images of Maia in her landsuit, like Little Red Riding Hood. I jolt upright. It's light out. The shouting continues. I push the covers off, and the cold air hits my bare skin like a slap. I slide my feet onto the rough wooden floor, open the door, and peer out. The blinding yellow of Beta's sun is peeking above the horizon, and a crowd has gathered over by the path to the shuttle camp.

I'm only wearing my thin sleepsuit. The familiar voices rise and fall as the wind shifts. I can't make out the words — I can only hear the panic. I don't need to be told what's happened. I can feel it in the horror of the crowd, in the hands clasped over mouths.

It's the creature. It's another body, ripped open like Orion.

I stumble over, barefoot. The mud is clammy against the soles of my feet. My arms are wrapped tight around myself, but the real chill is in my gut. I need to get to the crowd. I need to hear the story.

I need to know who's dead.

There's Sabik, at the center of the group, making wild shapes with his hands, unruly hair moving with the breeze and his gestures. Yuri, listening closely while his narrowed eyes skim over the people around him. Astra's back is to me, her whole body too straight, too tense.

At least they're safe. They're here.

Who's missing? Mom's not here. Celeste's not here. The voices get louder as I get closer. It's not a big group, yet. People are still sleeping.

Please let Mom be still at work. Please let Celeste be asleep.

Who else could it be? Vega isn't here. Cassius isn't here.

Cassius. Who was going to investigate the creature. Last night. Alone.

Oh no. No.

I check the crowd again in case I missed him. He should be here. He's the captain — someone would have summoned him.

I should have stopped him going. Why didn't I stop him?

I trip on the lumpy ground. Stub my bare toe, but keep going, hissing in an angry breath.

Sabik catches sight of me, and he stops talking. Yuri turns, following Sabik's gaze. His arm rises, as if by itself, finger pointing my way.

"Ursa!" he shouts, deep voice carrying while the others fade beneath the hiss of the trees around us. "She was screaming at him last night. I saw her."

And that's how I know I'm right.

Cassius is dead.

CHAPTER 10

Another trip up to the *Venture*. Another body heavy in the hold. Cassius's, this time.

The shuttle is packed. There's a compulsory ship's meeting, to be held on board tomorrow. My skin prickles with the suspicion around me. At least we're going home.

Sabik found the body. Not far from where Orion died. Not far from Maia's grave. Right where I sent him. My chest is tight from the weight of guilt.

Sabik sits next to me on the shuttle, leg jiggling as he tells me what he saw. "He was running away from something. There were normal footprints, but then they lengthened. More weight on the ball of his foot."

I don't want to hear this. It's my fault. I should have stopped him. I should have stopped Maia. My blood pulses in my ears. Mixes with the roar of the engines. The empty hum of the air circulation.

"Then there were knee prints. Handprints. Something attacked him. He was injured, trying to crawl away. And then there was his body."

I wish Sabik would stop. But I have to hear this.

"It ... the body ... barely looked like him. And there were bits ... missing."

Eaten. I close my eyes. The crew whispers in hisses around me, filling the shuttle, but their words are inaudible behind the blunt horror of Sabik's story. I know they're listening too, even as they pretend to talk among themselves. We're all good at listening.

Do they think I mutilated Cassius? That another enemy of mine is dead? I sink down in my bucket seat. Cassius wasn't my enemy. I should have realized how dangerous it was for him to investigate last night, but I was just glad he was taking me seriously.

Vega is at the back. Drugged again. She went crazy, apparently, shouting incoherently, and I don't blame her. First her husband, now her father. All she has left is her injured brother.

There's a lump in my chest, threatening to squeeze its way up to my throat. I don't know if it's a scream or tears. I just know I have to keep it down. I can't lose it here, in front of everyone.

Sabik keeps talking. "There were other prints, too. Coming from the forest. And that's where I found the fur."

That cuts through my daze. "Wait, fur?"

"That's what I said. Black fur."

Exhale. Inhale. There's no denying it now. There's a creature on the planet.

And it's killing us.

I BARELY SLEEP THAT night, even back in the safety of my cabin, walls close on either side, cocooned in familiars sounds and smells. The next morning, I head for breakfast, running my fingers over the engravings. But there's no comfort there, just cold metal cut into the shapes of the heaped bodies of the Great Virus.

I wonder how many of us will survive now. The Great Virus killed half the crew. We barely kept the ship's critical systems going. It took several generations to rebuild the population, even after they set the ratio to two women to each man to produce more children. The shortage of crew members created a backlog of repairs they were still dealing with in my father's time.

And once again, the bodies are piling up around us.

The corridors are crowded. Filled with conversation. But it's not the usual hubbub of ship's chatter and gossip. People are in pairs or small groups, holding hushed conversations against the walls. And there's no giggling, only the hissing and whispering of fear. I hear the word more than once.

Aliens.

But it makes no sense. The planet had nothing bigger than microbes before the first wave of seeding ships arrived. It was habitable only from a cosmic point of view, because most planets are boiling hellholes, frozen lumps, or gassy messes.

Beta had an atmosphere and liquid water, but was what they call a "scumworld." It only supported single-celled life. The genetically engineered microbes sent ahead of us had a tough job over hundreds of years. They tweaked the composition of the air and killed off anything that could hurt us. And when they died, they enriched the soil, making it ready for the next wave of seeding ships to start planting.

So how could something have evolved in isolation? What would it have fed on? How could it have survived our bioengineering?

Then there's the proximity to Maia's grave. I keep coming back to that. Keep wondering if she's restless in her dirt pit. Angry at being dumped there, the energy stored in her cells wasted. Clawing her way up to Beta's surface to get revenge.

Now I'm getting silly. Paranoid.

I reach the canteen. The tables are jammed together, and people try to squeeze past without dropping their meals on one another's heads.

Noise echoes off the walls. The metal amplifies it, turning it into loud gibberish hemming me in, compounding my headache. I forgot how full it gets up here when the crew is all on board. The room stinks of overcooked food and sweaty people. I shuffle between the tables, over to the serving vats, and grab a steel tray. I spoon goop from the giant tureens into my bowl. It's a choice of vegetable porridge or algae scramble. I pick porridge. It smells the same as always. I guess they were too busy to make it different this time.

Having everyone back on board makes me miss Maia. She should be here. She always used to insist on having exactly what I was having. We sat together. Sometimes it annoyed me, the way she was always there. Now I feel sick about how I treated her. Demanding time on my own, calling her clingy. She just wanted to be included.

If only I had included her on the day she died. If only I'd stopped Cassius going out alone. If only I'd given Orion the fixed landbike and stayed at the forest camp that night.

If only.

Once I've filled my tray I scan the canteen. Most of the seats are full, but in the corner a group of educators are leaving. I make a beeline for the empty table, squeezing down the narrow aisles as fast as I can. I plunk myself into a free seat and I'm shoving the tasteless porridge in my mouth when I hear my name in the din of conversation. I keep my head down.

"Ursa!" The voice is louder now. I look up.

Jovan. He points at the empty seat opposite me. "Can I join you?"

"Of course." I pull my tray over to make room for his. But as he slumps down into the seat, I realize he doesn't have any food.

"Are you okay?" I have to raise my voice to be heard over the clamor of the canteen.

"Yeah, just not hungry. All this death, you know."

I nod. He's quiet for a while, and when he speaks, it's hard to catch the words over the clatter of cutlery. "I can't help thinking about Celeste and the baby. And Vega and Perseus. They've lost so much. But the planet is dangerous."

"Cassius went to investigate the bird," I say. "He was there because I told him about it."

"Oh."

"I should have stopped him."

He looks at me. "This isn't your fault, Ursa. Don't blame yourself. Please, don't do that."

We're so close to each other. Unlike most people in the canteen, he smells clean and good.

"Blame our ancestors. They knew people would die. They sentenced my sister to death, and the others, too. I hate that people just go along with it. But we have other options."

I swallow. "We do?"

"We still have the *Venture*. We can move back to the ship, and stay here."

"At least while we investigate this creature and get used to Beta."

He waves a hand at the busy canteen around us. "But everything's fine up here. And everything was fine until we got here. We should go back to what works."

I poke at my porridge. He's reading my mind. "Things are a mess down there."

When I look up, he's staring at me. Those eyes still tie my stomach in knots.

"I should have talked to you right after Maia's death. We should be better friends. We have a lot in common."

A thrill runs through me. "Thanks."

"I wish more people on the ship were like you. We can't let anyone else die. And more will unless we get them off the planet."

"We need them to see the dangers. We can wait it out up here, at least while we find out what this creature is."

"And why should we ever leave the *Venture*? She's our home."

"She won't last forever."

Jovan puts his hand over mine. "With engineers like you, and the resources of the planet, I believe she can."

It's a nice compliment, but that's not how it works. I'm about to explain, but he rubs at his face and I notice how tired, how sad he is. He's still grieving for Maia, and the recent deaths have clearly upset him. Now isn't the time to make him face reality.

"I should leave you to get on with your breakfast." Then he stands. "We should hang out soon. Properly." And he's gone, through the crowds and out of the canteen.

I sit and stare at what's left of my food, congealing in the metal tray. We might get another fifty years out of the *Venture*, using the new resources from the planet. But she can't last forever, and she wasn't designed for long-term orbit. Our generation might not colonize Beta, but the next one will have to. Fifty years would be enough, though. The planet would be in better shape. The next generation will be used to all this. They'll know the dangers.

The clatter and hum of the canteen makes it harder to focus.

What about the creature? Will we ever get used to that? It's like a nightmare. An unseen monster that stalks the deep, dark woods. It makes no sense. It shouldn't exist.

My engineer brain kicks in. Occam's razor. The simplest explanation is usually the correct one. What if it doesn't exist? What if Cassius was right? Perhaps it could be a disguise, along with doctored DNA and manufactured fur. But why would anyone make up a nightmare like that?

There's only one logical answer: to cover up murder. Someone wanted to throw us off the scent, or frame me. I should look into this. But where to start?

I can hear my father's voice in my head. The way he told me to begin with any engineering problem.

Start with what you know, Ursa.

They have the fur in the genelab. And that's where they sequenced the DNA from Orion's body. If it was faked, it was faked there. A cold feeling creeps through my stomach. Jovan is a geneticist. He has access to the genelab.

No, wait. He stayed at the bonfire the night Orion was killed. There's no way he killed Orion and got back to the others without someone seeing. And he was back on the ship last night when Cassius died. In orbit, thousands of miles from the scene of the crime. I exhale. He's in the clear.

But I hate thinking like this. Hate suspecting my friends. Is the planet making me paranoid? The noise in here is overwhelming: the screech of chairs, the clatter of trays, the buzzing of conversation. I push my tray away. I'm not hungry anymore.

There's so much I need to look into on Beta, but I can't get down to the planet right now. I have to focus on the evidence I do have access to. The evidence on the ship.

As soon as I'm done with the meeting, I'm going to check out the genelab.

CHAPTER 11

The canteen fills with the sound of movement, of cutlery against meal trays as people hurry to finish their breakfast, start to move the tables away and pull out the benches in time for the meeting. I edge around the crowds out of the canteen, squeezing past people on their way in, heading in the direction of our habitation carriage, hoping to find Mom, Celeste, or Astra. I don't want to face this on my own.

Children move in groups down the hall, not looking where they're going. People pause on their way past to gawp at me or whisper. My stomach twists like an over-tight bolt. I'm relieved to see Astra with Celeste coming through the airlock to the next carriage, making their way toward me.

"Don't worry," Astra says as she approaches, as if I can switch off my anxiety. "They won't start the interviews today. We have to elect a new captain first. Your mother is with the rest of the executive now."

That makes sense. And it explains the compulsory attendance. The bolt in my stomach loosens a notch. Astra and Celeste both hug me, and we join the crowd flowing back toward the canteen.

I trail behind them, wishing Astra were big enough for me to hide behind.

She pauses as we pass the engraving of Dad. Touches his face.

"Be strong, Ursa. This is your father's ship," she says. "Filled with his fingerprints, his innovations, his fixes. This is his world, and he's watching over you here."

She always knows what to say. I walk a little taller as we head into the council room. It's mostly set up now, seats rearranged in rows, tables stowed. We help move one of the last benches into position and sit down, but soon have to shuffle up to make room for more people. I end up pressed against the metal wall to my left, with Astra to my right and Celeste on the other side of her. The rivets of old repairs dig into my arm.

The room fills to bursting, the space warming with the body heat of five hundred crew members. The air circulators hum at full power, but they can't cut through the stuffiness. The murmur of conversation tails off as the heads of each section file in: engineering, medicine, genetics, agricology, education, and construction. They take their places either side of Cassius's empty chair, all wearing faded black armbands.

Antares, Head of Engineering, steps forward. At fifty-five in Alpha years, he's the most senior of the executive. His age shows in his stooped figure, his slow movements.

He bows his head. "Cassius was our leader during a time of great change. He will be remembered as a man who was strong in trying to shape our future. He was fearless in pushing ahead on the colonization of Beta."

Fearless was right. But perhaps a little fear is necessary. Perhaps it would have saved him. I peek around at the packed room. A few people are wiping their eyes. Vega sits at the front, back straight.

"We will hold a memorial service with full honors on Beta when the investigation is complete." Antares takes a deep breath. "But

Cassius did not believe in wasting time, and he would want us to move on as soon as possible."

There are a few sad grins among the section heads.

"I will open the floor for nominations for the position of captain."

An agricologist stands immediately. Almach.

"I nominate Yuri, Head of Agricology," he says.

Yuri steps forward, his bulk imposing in the small room. "I accept the nomination."

No. Oh no. Don't let it be Yuri.

Medic Guion is on his feet too. "I nominate Nashira, Head of Medicine."

My mouth falls open. It never occurred to me that Mom might end up as captain. But she doesn't seem surprised at all. She nods, perfectly composed. "Thank you, Guion. I accept the nomination."

There's a thrill through me. Please let it be Mom.

One of the geneticists stands. "I nominate Merope, Head of Genetics."

But Merope shakes her gray head. "Thank you, but I will be supporting Nashira." No surprise there. Merope and Mom have been best friends for years. Their sectors often overlap, so they frequently work together. When Capella, Head of Construction, is nominated, she turns it down too, in favor of Yuri.

People shift on the crowded metal benches, peer around at each other. Antares waits for another minute as whispers hiss through the council room. But no one else stands to nominate. If he's disappointed that no one named him, he doesn't show it.

"Could I have a motion to close the nominations?" Antares asks. Several hands go up. "Any objections?" The hands fall back down. "Then I declare the nominations closed." He taps on his display pad.

"Ballots have been sent to your linkcoms. Please vote. You have five minutes."

I don't bother to check mine. I won't have a vote until I'm of age. But all the adults pull theirs out. Some hunch over them, so no one can see their selections. Some hold their linkcoms up as they press, displaying their allegiance to anyone who is paying attention. Astra hits the panel for Mom. I see it glow as the vote is registered.

Everyone is done long before the five minutes are up, so people sit in silence, fidgeting. A baby wails. I cross my fingers. Mom, please, let it be Mom. She'll let me work on the *Venture*. She'll be in charge of the investigations into Cassius's and Orion's deaths. She'll release the DNA report. She's reasonable. She might even delay the settlement. I can't see Yuri doing any of that.

A child a few rows in front has tilted her head back in boredom. Her mouth is open as she stares at the ceiling. She has no idea how important this is, how this vote will shape her life.

"Has everyone had an opportunity to vote?" Antares asks, his unsteady voice ringing through the room. Murmurs and nods greet him. "Did anyone have any problems casting their vote?" Shakes of the head. "Merope and Capella, will you confirm the results?" He hands them his display pad.

They both peer at it, murmuring to each other, voices too low for us to hear. Astra takes my hand and squeezes it tight. Merope and Capella glance at each other. Does Capella look happy? Or upset? It's impossible to tell with her.

It's Merope who steps forward. "The new captain, with fifty-two percent of the votes, is Nashira."

I close my eyes. Breathe. Listen to the mutterings and rustlings. People clap.

First Dad and now Mom. Captains of the *Venture*.

But that was too close, the ship split down the middle. I can't believe so many people voted for Yuri. When I open my eyes, Mom is already stepping forward, smiling. Yuri's mouth is open. Clearly, he thought he would win.

"Thank you," she says. "It is my great hope we can all work together. We need unity, above all else. We have many challenges ahead, and without each other we will not survive."

Some smiles around me. But a few people stare, making no attempt to hide their hostility.

Mom holds her display pad up. "Our first order of business is to vote on a new Head of Protection and then open the investigation into Cassius's and Orion's deaths."

Yuri steps forward. "I have an urgent motion for the full colony to vote on."

"The unexplained deaths on the planet are our clear priority —"

"Exactly," Yuri says. "My motion is for you to be removed from the investigation into Cassius's and Orion's murders."

My heart is in my throat. I barely hear the cries around me.

But Mom's voice is calm. "I am the captain, Yuri. You can check the votes yourself. Investigations come under my purview."

"You're Cassius's successor. You're related to Orion's wife. You're Ursa's mother. You're too close to the victims and the prime suspect."

There's a jolt through me at the words "prime suspect." He means me, of course. I shouldn't be surprised. But it's still shocking to hear it said out loud.

"Now you're slandering a crew member," Mom says. "And you did not complain when Orion's father-in-law was investigating his death."

"Ursa was the last one to see Cassius alive, and I witnessed her screaming at him. Her DNA was on Orion's body."

"There is evidence that points to a possibility other than homicide."

"Which is so unreliable the executive voted not to release it."

"That will be revisited, in light of events since then." Mom's voice is level, reasonable. But her hands are clutched in fists.

"You're out of order, Yuri," Merope says. "I trust Nashira to lead this investigation, and clearly, so does the crew."

Mom turns away from Yuri, back toward the crew. "There is new evidence from the scene of Cassius's death and I'm sure the investigation will reveal —"

"I second the motion for Nashira to be removed from the investigation." A voice echoes from the metal walls. Vega. She's standing in the front row, looking straight ahead at the council. "Orion was my husband. Cassius my father. They have been murdered. I demand an impartial investigation."

There's silence at this.

"I will certainly give you both full access to observe the investigation," Mom says. "Will that satisfy you, Yuri? Vega?"

"No," Vega says. "Ursa blamed Orion for Maia's death. She wanted revenge. And you just got my father's job."

There's a collective intake of breath from the audience. It's like they're sucking all the oxygen away from me. I spot Sabik in the crowd. His hand is across his mouth.

Vega turns, and I see the hate in her eyes. She jabs a finger toward me. "I want Ursa to face a trial. To face justice for what she did."

"I didn't do anything," I say. But I'm too quiet.

"We need to complete an investigation before putting anyone on trial," Mom says.

Yuri shakes his head. "Even before Cassius died, you were trying to push the investigation in another direction. If you're in charge, you'll make sure Ursa never faces trial."

My breath is stuck in my throat.

"I am following evidence, Yuri," Mom says. "DNA evidence. Footprints. The fur. You know this."

"All of which makes no sense. It must have been made in the genelab and planted."

A prickle runs up my back. I was thinking the same thing.

The muttering in the crowd is growing louder. Some people are getting to their feet.

Merope steps closer to Yuri. "Is that why you were skulking around in our carriage earlier, peering in the rooms? Checking up on us?"

Yuri towers over her. "Someone has to."

Mom pinches the bridge of her nose. "Why on Beta would anyone plant impossible DNA?"

Vega again. "To cover up Ursa's killings. To protect your family."

"Your family always stands together," Yuri says.

My pulse is pounding in my ears. I push myself up. All eyes turn to me. It takes a moment to find my voice. "I had nothing to do with their deaths. I swear."

"You hated my husband." Vega's voice cuts through me. "Dad was investigating you, an investigation that was ended by his death. You found Orion's body. You were the last person to see Dad alive."

"Cassius was fine when I last saw him! He went to investigate the creature!"

"This is insane, look at her!" It's Jovan's voice, from off to the side. I turn around. He's on his feet too, on the other side of the aisle, waving a hand at me. "Orion and Cassius were much bigger than she is. How do you suggest she overpowered them?"

He's as outraged as I am. My heart swells with gratitude.

"She's an engineer," Yuri says. "Someone was seen smuggling equipment out of the engineering shed and into the forest. Ursa could have made a weapon. She was seen cleaning landclearer blades. Probably to hide evidence."

"I was sharpening them!" I say. Then I realize that doesn't sound any better. I drop back down into my seat. This is ludicrous.

Yuri pulls himself up to his full height. "Captain Cygnus believed in killing crew members to make a point. His daughter is following in his footsteps."

So that's what this is all about: revenge for Yuri's father. Astra grabs my hand again and clutches it tight. I turn to her and see my own anger mirrored in her eyes.

Mom's wide nose flares. "This is news to me — engineering equipment being smuggled into the forest." She turns to Antares. "Is there anything missing from the engineering hut?"

"I ... don't think so. I'll check the inventories."

"Make it a priority," Mom says. "Yuri, I need that witness to testify in the investigation. If you have any more information you are hiding, you must let the executive know."

But Jovan is still standing. "You can't seriously think Ursa built something. What about the genetic evidence? What about the fur?"

"I know you're on her side," Yuri says. "I've seen you heading into the forest together, gazing into each other's eyes."

I suck in a breath, horrified and embarrassed.

"What do you mean, on her side?" Merope says. "Jovan is not the only geneticist working on this. Are you accusing the whole genetics section of being part of a cover-up?"

"If this continues, I will have to disband the meeting," Mom says.

Yuri stares at Merope. "If the cap fits. None of you liked Cassius or Orion, or the fact that the agricology section was finally getting the respect it deserved."

"We are professional and unbiased, Yuri," Merope says.

There's mocking laughter from the agricologists at the back.

To my surprise, Pisces, Head of Education, speaks. "Some ... some of my section have reported hearing howling on the planet at night."

A prickle works its way up my spine.

"It's called the wind," Yuri shouts. "And you'd better get used to it!"

More laughter.

"No," Pisces says. "I don't think ..." but he's too timid.

Mom shakes her head. "Is there anything that will convince you, Yuri?"

"Nothing that comes through you or the genelab."

"Then how am I meant to investigate?"

Yuri shrugs. "Not my problem. As you were so keen to point out, you're in charge of investigations now." Then he turns and starts walking away, down the aisle of the council chamber. "I'm the only person who will look out for people down on the planet. You just want to protect your own family."

"That's not true!" Mom says, but her voice is lost in the clamor of the room.

"I'm going back to the surface. There's a lot of work to do there." Yuri opens his arms wide and shouts, his voice cutting through the commotion. "Come with me if you want to live on the planet in the wide open spaces of our future. Or you can hide up here, listening to lies crammed in with this killer." He points at me. "It's your choice."

"But I —" My voice is drowned in the noise of people standing. A lot of them.

Yuri strides toward the doors, Vega following, the two of them pulling people behind them like they're caught in a gravitational field. Agricologists, mainly, and the Head of Construction and half of her team. Celeste stays seated, but her eyes follow her colleagues.

"Wait," Mom says. "We need to vote on the Head of Protection —"

Sabik is one of the last to get to his feet, and on his way out he pulls out his linkcom and types. A message buzzes on mine as he's walking through the door.

Don't worry. I'll speak to Yuri, it says.

He looks back and gives me a little wave. He's still leaving with them, though. I doubt he'll be able to make a difference.

Yuri has made up his mind, and the ship is tearing itself in two.

CHAPTER 12

Mom dissolves the meeting, but calls an emergency discussion of the executive to be held in a side room. Astra hugs me tightly as the audience files out, muttering among themselves, some peering at us with naked suspicion, some giving us sympathetic smiles. I hide in her arms until Mom comes over and stands next to us. She pats my shoulder, awkwardly.

"I'm sorry you had to go through that," Mom says. "I wanted to stand up for you more. Actually, I wanted to scream. But they already think I'm biased. It would have made it worse."

I clutch my hands together.

"Don't worry. We're sticking to the truth, and as more evidence comes to light, I know it'll clear you."

Astra speaks for me. "But what do we do until then?"

"Keep investigating," Mom says. "And I'll send down the chickens today as planned, and continue with the release schedule. We'll prove we care about the people on the planet. Then we'll have a better chance of uniting the ship."

"I don't know how, if Yuri keeps spreading his hateful lies," Astra mutters. "He's shattering this crew into factions."

"Have some sympathy for Yuri. You know what he lost."

Astra breathes in through her nose. "He lost a selfish father. Charon knew the law on stealing food."

"He did it for his son."

"He was stealing food for Yuri?" I didn't know that.

Astra nods, puts a hand on my shoulder. "It was sad, but an example had to be made."

"Let's not go over this again," Mom says.

But Astra ignores her. "We were hanging on by a thread. Everyone's children were hungry. More theft would have endangered us all. Cygnus had to make an example of someone. Sacrifices have to be made to save the ship."

Mom sighs. "I have to focus on the present. Astra, I'm appointing you Acting Head of Protection. I need someone I can trust."

Astra's mouth opens. "But there hasn't been an election."

"And there can't be, until we can get the crew back together. You'll only be Acting Head until then. Okay?"

Astra pauses for a moment before she nods. "Whatever you need."

Mom turns back to me. "You should take the morning off. You've been put through a lot in the last few days."

"Okay," I manage.

"I have to join the rest of the executive." Mom sways, and I notice the dark circles under her eyes. "Look," she says. "I know this is a tough time, but I'm here for you, and Astra's here for you. Okay?"

She's staring at me intently.

"Okay."

"I love you, Ursa. Ping me if you need me."

"Love you too." Then she's gone.

Astra turns to me. "I have a little time. Do you want to talk about what just happened?"

"You're Head of Protection. You can work on the investigation, right? That's what's going to help the most."

Astra nods, and I wonder if she's been thinking the same thing. "If you're sure."

"I'm sure."

Astra wraps her arms around me. Squeezes tightly. "I love you, Little Bear. So much." And she leaves, filing out with the last of the stragglers from the meeting.

I'm soon all alone in the echoing metal room. I have to get to the bottom of this. Who is trying to frame me?

Vega hates me. But would she kill her own husband and father?

Yuri clearly thought he'd become captain after Cassius's death. He and his team know the planet better than anyone. They'd know exactly how to get away with it. I want to see what's down that path Sabik was hiding. He's close with Yuri. Although it's hard to believe he'd try to frame me.

But I never thought he'd lie to me, either.

I push the thought away. That investigation will have to wait until I'm next on the planet. I have an unexpected morning free, and I can get to the genelab. See if there's anything amiss there. There's a twinge of guilt that I'm looking there first. It's Yuri and the agricologists I should be investigating, but there's no way I can go down to the planet now.

I can't just wander into the genelab either, of course. It's a clean zone. No one is allowed in unless they have work there, and even the geneticists have to wear full protection to prevent a skin cell falling into their test tubes and petri dishes.

That's not a problem for me, though. This is my ship, and nowhere was off limits for Maia and me. I just need my screwdriver, the remote control Maia and I made, and a quiet spot near the genelab.

I GRAB MY GEAR bag and the remote hidden in my clothes closet, then take the elevator up to the engine room. I tell Aldrin, the engineer on duty, that I'm checking on the air circulation feed data. Once I've made a show of doing that and he's distracted, I kick off the wall, float across the space, and take the elevator down to the genelab carriage.

I slip down the corridor and into the carriage's washrooms. I wait in one of the metal cubicles — it stinks, but it's quiet. I climb up on the toilet, reach up to the vent above me, and unscrew the cover, praying that no one comes in.

This is the first time I've done this alone, and it's hard without a lookout. Maia should be here, giggling as she keeps an eye on the corridor, whispering at me to hurry. It's so wrong she isn't. I pause and wipe my eyes on my sleeve.

Then the screws are undone. The only sounds are the toilets flushing in another cubicle and the air circulators spinning. I flip the cover off and heave my torso up and into the vents, scraping my hip against the metal edges as I wiggle in. Once I'm up there, I turn around and position the grille behind me so that, at a glance, it looks like it's closed.

I twist myself onto my hands and knees, careful not to bash the metal panels either side, and start crawling. Stale air blows in my face. It's gray and dark, the only light glimmering through the grilles spaced along the left side, a few meters between each of them. As I crawl by each one, the light casts stripes on my arms and side.

This is how Maia and I used to explore the ship: eavesdropping on the habitation cabins, hiding in the ecocarriages. The vents are big enough for a large person to move through. When we were little, Maia and I could crawl side by side, although in the last few years, we had to go single file. When I took the lead, Maia would always complain I was too slow, pinching at my ankles to make me go faster.

The loneliness closes in on me like the thick alloy sides of the vents.

As I approach the first fan, I pull out the remote Maia and I made. It's a simple white box, the size of a linkcom, but it looks gray in the dark of the vents. I slide the black switch. That hijacks the signal from the engine room, the one we use to shut down the fans when we're doing maintenance. I hit the red button and wait. Slowly, the fan stops spinning.

Once it's come to a halt, I squeeze between the blades, onto the other side, and continue crawling down the vent. When I'm a couple of meters away, I hit the green button. The fan behind me restarts, slowly at first, then picking up speed, blowing air at my feet and legs.

"We were a great team," I whisper, then pause. "I miss you."

I took Sabik into the vents, too. He stole some seeds from the agricology stores and set up a planter in here. But I guess there wasn't enough light. The plants never became more than shoots. Little green blades that slowly turned brown.

I keep crawling through the fans, stopping and starting each one as I go.

Air blows in my face from the next grille. I must be at the lab itself. It has a positive pressure system, pushing air out from the lab to prevent contaminants coming in. It's noisy here too. There's screeching, scraping, and cawing, and someone is shouting that they can't find the spare accelerated cell division unit and demanding to know who used it last.

I peer through the grille. The genelab is huge, brightly lit and crowded with people hidden behind matching white lab coats and masks. Most of them are bent over microscopes and centrifuges, working with pipettes and petri dishes, but some attend to a huge bank of cages, sealed off from the rest of the room with a glass wall.

The cages are full of animals, from small rodents to rabbits and larger birds. I guess that's where the bad smell is coming from. It reminds me of the water recycler when the pipes get backed up. There are no chickens there, so they're probably already in the cargo bay waiting for the next shuttle down to the planet.

I hear a humming below me where the womb units are. It's warm, even from a few meters away. Dozens of red spheres hang from the wall, like huge red bubbles, tubes feeding into them, all glowing to indicate they're in use. They pulse as the artificial circulation feeds nutrients and oxygen to the growing creatures. They can grow populations in less than a third of the natural gestation times, and we only lose about fifteen percent to genetic replication errors. It's an acceptable level for animals, but not for humans, which is why we stick with implantation for our reproduction, even after the Great Virus. Each of the wombs is small now, but they can stretch to accommodate any animal. There will be cows and horses one day.

For one mad moment, I wonder if the creature could be real, could have been grown here, but there's no way to hide something that big in the crowded genelab. It would be too obvious as it grew far bigger than any of the other creatures in the artificial wombs. And how would they get it down to the planet? Everyone would have noticed a monster on the shuttle.

The rest of the carriage, to my right, is the Genebank. Part freezer, part ark. Most of it is animal genetic material, everything that we need to introduce to the planet to create thriving ecosystems. Hundreds of columns filled with tiny rows of drawers, each with hundreds of samples of DNA. Thousands of each species, to ensure genetic diversity.

The far section is the human DNA bank. Over sixty thousand people are represented there, all anonymous. Selected from Alpha Earth for their health, intelligence, and lack of family history of disease. And over the voyage, the Genebank has been expanded with the genetic material of four hundred years' worth of the crew. When I'm of age, they'll save some of my eggs, too.

Our history is also our future.

Each of us is randomly created from two donors to keep the gene pool wide. I've studied myself in the mirror for clues about my genetic parents. Checked images from Alpha Earth. I'm guessing one of them was from Africa, ancestrally at least. Sabik looks like both his genetic donors might be from Asia, and Maia was as pale as the Europeans in the vidstreams. But most of us are harder to place.

In the lab, no one is working on any fur that I can see. And other than that, I don't know what I'm looking for. There's too much going on in here: the creation of antibiotics, modified yeasts for the fermentation vats, vaccines and bacteria that deal with any dangerous organisms that develop on board, and solutions for autoimmune reactions to our new environment. Although now they're mostly focused on the animal program.

How would I identify the staff who are investigating the deaths, and how could I tell if they were doing it wrong? It was dumb of me to come here. What did I expect? A workstation with a "How to frame Ursa" flowchart on a display screen above it?

I sit back on my haunches in the vent.

This has been a wasted trip. And a lonely one, without Maia.

I stare for a moment at the bustle of the genelab. The white-coated people move around each other, impossible to identify in their masks and suits. A pair of them stare at a microscope together. Two others are chatting. One leans back, puts a gloved hand on their stomach. Their eyes crinkle with laughter.

The vent stretches out either side of me. Empty.

After a while, I start crawling back, working my way down the vent, keeping my movements as quiet as possible. My knees and hands are cold from the chill of the metal floor. I'm soon into a rhythm, using the remote to shut down the fans, crawling through and starting them again. But as I crawl over the air recyclers for the carriage, I bump my left elbow hard.

I stop myself from crying out, then sit, breathing in air through my teeth and twisting my arm to peer at my elbow. My overalls aren't ripped, but I hit the funny bone. I close my eyes until the pain has eased, then check the side of the duct.

There's a bump on the wall. A flat rectangle, the size of a meal-pack, easy to miss. I didn't notice it in the dark on the way out. It's featureless apart from screws at the corners. I pull my linkcom from my gear bag and shine it on the object.

"What is it?" I ask Maia. And I know what she'd say. *Only one way to find out.*

I quickly loosen the screws on the outside and pop it open.

My breath stops in my throat.

Wires, forming a circuit I only know in theory, leading from a remote sensor to a lump of white putty.

This is a bomb.

CHAPTER 13

I push myself back against the other side of the vent. The bomb has no lights or countdown on it, but that's not reassuring. It could be set off at any time, remotely. I force air into my lungs. In. Out. What do I do? Okay. Okay. I can deal with this.

Breathe. Breathe.

I pull a wire cutter from my gear bag. It's a simple circuit. I can disarm it. I'm sure.

Mostly sure.

Should I leave it? Get help? But what if it's triggered in the meantime? There's a chance it could blow a hole in the hull and decompress this part of the carriage.

My mind whirrs through an assessment of the likely result. The Genebank is far enough away to be safe. It's mostly storage and changing rooms here. I'm right above the machinery for this carriage's air circulation unit. It's a low population area.

If the bomb triggered a hull breach, the emergency doors would seal automatically. The air circulation backup in the engine room would kick in and take over pumping in fresh air through the spokes to the rest of the ship until we repaired the damage and normal air flow could resume around the rim. It's unlikely anyone would be hurt, except me, and they couldn't have known I'd be here.

So why would someone plant a bomb here, where it could only take out the air recyclers?

Cold itches up my back.

There's only one reason I can think of for taking out the air recyclers.

If an air circulator went out in one of the carriages, then something went wrong with the backup in the engine room, the ship's air flow would be compromised. It wouldn't be able to circulate around the rim or down the spokes. Carbon dioxide would build up in the inhabited areas, and dangerous pockets of oxygen would form in the ecocarriages. The *Venture* would trigger the emergency protocols to prevent suffocation or explosions. All the carriages would break away from the spokes that connect them to the engine room and descend to Beta.

It's a failsafe, now that we're in orbit. If anything threatens survival up here, the ship will automatically initiate Betafall. The ship would be destroyed, but the individual carriages will land in the breathable air of the planet, saving the crew and the crops. It's what the ship's designed to do — bring the carriages with all their metal and tech down to Beta, once we're ready.

But we're not ready. If I'm right, whoever planted this must intend to force the *Venture* down to Beta. Now.

There might be other bombs. They'd have to destroy the backup in the engine room, and they can't be certain this one would take out the air circulation unit. They may have planted another bomb in the vents near a different air circulation unit to be sure.

My throat is dry, but my hands are steady. I pass the wire cutter back and forth between them. A red wire runs from the explosive to the remote sensor. The remote sensor is a simple one, like we use on doors. A binary device. Only two states: on and off, open and closed, wait or explode.

There's no time to get help. It could be detonated from anywhere on the ship, at any moment. And I need to look for other bombs, too.

Okay. Okay. I can do this.

I reach for the wire. Put the cutters around it and pause. It's too simple. Probably because they didn't expect this to be found. But if it's a trick, and I get this wrong, I'm dead. Plastered all over the inside of this vent.

But what choice do I have?

I close my eyes and squeeze the wire cutters closed.

Nothing.

I open my eyes.

The circuit is broken, wires hanging loose. I did it. I sit there, breathing in and out, feeling my blood pulsing through my skull. The box is harmless now. It's still attached to the wall from the inside, so I unscrew it and pull it off the side of the vent. Someone will need to examine it. Check for evidence.

Now what? Who planted this? Who can I trust? We have to keep this secret, at least until we check the ship. If there are other bombs, and they know we're on to them, they could detonate them right away.

I should tell Mom. Thank Beta she's captain. I put the box under my arm and start crawling as fast as I can. I get to the next fan. Hit the button, wait for the fan to stop. I shove the remote in my gear bag, then start climbing through. It's awkward because I'm hurrying and holding the bomb. There's a clatter. I must have kicked something. I need to be quieter. I can't draw attention to myself now. I ease my top half through the fan, but kneel on a hard object before I get my legs through.

There's the hum of the fan rebooting.

No. Oh no.

I lunge forward through the blades before the fan can start turning and crush me.

I twist around and stare at the fan. It's starting now, picking up speed. I breathe hard and check my arms and legs. Unscathed, thank Beta. But how did that happen? Does someone else have a remote? Do they know I'm here?

It's only when my heart stops racing that I realize how dumb I am.

The clatter was the remote falling out of my gear bag. I must have knelt on the green button, or kicked it. Or perhaps it just landed face down and the weight of the unit was enough to press the button. I peer through the fan, the blade spinning so fast it's invisible. I blink against the air it's blowing in my eyes. Yes. The remote is lying on the other side. Without it, I'm trapped in this section of the vent, between two sets of whirling blades. I can't stop the fans. I can't get back to the washrooms.

I drop my head into my hands. Think, Ursa. Use that logical brain.

How do I get out? What will people think if I'm caught in here with a bomb? Will they believe I found it?

I doubt it, after what Yuri said about me at the hearing.

Okay. Deep breathing again. Where am I? There's only one grille between these two fans. It doesn't stink here, so I haven't reached the washrooms yet. I swivel myself around in the narrow space and crawl to the grille. I peer through.

Four stained metal walls. A door that must lead out to the corridor. A protective suit hangs on the wall, but there's no one in the room. Thank Beta. It's a changing room.

There's no time to be careful; someone could come at any moment. The screws are on the other side, of course. But that shouldn't be a problem. The threads on many of them are stripped from overuse.

I listen, but it's hard to hear anything over the whirr of the fans. I just have to go for it.

I kick the grille hard. It bends, and one of the corners pops out. Bingo. There's enough room to get my hand through, so I pull out my screwdriver and work on the other three screws as quickly as I can. They tinkle as they hit the floor. I grab the grille before it can fall and pull it into the vent. Good. Stage one done.

Now to get out of here. I shuffle around again. Slower this time, careful not to bash the sides. I don't want to attract any attention.

I wiggle my legs out first, jump down to the floor, then reach back into the vent for the grille. I grab the screws from the floor and have two of them in when there's the creak of a door handle.

There's no time to get the screws back off and get in the vent. I shove the screwdriver in my gear bag and am wondering what on Beta I'm going to say when someone enters the small room.

A tall figure. Dressed head to toe in a protective suit.

"Ursa," he says, deep voice muffled by the mask and hood. "What are you doing?"

Good question.

"Hi." I try for a casual voice and slide the bomb behind me. "Just some engineering fixes. All done now." I try to slip past, head for the other door before he can wonder what engineering fixes are needed in a changing room.

"It's good to see you." The figure pulls off his hood and loosens his mask so it hangs around his neck.

Jovan. Thank Beta. I should have recognized those eyes. I let go of the door.

"What's that behind you?" he asks.

"What's what?"

"The box you're hiding behind your back, Ursa."

I might as well be honest. If he planted it, he already knows what it is. I pull it out.

"It's a bomb."

He takes a step back, and his expression tells me it's not his, at least.

"Don't worry. I defused it. Someone put it in the vents. I think they're trying to force an early separation and descent."

"What?" His mouth falls open. He stares at me for a long moment, then looks at the bomb again. "Are you sure it's safe?"

"This one is: I defused it. But there may be more. I need to take it to Mom."

"Is she still meeting with the executive?"

I close my eyes. "I forgot about that. I can't just turn up to their meeting with this. I need to speak to Mom alone."

Jovan glances at the bomb. "Will the person who put it there know you found it?"

"It was a simple bomb. No feedback circuit. I'm hoping they'll assume it's still functional until they try to detonate it."

Jovan nods. "Then we have to get you to your cabin without anyone seeing you. You can talk to your mother when she comes home, in private. I'll help."

I exhale and fight the urge to hug him. "Thanks. I'd better get this grille on properly. You watch out for anyone trying to come in."

Jovan moves into place, between the two doors. It takes me only a few seconds to finish screwing the grille in place. It's good to have a lookout again. Once it's done, I slide the bomb into my gear bag.

Jovan grabs the suit from the wall. "Get this on. It's better if no one knows you were here. Mask first." He holds it out, and I snap it into place around my mouth and nose.

Then he kneels in front of me and holds out the bottom half of the suit, looking up at me with his deep, dark eyes. "Here you go."

I look away and concentrate on getting the rest of the suit on by myself.

Jovan pulls open the door to the carriage and checks outside. "Follow my lead. Act casual." And he's out. I head through the door, trying to walk casually. How do I normally walk? Why can't I remember? I feel like I'm swaggering. That's not right. A couple of genelab technicians are heading our way. Zaniah and Lyra, arguing about something.

"You had the centrifuge last," Zaniah says. I glance at her hands as she approaches, at her long fingers. You can't tell she lost them to frostbite. Mom did a good job attaching the lab-grown replacements.

"And I put it away," Lyra says.

Then they both catch sight of Jovan. Zaniah quickly brushes a hand over her dark hair. Lyra tilts her head. "Hi, Jovan."

"Lyra, Zaniah." He nods at each as we pass.

I hope I'm not that obvious when I talk to him.

We reach the end-of-carriage doors, and I follow him through the airlocks into ecocarriage 4. I exhale. The main lights come on as we enter, switching from the UV growing lights to the full visible spectrum. There's no one between the tanks lining the carriage walls, so we hurry down the central walkway. We speed past murky tanks, each a different color, with kelp and algae at various stages of development. We hurry past sealed vats filled with genetically modified organisms that produce essential nutrients through fermentation. Our boots clang on the metal walkway, half muffled by bubbling of the oxygen and the hum of the water circulation units and harvester filters.

The generator carriage is next, with its mess of catwalks and corridors weaving in and out of the four main barrels that hold the cells and turbines of the reactor and the pipes of coolant. The main lights are on, so there must be someone in here. I check the feeds scrolling over each of the subsystems as we pass. All are normal.

We stick to the path on the left side and pass a couple of engineers in the center at the main control panel, tending to the system: Antares and Ida, his assistant. They barely nod at us. We reach the airlocks without incident and head into the humidity of ecocarriage 3. My habitation carriage is the next one around the rim.

The system is mostly automated, so it's quiet in here apart from the hiss of the mist feeding the plants. It feels like a long walk to the airlocks on the other side, but it's probably less than five minutes. We hurry down the narrow corridor, glancing at the thick purple plants in the foggy air on the other side of the glass, hanging in rows stretching the length of the carriage, from the floor to the ceiling, like an impenetrable purple forest.

Jovan is striding so fast I can barely keep up, but I don't ask him to go slower. I just listen to my ragged breath and the ringing of my boots as we hurry along the central corridor. When we're nearly at the airlock, Jovan turns to me. "Time to strip down." Then he shakes his head, and a cheeky grin spreads across his face. "Sorry, that sounded ... well, I meant we'll get all kinds of awkward questions if you're in a full genelab suit in a habitation carriage."

He's right. I pull off the hood and mask, then lean on him to take off the rest, wobbling a bit as I struggle with the legs of the suit. "Thanks so much."

"I barely did anything," Jovan says, and we start walking again. "I mean, compared to you. Defusing bombs, saving the *Venture*. Nice work, Ursa."

I turn to him. The ecocarriage corridor is narrow to maximize growing space. And he's right next to me. Our eyes meet. I can't tell if it's the humidity or his proximity that is making my cheeks warm.

Bomb. We have to deal with the bomb. Focus, Ursa.

We reach the end of the carriage and step through the airlock onto the stairs to the two levels of the habitation carriage. As soon as we're down on my level, we're back among the bustle. I try to walk normally, but I'm so far from normal right now. Luckily, my cabin is the first on the left. Jovan wrenches the broken door open. I stumble in, glad to be home. Jovan follows and shuts the door behind us.

I take the defused bomb out from my gear bag and look at it properly. Maybe there's a clue as to who made it or how they got it into the vents.

But something else occurs to me as I examine it.

"You weren't surprised I was in the vents," I say.

Jovan shrugs. "Everyone knows how to get into the vents. But it was obvious you and Maia found a way to get through the fans. You kept turning up in unexpected places."

I exhale. Of course he knew. Probably everyone knew. But if everyone knows, I'm going to be the prime suspect for planting this bomb. Perhaps this was another way to frame me.

"What's that?" Jovan says, pointing to the lump of explosive. "Is it from engineering?'

I crumble some of the white block between my fingers. Sniff it. It's pungent, with the sharpness of urine but also a faint smell like burning plastic. "It's not ours. Smells like ammonia and something else. It's pretty concentrated." I brush it off on my work clothes.

"They use ammonium nitrate as fertilizer on Beta," Jovan says. "It's got to be the agricologists. Yuri and his lot."

That makes sense. It's a pretty basic bomb. I'd have made a better one.

"I don't know how reliable it would be," I say. "If I were using it, I'd plant another on a different air circulator, just in case. I'll search the ship's vents for more bombs. I'll check the engine room, too, although I'm pretty sure it's clear. I'd notice if an atom was out of place up there. They must have not finished setting up the bombs."

"Are you going to tell your mom?" Jovan asks.

"She is captain, but ..." I trail off.

"But what?"

I swallow. "She's a stickler for rules. She'll follow the process. Report major incidents to the executive. If Yuri's involved, and there's another hidden bomb, he might detonate it right away."

Jovan looks pale. "I hadn't thought of that."

I slump down onto my bunk. "I don't know who to trust."

"We have to do something. Someone is trying to start a war."

I feel cold. As if a crack is opening up in my world. *War*.

Jovan sits next to me. "We have to defend ourselves and the ship."

"Yes, but not through fighting. We can't make the mistakes they made on *Venture 2*." I stare at the familiar cabin. Trying not to think about it blowing apart, about being sucked into space.

"But how do we stop it?" Jovan asks.

"We could tell Astra. She's Acting Head of Protection."

"She is? That's great!"

"But she's meeting with the executive now. And she'll probably tell Mom, and then we've got the same problem." I turn the bomb over, as if it could be hiding answers on the other side. White explosive. Black box. Red wire. Basic detonator. No new clues. "If we make the wrong move, we could trigger a war ourselves."

"We need to work out what the agricologists are up to. You dated Sabik, didn't you?"

"Yes, but I ended it." I showed him the vents, too. Could he have planted the bomb?

"Sabik's still hung up on you," Jovan says, cutting through my thoughts.

My cheeks get warm. I didn't know Jovan paid any attention to my love life.

"Does he trust you? Do you think you could get him to tell us about Yuri?"

I shake my head. "He's been lying to me. I think he was hiding a path in the woods."

"A path? What do you mean?"

"On the way back from fixing a landclearer. There was a path further into the forest, but he tried to distract me as we walked past it."

"Where is it?" Jovan grabs my display screen from a shelf. "We have to find out what they're trying to hide. We could get Astra to send a protector." He taps on the screen a few times, then passes it to me.

I take it from him and peer at the image. It's a map of Beta: the view from the shuttle simplified, turned into a harmless diagram. There's the shuttle camp, the village in the forest, the path between them, the graveyard, and the surrounding fields and woods.

I scan the picture, trying to make it match up with what I know of the surface. It's difficult. The map is too clean, nothing like the mess of a planet. And we never needed maps on the ship. I try to think of it like a schematic, but then I realize the path to the landclearer won't be on the map anyway, because it's not a real road.

"Sorry." I wave a hand over a large mass of woodland. "I know it's this side of the village, but that's all."

Jovan exhales. "I guess even if we knew where it was, we don't know if we can trust any of the protectors on the surface."

"I might be able to work out where it is if I were on Beta." I feel sick saying it.

"You're not going down to Beta. Things are too tense. You might get hurt. Yuri would definitely be suspicious."

"But we have to find out what they're hiding."

"Astra and your mother would never let you. Not now. And what excuse could you give for going there?"

"This is impossible. If we tell Astra, she might tell Mom. Even if she doesn't, and she sends a protector, we don't know if we can trust them, and I won't be able to explain where to look. How are we going to find out anything?"

Jovan pauses. Stares ahead for a moment. "Perhaps you could smuggle me down in something big, like an empty landclearer shell. I'd hide until night so they won't see me searching."

"You won't find the path if you don't know what you're looking for. And what about the creature?"

"Cassius, Orion, and the bird were all near the shuttle camp. I think it's safe on the other side of the village. And I'll take images," Jovan says. "Send them to you. You can tell me where to go."

"The trees all look the same to me. I'd need to be there."

Jovan shakes his head. He takes my hand. It makes my heart jump. The warmth of his skin. "I have to do this, Ursa," he says. "If they're planting bombs, they mean to start a war."

I think of the *Venture 2*. The bodies of her crew must still be floating through space somewhere, horror in their frozen eyes.

I breathe in, pull my hand away, and sit upright. "I'm not going to sit up here and wait for someone to blow up the *Venture,* and I'm the only one who can find the path. I'm going down there."

"Fine. I'll go with you. Protect you."

My stomach is warm. I wish we could do that.

"We'd be more likely to be caught if there's two of us. And even if that landclearer plan of yours would work, there'd only be room for one inside."

"You'd be in danger."

I clutch my hands together, think for a moment. "I know where Astra keeps her pulse gun. And you were right about the creature being on the other side of the settlement."

"But —"

"I'll ping my location if I get in trouble. I'll upload any evidence as soon as I find it."

Jovan shakes his head. "Send you down with a weapon? What

if you get caught? That'll give Yuri too much ammunition for his conspiracy nonsense."

He's right. It's one thing to be caught investigating in the forest, another to be caught with a stolen weapon. But a pulse gun is a small neon green cylinder. There has to be a way to hide it.

"My blowtorch," I say, finally.

"What?"

I pull it out of my gear bag, hold it up. It's a dark metal tube, just bigger than a pulse gun. "I can adjust this, take out the energy cylinder. Slide the gun into the body of the blowtorch. If I get searched, all they'll find is an innocent-looking tool."

Jovan's Adam's apple bobs. "There has to be another way. I don't want you to go, Ursa."

"You said it yourself, we have no evidence and no way of knowing what Yuri is going to do next. We can't just wait for him to destroy the *Venture*."

Jovan meets my gaze. "I don't have a choice, do I?"

"No. Because this is my decision. The landclearer thing is a good idea. There's one due to go down in a couple of days. But I can work on it tomorrow, get it finished ahead of schedule, so it's ready for the next shuttle down."

Jovan puts his hand on my shoulder. Our eyes lock.

Deep breath. "Let's do it," I say.

CHAPTER 14

I make a new remote as quickly as I can and spend the rest of the morning checking the vents and the engine room. They're all clear, which is good. I guess Yuri hasn't gotten around to planting another bomb. Or maybe he didn't think of planting two. He's an agricologist, after all. They're pretty dumb when it comes to the basics of engineering. He probably knows nothing about the principle of redundancy.

Then I try to do normal things. Lunch. My afternoon shift, then an extra evening shift, working on the landclearer. I'm exhausted by the time I pad back along the narrow corridors to my habitation carriage and down the steps to my cabin, avoiding the gaze of the people I pass.

I heave open our cabin door and squeeze through. Mom's in there, just sitting on my bunk. She smiles and stands when I come in, but I slink over to my bed and sit down, slouching forward so I don't hit my head on the bunk above. Mom leans against the bathroom unit, and I stare down at our feet.

"How are you?" she asks.

The air in the room is so still with no breeze to move it. Everything is limp and dead around us, the air filling with our bodily odors. I try to block it all out. Concentrate on what I have to say.

"I'm going to be working some double shifts over the next couple of days," I say, feeling guilty. "Including an overnight. There's a lot to do, since people have gone down to the planet. I won't be in the cabin much."

It's the excuse Jovan and I came up with.

Mom frowns. "I was hoping we could spend some time together. I don't want you to think that because I'm captain now, I don't have time for you."

"It's fine, Mom. Working is the best thing for me. Can you tell Astra that I'm going to be busy?" I don't want to tell her myself. She can always tell when I'm lying.

She sighs. "Okay."

"How's the investigation going?"

Mom shrugs. "I don't know. Antares had the engineering equipment checked. There's nothing missing from the hut."

"So, Yuri was making it up? What are you going to do?"

Mom shakes her head. "I can't do anything without evidence. I just have to keep digging."

At least I can help with that.

Mom sighs. "I wanted to see you. I've missed you. But I should probably get back to work. See if there's a new angle on this I can come up with."

"Okay." I start changing into my sleepsuit. I can't meet her eyes.

"Well, good night then." She sounds sad. She pushes the door open and is gone.

Once I'm ready, I lie on my thin mattress, breathing in the air of the ship. Listening to her creaks and clunks. The hum of the air circulation system. The murmur of the boosters correcting our position and spin. My home. My cramped and crowded oasis in the heavens. Tomorrow I will be flung down to Beta. And who knows what will happen there.

I squeeze my eyes tight shut and try not to think about it.

I don't want to go down to the planet. But I don't want us to go to war, either. What's happened to us? To this crew? I used to know them all so well. But they're becoming strangers, nursing secrets and suspicion. It feels as if the ground is fracturing beneath my feet, like Maia on the ice.

I try to swallow the lump in my throat, but it sticks there. When I start crying, it's like it's going to choke me or make me sick. I sob into the bedclothes. It's not pretty, and I'm glad no one is here to see.

THE NEXT DAY SPEEDS by. I work around the ship, mostly tinkering. Patching up insulation, checking on the magnetic shield, and fixing the leak in habitation carriage 2. I soak up the drops on the floor after I've tightened the gasket, and then I transfer the water to a vial to put back into the system. It's only when I'm finished that I remember I don't need to do that anymore.

At lunchtime, when I know the cabin and corridors will be mostly empty, I creep in to take Astra's pulse gun. I'm not supposed to be able to get into the crew's personal safes, but I learned how to hack the emergency opening mechanism years ago. And there, in Astra's small safe, is the neon green of her pulse gun. It's slim and cold in my fingers. I change the setting on the gun from green to red. Lethal. If I'm going up against the creature, I doubt the stun option will be enough.

Astra won't check the safe while I'm away. She never uses her gun. She's more of an investigator and interviewer these days. I slip it into my gear bag and head back to the main engineering workshop. The energy cylinder is jammed in the blowtorch. I hit it with my wrench, and the strike rebounds on the pulse gun sitting next to it on the workbench, chipping a corner off the pulse gun casing.

But it does the trick. The energy cylinder slides out of the blowtorch, and the pulse gun slides in perfectly. I only hope I haven't broken it. Lunch is almost over, and I can't risk testing it in the engineering lab when anyone can walk in.

Once that's done, I double-check what Mom told me last night, scanning through the engineering supply lists, the manifests of what went down to the planet, and the checklists of what's still in the engineering supply hut. My head spins when I try to focus. But Antares is right: no engineering equipment is missing. Yuri did make that up.

Jovan pings me to let me know he's switched his shift. Now he's scheduled to pick up the animal transport pod when it comes back up on the shuttle tomorrow. The chickens are going down in it today, but it'll be empty coming back. That's my ride back sorted. If all goes well, I'll spend one night on the planet, hide in the animal transport pod, and be back on the ship before my disappearance is noticed.

I don't want to think about what will happen if all doesn't go well.

AFTER MY SHIFT, I pack my landsuit into a small bag and leave the cabin. Jovan meets me at the cargo loading bay. We wait until the corridor clears around us before opening the doors.

"Ready?" he says. I nod, and he hits the button.

The doors swish open. There are heaps of equipment in the cargo bay, ready to go down to the planet. Right in the middle stands the empty casing of the landclearer I fixed yesterday. Jovan heads straight for it and swings open the side hatch. I join him and we peer into the dark.

"It's cramped, but you'll fit okay. It's good that you're petite. Probably best to brace yourself against the sides as much as you can. It'll be a bumpy ride."

I switch from my gray ship's overalls to my warm landsuit while Jovan keeps watch, back turned out of respect. Then I climb into the landclearer. It is tight in here. Metal corners stick into my back as I try to find a comfortable way to sit.

Jovan is framed by the hatch. "Stay safe. See you tomorrow."

"See you tomorrow?" It comes out like a question when I say it.

Jovan looks like he's about to say something else, but there's the buzz the cargo bay doors make when they're about to open. Jovan closes the hatch quickly, shutting me in the body of the landclearer.

There's a voice. Aldrin. "What are you doing here?"

"Just checking on the chickens," Jovan says. "They're ready to go."

"They'd better be." Aldrin sounds tired. "Because I have to load them."

Jovan's footsteps fade, replaced by the sound of Aldrin clumping around, readying the loading cart. The hydraulics buzz, lifting me into the cargo hold of the shuttle and bumping me against the inside of the landclearer. Once I'm in place I can see out of the crack around the edge of the hatch, if I put my eye right against the cold metal. I see the animal transport pod and a few other boxes loaded into the hold, then the shuttle cargo doors close and it's pitch black.

It's not long before the shuttle leaves. It's hard to brace myself as gravity lifts, then returns. My eyes strain at the blackness, desperate for something to focus on.

I'm not the only live passenger in the cargo hold. The dark around me is filled with the alien sounds of clucking and squawking. I know chickens are harmless, but it's hard to remember that when their screeches and bawks echo through the black. Soon the stuffy space fills with a stink worse than the washrooms. The smell of panicked poultry, I guess.

The shuttle is a smooth ride if you're in one of the bucket seats, but by the time we land, I'm bruised and battered, muscles aching from the strain of pressing against the casing, trying to steady myself. Skin hot from where I hit the sides too many times. I'm glad of the extra padding of my landsuit, but sweaty because of it.

A little while after we land there's a whirr. A gray line appears in the darkness, the outline of the landclearer's hatch. The air is suddenly fresher; the shuttle cargo hold doors must be open, releasing the chicken-stink into the outside world. There's the hum of the hydraulics, more bumping as the landclearer shell is unloaded, then proper light through the crack. I exhale and breathe the cool air in deeply.

There's the rhythmic patter of rain on the landclearer casing. Some lurches and bumps, then acceleration. I must be on the trailer of a landbike. I tense against the metal as we jolt along the forest path.

It's not long before we halt, and there's tipping and tilting, then the tapping of the rain stops. A painful thump bangs my head hard against a metal corner, and I'm still. I bite my tongue to stop myself screaming and count to ten silently as the pain in my skull crests then subsides. I rub my bruised head, put an eye to the crack around the edge of the hatch, and see the hulking shadows of equipment around me.

I've made it to the equipment hut.

I wait, listening. No voices. No chickens; they'll have gone to their new homes. No sound but the thrum of rain on the roof high above me. I need to stretch my cramping legs. I ease open the hatch and peer out. My landclearer has been set down next to some digger parts, so I'm hidden even if someone enters the hut. I climb out, grateful to ease the pressure in my legs and body.

I stretch, rubbing my aching limbs and bruises and waiting until the pins and needles have gone, then creep across the hut. The packed, dry dirt of the ground and the rain on the roof muffle my steps, but I kick up dust. Some gets up my nose, and I pinch it until the urge to sneeze fades.

Nearer the door, the dirt darkens into mud, and there are voices from outside. I tiptoe over to peek through the crack. Agricologists and builders huddle there, using the overhang of the hut as shelter from the downpour: Sabik, Almach, Phoebe, and Cassiopeia.

My nose itches again. A sneeze forces its way out as I'm still raising my hand, but I manage to muffle it with my palm. Only a quiet "chuff" sneaks out. I check outside. None of them have turned around. There's not even a break in the conversation. The sound was probably drowned out by the drumming rain on the roof above.

The sun is setting, and there are gaps in the clouds. The tapping on the roof grows sporadic, then stops altogether. The crew members wrap up their conversation and go their separate ways. Three of them head toward the habitation huts. Sabik heads the other way, behind the equipment hut and out of sight.

My plan is to head out when it's dark, so I sit down on the dusty ground and wait, peering out the crack in the door. Slowly, the weather clears. There are still clouds, smeared over the darkening blue. The setting sun colors them shades of pink and purple before sliding below the horizon, soaking the forest camp in the mauve-gray of twilight.

I guess this planet would be kind of pretty if it weren't for all the danger.

I scratch my arms. This weather is drying it out my skin, making it flake like rust. My lips are dry too, and I bite at them as I wait, peeling the upper layer off like old glue.

People should be back at their huts now, settling in for the night, lifting their feet into bed and silencing the creak of their floorboards. My limbs ache with exhaustion. I wish I could slink to a hut and rest. But instead I wait until the last of the light drains from the sky.

I creak the door open. Pull up the hood on my landsuit. There's a chill to the air, and it's still damp after the rain. I head for the habitation huts nearest the fields, moving carefully from the shadow of one hut to the next, keeping my face turned away from the village as much as I can. There are cracks of light visible at some of the windows. I try not to creep. I don't want to draw attention to myself. I'm just a shadow in the dark. A late worker returning home.

I reach the edge of the huts and head out over the fields in what I hope is the right direction. The planet is almost unrecognizable in the night. I know it's just because of the way the rods and cones in my eyes react to low light, but it turns Beta into a different place.

Some plants are already growing in the fields surrounding our small town. They're ankle high, the green stalks looking gray in the starlight. The galaxy is spread out above me. Familiar constellations of light in the blackness of the heavens. The stars extend around me on all sides, like an inverted blanket. They twinkle here. The effect of the atmosphere: stellar scintillation. The only sound is the tramp of my feet on the soil and the pant of my breath. I try to look purposeful, in case anyone is watching.

I reach the dark edge of the forest and pause, trying to remember where I went with Sabik. I'm pretty sure I turned left, so I head that way, keeping close enough to the woods that my figure should fade into the darkness of the trees. At least that's what I hope. The glowferns could be outlining my silhouette.

I try not to think about the creature. Remind myself it was on the other side of the village. Far away from here. But I still pull the blowtorch from my bag and slide out the pulse gun, feeling the sharp edge of the chipped casing in my palm. Clutching it tightly, I walk up and down along the tree line a few times. No path. What if I can't find it in time? What if I'm searching all night? I move further along, into the next field, and I'm starting to think I'm heading in the wrong direction when I spot it.

It's just another gap between the trees, slightly wider than the usual. A dark tunnel. The relief of finding the path evaporates as I realize what that means.

I have to go into the woods. Alone. At night.

I check back over the fields, wondering if I sensed a movement. Nothing. Barely even the sway of the plants on this still night. Deep breath. Gun gripped in my hand, I step between the trees.

The first few meters are the hardest. My heart pounds. The cold I felt in the fields morphs into a clammy sweat. I don't want to turn on my linkcom's light until I'm well into the woods, out of sight of the village. Thin branches are invisible in the dark, and they whip into my face, scratching my cheek. It's easy to imagine them as claws. I bite my tongue so I don't cry out. Roots trip my feet. But soon I've blundered enough into the darkness for my light to be hidden by the thick trees. And anyway, I can't take this anymore, so I flip my linkcom's light on.

The glare makes every branch and needle stand out, and for a second I blink in the light before forcing myself to continue. I swallow down the acid of panic in my mouth, aware that I'm illuminating myself as much as the path and that there's a killer down here on the planet, somewhere.

An alien.

No. That's impossible. And anyway, I know if there's a creature it's probably far away, the other side of the village. But rational thought is hard as the shadows of the trees jump and move in my linkcom's glare. It was about an hour into the walk that I noticed the path last time; I set an alert on my linkcom to go off just short of that. I check the red light on my gun. It's a high enough pulse to kill a human, but will that be enough against a monster in the forest? I run my thumb over the chip. What if I broke it when the wrench blow rebounded in the engineering lab, and it doesn't fire at all?

I keep peering behind me. But there's only the hiss of a gentle breeze stirring the branches, like an invisible body moving between them. Time passes too slowly as I slog through the forest, twitchy and tense. Why did I agree to this? Why did I insist upon it? I check my linkcom several times, worried I've missed the alert, but each time, only minutes have passed.

I think of Maia. Her body rotting in the cold ground of Beta. All that potential energy locked up in her corpse. She always came with me on adventures. What if she comes this time? I can almost hear her dead feet dragging behind me.

No. That's the wind. I'm being irrational. I need to focus. But I can't shake her from my thoughts.

I push on. I can only see a few meters into the tangled trees either side of me, and my mind is quick to project horrors on the dark, so I stop looking. Concentrate on putting one foot in front of the other.

I want to talk to Maia, but I'm scared she'll answer.

I nearly scream when the alert pings in my hand.

One hour. I wait for my thumping heart to calm before I carry on walking, looking around more carefully now. What if there is no path, and Sabik was telling the truth? What if it was just a trick of the trees?

I'm starting to think I've made a huge mistake when I trip over a raised lump in the land. I assume it's another root until I look down at my feet. It's a mound of earth around the trunk of a tree, protruding slightly onto the path.

That's odd.

It reminds me of something. I shine the linkcom's light on the tree. It's not like the others around it. It's shorter, and its needles are drier. They fall off at my touch.

I realize what the mound reminds me of. Next to some of the

huts, people have moved plants from the forest, ones that are meant to produce flowers. They're trying to mimic gardens on Alpha. Each of those plants has a little mound around its base where the soil was heaped after they were put in the dirt. Most of them are growing well, but a few are dying, turning brown. They didn't survive the move.

Like this tree. It was replanted here.

I step back and peer behind it. Darkness between trunks. I aim my linkcom's light at the ground. The undergrowth behind the mound is trodden down.

It's the hidden path.

This tree was planted to hide the trail. Probably because of the questions I asked. I swallow. There's no doubt now. Sabik was lying to me. But what was he hiding? I'm about to squeeze by the new tree when a noise catches my attention.

Was that the crack of a twig?

I pause. Just the gentle rustle of the trees. The creak of bending branches. But still I lift my light, peer back down the path. Why do I feel like something is following me?

Because I'm paranoid. Or because there is something there, just out of sight. Perhaps it's whoever killed Cassius and Orion. Or the corpse of my best friend, dragging her dead limbs through the forest. Or a bloodthirsty alien. Or the big bad wolf.

I used to be so rational. What happened to me? Why can't I stop thinking like this?

I wait for a long time, my heart in my throat, but only the trees move with the wind.

Okay then, down the secret path.

I push by the new tree. The path is narrower than the one left behind by the landclearer before it broke down. But it's more recently made, following the natural gaps between trees. If I look carefully I can spot the red stumps where branches have been cut back to make the way through easier. The red sap of the tree has dried in trickles, like blood running down the black trunks. I hope I'll find whatever it is quickly. Hope there won't be anyone, or anything, there. Hope I can upload evidence to Jovan and get out of here.

The branches above thin out a little, so I catch glimpses of the sky. I wonder why, until my linkcom light highlights the red of severed trunks in the undergrowth, scattered among the still-standing trunks. Someone cut down these trees. What for? I'm staring down at the rings of the last stump, so I almost walk into it.

A cottage, hidden in the deep, dark wood.

It's more primitive than the huts in our village. The timber isn't cut into planks or finished. The logs intersect at the corners, like a cabin out of a history vidstream.

I walk around it, the unreal feeling of the night compounding. I almost expect it to be made of gingerbread. There are no windows breaking up the crude walls. What is this?

I head to the door. Try to push it open. But it's jammed. I shove at it, harder. No joy. I step back and am about to kick it when my linkcom light catches the gleam of metal in the gap between the door and the frame. I'd never have noticed in daylight.

I get down on my knees and put my eye to the gap. The corner of a remote sensor shines between the door and the frame. It's clever. A remotely controlled lock. Perhaps calibrated to someone's linkcom. A binary circuit, just like the bomb. Open or closed.

And I know how to open it.

I pull out the pulse gun, press it to the millimeter of metal I spy through the gap, and hit the button. There's a spark and a quiet zap as I blow out the sensor. Then I give the door a shove, and it swings open. I tiptoe in, glad the ground is just dirt. There are no floorboards to creak. No feeling that someone is following me around the room. But still, I check over my shoulder.

There's one chest in the center of the room, and others pushed against the walls around the edges. I head for the chest in the center, and I heave open the heavy wooden lid. I shine my linkcom's beam inside and see the fuzzy shapes of clothes.

I move across the room to the first chest against the wall. This one is filled with dried beans. I lower the lid and move to the next trunk. The familiar shapes of tools in that one. I work my way around, open all the chests, but they're the same: dried soya noodles and kelp, chickpeas and more tools. What is going on here?

I'm about to give up when I turn back to the chest in the middle of the room. I stare at it for a while, wondering about its placement. Why is it there? It can't be in use as a table — there are no chairs around it. And there's room for it against the walls with the other chests. Think, Ursa. What's different about it?

It's the only one filled with clothes, not heavy tools or dried food. It would be easy to move. Hmm. I give it a heave, and yes, the dirt looks different underneath. A shade lighter. Like it's been disturbed. I stomp on it, and there's a hollow noise.

I crouch down and dig my fingers into the ground. Immediately they hit something hard. I sweep away the layer with the side of my arm, and there it is. Another trunk, buried under a thin covering of dirt. Unlike the others, the lid of this one is nailed shut.

Like that's going to stop me.

I turn back to one of the tool chests and rummage until I find a crowbar. I pry the lid off, and my linkcom's light reveals the shine of neon green. Pulse guns. Four of them. And below them axes, hammers, and explosives. There's wire too, and casings from the printers. Everything you need to make the bomb I saw on the ship. To make several bombs.

This is an arsenal. Enough for war.

I swallow down the bile that rises. I need to focus. I've found what I was looking for: hard evidence. I pull up the display on my linkcom. Take photos and upload them to the ship's engineering databanks, along with the coordinates, in the file I've already agreed upon with Jovan. I save them in the format we use for the maintenance logs, and label it only with the date and time. If anyone's checking on the systems, it'll look like a routine engineering file.

But that's not enough. I can't wait until I'm back on the ship, not since I've seen this. I doubt I'll be able to rebury this neatly enough. They'll know someone was here. I have to tell someone now. But who? And what can I say? Someone could be monitoring the pings.

And then I know. Astra. I've found the evidence. She's Head of Protection. It's time for her to get involved. I type a quick ping to her. *Jovan wants to show you something in the databanks. Now.* That should sound innocent, in case anyone is listening in, and Jovan will understand when she asks.

The adrenaline is draining from my system. I stare down into the chest, chilled by the horror of it. Someone put all these here. Someone who planned to murder their fellow crew members. I was wrong. It's not cracks opening between the crew. It's chasms.

Astra's reply comes in quicker than I'd have expected.

You should have spoken to me earlier. Sending people to help with the issue now. Don't go anywhere.

I am in so much trouble when I get back on the ship.

If I get back on the ship.

But I've done it. I've found the evidence. My joints ache with weariness and the bruises from my descent. I sit down on the cold of the hut's dirt floor. My head is pounding. I lean against the chest, but the edges of the wood dig into my back. I pull some of the clothes out and put them on the ground and against the chest, cushioning it.

I settle into my new seat and wait. Make sure my pulse gun is in my hand, my focus on the open door. But my grip is growing weaker. The dizziness of exhaustion is creeping in. And I close my eyes. Just for a moment.

I don't know how much later it is when I open them again. I just know a noise wakes me. Twigs snapping outside. It'll be the people Astra sent. People she trusts, no doubt. Thank Beta.

I push myself up and hurry out of the hut to greet them. Then I freeze.

It's not people at all.

It's only one person, standing in the shadow of a tree, face in darkness.

CHAPTER 15

I lift the pulse gun.

"Who's there?"

The figure steps forward, into the starlight, pushing his floppy hair from his eyes with a bandaged hand. Sabik.

Astra would not have sent Sabik.

"It's me. What are you doing here, Ursa?"

I keep the gun raised, but my hand is shaking.

"Don't come any closer."

He takes another step. "What?"

"You heard me! Stay there! I will shoot!"

He raises his arms. "Is that thing on red? Put it down, Ursa. It's me."

"Don't play innocent. I saw your arsenal."

"What arsenal?"

"You know full well! You're the one who tried to hide this place from me!"

"Whoa." He keeps his hands up. "Yes, I hid this place from you. But there is no arsenal here. This is a refuge."

"Some refuge! There's enough explosive to blow up the ship. Enough weapons to kill half the crew."

His brow crinkles. "What?"

"I found the hidden chest, Sabik."

"I don't know what you're talking about. I promise."

I almost believe him. That's the dumb thing. It's hard to read his expression in the dark, but his face, his stance, is so familiar, and I remember when I loved him. I use my other hand to steady the gun, keeping it trained on his chest. Could I shoot him? I must be ready to. He's betrayed me. He's betrayed us all.

He puts a hand out. "Why don't you show me, Ursa?"

"I'm not falling for this."

"I would never hurt you, Ursa. You have to know that." His hands are palm up now. "Please, show me what you're talking about."

"This is a trick."

"It's not. You have a pulse gun. My hands are empty. Just show me."

He steps forward, and I can see the plea in his eyes. A bit of my resolve crumbles.

"If you make any sneaky moves I will kill you."

"I believe you, Ursa." He looks sad when he says it.

"See for yourself." I keep the gun steady. "Walk inside. Slowly. The gun is pointed at your back. If you make a move for the weapons I will shoot."

He does what I say, following the light I cast on the dirt floor ahead of him. He's only taken one step inside when he spots the excavated chest. He gasps, takes a step back.

"I … I didn't know about this. I promise, Ursa. You know me, I wouldn't have had anything to do with this." He turns around. I shine the light on his face. He blinks, but I see shock in his dark eyes.

Is it possible Sabik didn't know about the arsenal? He can't be that naive. He couldn't spend all this time with someone like Yuri and not know what he's up to.

"Then what on Beta is this hut for? You tried to hide it from me."

"It was a clubhouse at first, just a place to hang out."

"What?"

"Yuri, me, a few of the agricologists and builders. For fun. On the ship, there was never any privacy. Never a place of your own." He looks at me. "You understand, right? You had the vents."

"You said it was a clubhouse *at first*. Then what?"

Sabik drops his gaze to the dirt floor. "Yuri thought there were people on the ship preparing for war, so we stocked this place so we'd have somewhere safe to hide if we needed it."

"Yuri's the one who wants to start a war."

Sabik's gaze snaps back up to me. "We saw people smuggling stuff out of the engineering hut in the middle of the night. Just like the *Venture 2*. Weapons made out of engineering equipment, remember?"

"There's no engineering equipment missing."

Sabik stares. "What?"

"I checked. Yuri made that up to justify his war."

"No. You don't understand. It wasn't Yuri who saw people smuggling equipment from the engineering hut. It was me."

I pause. "Then you got it wrong."

"No ... I didn't ..." He stops talking and tilts his head, listening.

Then I hear it too. More footsteps, coming through the forest.

I've been stupid. I've let Sabik get between the weapons and me.

"Get away from the chest!" I shout.

Sabik jumps back, almost colliding with me. I stumble, then rush to get to the other side of him, nearer the chest. I switch off the linkcom's light, but keep the pulse gun focused on Sabik, hand shaking.

"Step outside. Lie down! Face down! Now!"

I'm nearly incoherent, words slurring together in my panic. But Sabik does as I say, lying down on the dirt outside the hut's door. I take a step back and position myself in the hut, behind the open door, heart racing. I'm hidden in the shadows. I can see anyone long before they get to the hut. Can shoot them before they can get me or the pulse guns.

I watch the sliver of the forest I can see. Listen to the hiss of the trees. The tips of them bend and bow in the breeze like dark flames. Then two figures appear, stepping out of the black between the branches, staring at the hut, the tree stumps.

A woman first, shoulders back, head twitching around at high attention. It's Protector Leda. Behind her there's a skinny male figure, slouching and breaking twigs as he stomps into sight: Protector Sirius, still new at this. They see Sabik first, and Leda's pulse gun is out in an instant, pointed at him.

"What's this hut? Where's Ursa?" she demands. "Astra said she was here."

I exhale and lower my gun. They're my rescuers. Thank Beta. Astra's smart. I should have known she'd put people she trusted on the planet. They probably came down on the same shuttle as I did, cradled in the bucket seats, while I was thrown around in a landclearer shell in cargo.

"I'm in here," I yell. "Yuri built this camp. And he was hiding this."

"Cover him," Leda says to Sirius, pointing at Sabik, still lying on the ground. Then she strides over, stepping around him. She peers through the door and shines her linkcom's light on the arsenal.

I nod at Sabik. "He claims he didn't know about the weapons. They were buried."

"I didn't know," Sabik says. "I swear."

She breathes in through her teeth. "Do you think he's telling the truth?"

Sabik looks at me, face smeared with dirt.

"Maybe," I say. "It would be out of character for him to hide weapons. But I'm not sure I know him anymore."

Sabik lets his gaze drop to the ground again.

"We need to hide Sabik while we interview him. We can't risk Sabik letting Yuri know that we're on to him."

"Aren't we going to arrest Yuri?"

"Not now. There aren't enough of us," Leda says. "We'll get you two somewhere safe. There are some empty cabins in the shuttle camp. We can hide you there, if Sabik cooperates."

"I'll cooperate," Sabik says, his voice quiet.

"We'll gag him to be sure," Leda says, "since we have to get back through the camp without attracting attention. We'll bring down reinforcements on the next shuttle."

Sirius pulls some fabric from his pocket and holds it out. Sabik opens his mouth obediently. Lets Sirius silence him.

"Switch your pulse gun to lethal," I say. "There may be a creature in the forest."

Sirius hesitates, but they both pull out their guns, and the buttons change from green to red as they adjust them.

We're quiet as we trek back through the wood, Leda in the lead, Sabik ahead of me, my gun trained on his back. Sirius brings up the rear. For a long time, I hear nothing but our panting and our feet crunching on the forest floor.

I'm dizzy with exhaustion and the stress of all this. But I'm glad to be walking in the middle of the group. The trek feels shorter with company, and my fears about monsters, ghosts, and wolves seem stupid now. We pause as we get close to the fields, turn off our linkcom lights, and proceed in darkness. We tread carefully, skirting the edge of the fields, keeping to the shadows.

We're passing the first of the habitation huts when I see it.

A shadow behind the building, twitching movements in the

darkness. Just above waist height. Too low to be a person. And it doesn't move like one.

I grab Sabik, wave desperately at where I saw the shadow move. He glances behind the huts and shakes his head.

"I saw something," I whisper, as quietly as I can.

Leda stops, looks back over her shoulder. She raises a finger to her lips.

I stare into the darkness. What if it's the creature, here in the forest camp? It could kill us, or get into a hut and rip apart a family as they sleep.

I point my gun at the gap. The red button glows.

Another movement in the dark.

"Look!" I whisper. "It's there!"

Sabik tilts his head urgently in the direction we were moving. His eyes are wide. Leda is waving me on. But if the creature is there, it'll attack us from behind.

A screech from the darkness behind the hut.

A cry bursts from my throat before I can stop it. I press the button. The scene lights up for a second, bright as if I'd used my arc welder. I see a flash of a cage, with perches in it, plump shapes on each. One of them falls, thumps against the ground.

Chickens. Oh no. I'm an idiot.

The birds cluck and squawk. A light goes on in the hut, illuminating the cage properly. The other chickens are awake now, screeching and flapping, madness in their beady eyes as they twitch their heads from side to side to look at me and at the chicken I killed.

"Who's out there?" Phoebe's voice calls from inside, then a child starts wailing behind her. "You're scaring the chickens and Aquila. What was that flash?"

"Come on!" Leda hisses, and we're off, running as silently as we can, heading for the path through the forest to the shuttle camp.

I peer back over my shoulder. The door of the hut opens.

"Hey, what's going on?" Phoebe says. "Leda, Sirius, what are you doing? Sabik? What's going on?" She peers at the cage. "Did you kill one of the chickens? Why on Beta?"

I duck behind Sirius, but it's too late.

"Ursa!" Phoebe yells. "What are you doing down here?"

Lights come on in other huts. Shouting.

We're in trouble.

CHAPTER 16

There's no point in running now. People come out of their huts. Voices are raised in alarm and anger when they spot me with Sabik, cuffed and gagged.

Yeah. This doesn't look good.

"What do we do?" I ask Leda.

"We tell the truth." She's backing up, hand clutching her gun. "We're following the law. We have to hope that still holds some sway down here."

Sabik makes a "mmmf" noise. Points his eyes down at his gag. People are coming nearer. We're at the edge of the forest camp, our backs to the path toward the shuttle. We'd have made it if I hadn't been an idiot.

"What's going on? Why is she down here?" a man shouts. I can't tell who. He's in the shadow of a hut, just a dark shape.

"They killed one of our chickens!" Phoebe yells.

"I'm sorry, that was an accident."

But other voices join the hubbub, drowning me out. I take a step back and keep my gun low. Not pointed at anyone.

"What are you doing with Sabik?" A big man is running toward us through the darkness, with a second, smaller man right behind him. Leda raises her gun. It takes me a second to recognize them in the low light.

Tabit and Rigel. Sabik's dads.

"Stay back!" Leda shouts.

Tabit is getting closer, eyes wide as he runs. Rigel's arm is reaching out toward his son. There are others behind them, agricologists and builders.

"Mmmm!" says Sabik, straining on the gag.

"Tabit and Rigel won't hurt us," I say to Leda. I reach out and push her gun down.

"Ursa?" says Tabit, slowing down, taking in our weapons. "Why is he gagged?"

I pull the gag out of Sabik's mouth. "I'm okay, Dad," he says.

Rigel catches up, rests his hands on his thighs. Pants. "What's going on? Where are you taking him?"

"To the shuttle camp," Leda says. "He's under arrest."

"Why?" asks Tabit.

"Suspicion of involvement in treason," Sirius says.

There's a gasp from the growing crowd. Tabit takes his husband's hand. More people are gathering. No sign of Yuri. But this lot is threatening enough.

I look around, trying to orient myself, figure out where Yuri's hut is. There. The cabin with the chickens. Phoebe's in the crowd, clutching Aquila, but Yuri isn't. There's a light on in their hut, but the door is closed.

"You can't be serious," Rigel says.

"They found weapons at the hut in the woods, Pa," Sabik says. "I didn't know they were there."

I scan the faces before us. Sabik's dads seem surprised, as does most of the crowd.

"You can't take him," says Almach, who nominated Yuri for

captain. "There's no justice on board. Ursa's family runs the ship. Nashira just made Astra Acting Head of Protection."

Murmurs of agreement. Hands clenched in fists.

"We'll defend Yuri," someone shouts from the back of the crowd.

"With what?" Sabik asks. "They're armed."

"There's more of us," Tabit says, straightening up.

"Please, Dad. It's okay. I don't want anyone getting hurt."

There must be a hundred people here in the darkness. Too many for us to take on. And I feel unsteady in this mud. I peer down at my gun and notice it's red. Time to switch it to stun.

But a door slams from the direction of the lit hut. No one comes out. That must mean someone went in when I wasn't looking. Who? What if there's an arsenal in there, like in the forest?

"I saw the weapons myself," Sabik says. "Yuri lied to us."

A few people pause. Phoebe bites her lip, arm around her daughter Aquila in front of her.

A flicker in the window of Yuri's hut, as someone moves in front of the light source.

"Sabik's lying! He probably planted the weapons, and planted the fur near Cassius's body!" shouts Almach. "He's working for his girlfriend!"

"She's not my —" Sabik starts, but people are moving closer. The hiss of outraged whispers mixes with the sound of the trees and the breeze, crowding me. I look away from the hut. Next to me, Leda and Sirius raise their guns.

"Stop! Stay back, please!" Sabik says.

"Don't come any nearer!" Leda shouts.

But they're not stopping. I swallow. Point my gun at the nearest person. It's Chara, a builder. She's only three years older than me. We were in the same cohort in basic training. Got yelled at for whispering to each other during Pisces's dull, droning lectures.

I can barely keep the gun straight. Then I realize the button is still red.

"Please! It's set to full power!" I say.

She doesn't break her stride. Our eyes are locked. Cassiopeia, her older sister, emerges behind her, running toward us, shouting and shoving her way through the crowd. Her arm is stretched out to Chara, but she's too far away to grab hold of her.

"I don't want to shoot!" I say. My hands are shaking. I fumble to find the button, wishing it were green. Soon she'll be close enough to snatch it from me. I can't let that happen.

But I can't kill her, either.

"Stop!" A commanding female voice from the back of the crowd.

Chara freezes, then looks back over her shoulder.

There, in front of his hut, is Yuri. His hands are cuffed behind him. Vega is holding his elbow in one hand and pressing a pulse gun to his head with the other. The button is red.

"Step back," Yuri says. "I don't want anyone to get hurt."

"If any of you move, I'll shoot," Vega says. "I heard everything. Yuri is under arrest."

Leda exhales next to me. "Thank Beta."

No one is moving any closer. But they're not backing up, either. Cassiopeia has reached Chara's side and puts a gentle hand on her shoulder. Chara still doesn't move.

The hissing of the trees gets louder, as if they're discussing us.

"This is a misunderstanding," Yuri says. "I'm happy to clear it up." His head is over to one side slightly. Vega is obviously shoving the gun hard against it.

"Smart decision," she says. "We'll clear it up on the ship. And unless you lot want to see me zap this guy, I suggest you back up."

There's a long pause, then Chara takes two steps back. Cassiopeia wraps her arms around her younger sister and clutches her tight. I breathe, grateful for the space she leaves. The rest of the crowd shifts too, creating a corridor between them for Vega to pass through. She strides forward, pulling Yuri by his elbow, not moving the gun from his skull.

"Can we trust her?" I ask Leda, quietly.

"She's a good protector. And I think this is proof that we can. Don't you?"

I don't answer. Vega isn't looking at me as she joins us.

"Get me a landbike and a trailer," she barks at an agricologist.

"Why are you siding with Ursa?" Chara asks.

"I'm not." Vega glances at me, and there's anger in her eyes. "Ursa has to face justice. But this is about us, not her. We need to know if Yuri lied to us."

Everyone around us is still. Vega pushes the pulse gun harder against Yuri's head.

"Ow!"

"Landbike and trailer, now!" she orders.

At the back of the crowd, Almach heads toward the parked landbikes.

If everyone stays calm, we might all survive this. I keep my pulse gun pointed at the crowd. The landbike pulls up beside us with a hum, and Almach gets off. Vega shoves Yuri onto the trailer at the back.

"I'll drive," Leda says. I nod toward the trailer, and Sabik gets in beside Yuri. I follow him, clambering my way to a seat. Sirius brings up the rear, pulse gun still pointed at the crowd.

"They won't give him a fair trial!" someone shouts from the shadow of a hut.

For a moment, I think it's going to turn ugly, but Vega fires a pulse into the air. The zap lights the scene for a second. A freeze-frame of familiar faces warped by shock and anger, the village dark behind them.

"I'll make sure he gets a fair trial," Vega shouts. "I won't let them cover anything up."

There are some murmurings in the crowd, but this seems to reassure them.

Vega climbs into the trailer. "Let's go," she says quietly. "They could turn on us any minute."

Leda revs the engine, and we jolt in our seats as the bike lurches forward, through the darkness, toward the shuttle camp. The launch isn't scheduled until the morning, but Sirius pings Mom back on the *Venture*, and she authorizes the early takeoff. I guess Astra told her everything.

She is going to be so mad at me.

We bump along the path. Sirius sits and stares back toward the forest camp. "No one's following."

I try not to look at the trees as we whip past them. Try to ignore the glowferns and focus on keeping an eye on Yuri, Sabik, and Vega.

Yuri leans forward, addresses Sabik. "Why were you snooping around at the peace camp? Didn't you trust me?"

"I trusted you." There's hurt in Sabik's eyes. "I was following Ursa."

My mouth drops open. "You saw me?"

"Heard you. Your sneeze, from the engineering shed. I hid out of sight and waited until you came out."

Yuri laughs. "You recognized her sneeze? You're still hung up on her."

Sabik doesn't respond. My cheeks are warm against the cold breeze.

"I bet you never told her about Maia." Vega's speaking too loud. Smiling too wide.

Sabik's head snaps up. "Don't."

"What about Maia?" I ask, not sure I want the answer.

The landbike jolts over a rut in the path and we all bounce in our seats.

"Leave it," Sabik says.

"She was after Sabik," Vega says. "Always putting moves on him. Whenever your back was turned. Everyone knew." There's triumph in her voice.

My blood has frozen. "Sabik, Vega's lying. Right? Maia never tried to steal you."

"She wasn't trying to break us up."

Then I understand what Sabik is not saying. "She wanted us to share you. Wanted to be your secunda."

Another laugh from Vega. She tilts her head back, closes her eyes as the wind blows her dark brown hair around her face. It's loose, twisting like snakes behind her, not tied up in her usual neat ponytail. I guess she's not on the sedatives anymore.

"Please, don't be angry at Maia," Sabik says. "It wasn't about me. She saw how you and your sister drifted apart when Celeste got married. She thought it was the best way to stay close."

My hands curl into fists on the bench. Sabik's trying to be kind. Trying to protect my memory of her. But Maia knew how I felt about being one of two wives. Couldn't she let me have one thing to myself?

That's why Sabik never liked Maia. And on some level, I knew. I tried to keep her away from him, hung out with them separately. I saw how she smiled at him. But since she died I've made her into my perfect imaginary friend. Forgotten what she was really like. She always had to have the same marks I did in exams, even if that meant looking at my answers. She wanted the exact same food at lunch, and would whine and make me share if she didn't get it. She always tried to muscle in on the times when I hung out with Sabik.

Sabik looks up, floppy hair blown back off his face by our speed.

He turns his glare onto Yuri. "And what about you? Lying to me, all this time? You said it was a refuge."

"We had to be prepared," Yuri says, deep voice calm. "Someone has to look out for the people on the planet."

Sabik's jaw clenches. "Why didn't I get to know about the weapons?"

"Because you're too trusting. There's a conspiracy to scare everyone back on the ship. We need the tech to survive. What if they retreat to the *Venture* and take the medical equipment Perseus needs?"

I glance at Vega. Yuri's clearly trying to win her over. Her jaw clenches. I'm not sure if she gives a little nod or if it's just the bumping of the landbike.

"You're the one who's scaremongering," I say. "We're not taking Perseus's equipment. Some of us just want to take more time with the colonization."

Yuri turns his glare onto me. "We can't split the crew. Can't keep up the flights. A decision must be made."

I think about the bomb. Yuri decided to make that decision for us.

He turns to Sabik. "I want peace, but it's my responsibility to defend this colony."

"I want peace too," I say.

Yuri ignores me. "Whoever killed Orion and Cassius will keep killing as long as they have the ship to defend. I have to make the hard decisions so people like you don't have to, Sabik."

"That's so patronizing," Sabik says.

But now Yuri is staring at a patch of the woods, his head swiveling as we pass to keep it in sight. I try to see what he's looking at, but there's nothing. Just glowferns, trunks, and branches.

"What is it?" But Yuri closes his mouth. I guess he's just trying to distract me.

Still, I'm glad for the silence as we jolt our way over the rest of the route to the shuttle. I keep a close eye on Yuri and Vega, but neither of them moves. Yuri stares into space, and Vega glances between him and me, her gun drawn.

When we pull onto the runway, the reassuring bulk of the shuttle is ahead of us. We climb off the trailer, and I keep Vega in front of me, covering her, Yuri, and Sabik with my gun. We head up the clanging steps and onto the shuttle. Leda and Sirius go into the cockpit, and I stay close to Yuri and Vega. I watch closely as she uncuffs Yuri's hands from behind his back and recuffs them at his front so she can strap him into his bucket chair. Yuri doesn't resist. He looks limp, deflated. I do the same with Sabik, then strap myself in next to him. I keep one hand on the latch of my strap, ready to undo it at any sudden movement. In the other, I clutch the pulse gun.

The flight is longer than usual, as we didn't time the launch to coincide with the *Venture*'s next overpass. Yuri stares out the window next to him, concentrating on the sky as if it holds the key to a tough puzzle. Vega is breathing too fast, eyes shining. Sabik slumps in his chair.

After a while, climbing through the atmosphere, it gets harder to focus. I'm so tired. I haven't slept properly in too long. The scene grows fuzzy. My eyelids are heavy, trying to close. My crowded thoughts grow more confused, threaten to slide into the nonsense of dreams. I squeeze the latch tight, letting the metal leave red marks on my palm, but the pain wears off too quickly, the exhaustion creeping back. I can't fall asleep now. I have to watch Yuri. I have to watch Vega and Sabik. I can't trust any of them.

I exhale when the *Venture* appears, glinting through the window. Our home. I made it back.

We pull alongside the ship, match the rotation and dock, and gravity kicks in again. I stand up in a daze and uncuff Sabik.

Vega does the same with Yuri, then she spins around, pointing her pulse gun at my head. There's a wide grin on her face. I fumble with my own weapon.

Sabik kicks me in the back of my knees, hard. I drop the pulse gun as I start to fall.

Vega shoots.

CHAPTER 17

I twist as I fall. I smack into the ground — first knees, then hands, then chest. I land between two bucket seats, and my breath is knocked out of me. I can't see Vega and Yuri. My pulse gun rolls under a chair. Pain in my chin where it hit the metal of the shuttle floor. I've bitten my tongue, and my mouth fills with the sharp taste of blood.

"What'd you do?" Sabik shouts at Vega.

I'm not stunned. The zap from Vega's pulse gun must have gone over my head and grounded itself in the ship's body. I knew I couldn't trust her. I should have had my gun ready.

Muddy boots appear in front of me. Then a face, leaning down into my field of vision. Sabik. He betrayed me. Why didn't I see it coming? I'm about to grab him, scratch his eyes out. I'm going down fighting. I'll take him with me.

Then he winks and his fingers go to my neck, taking my pulse. Sabik keeps staring at me. I'm blinking. I'm clearly not even unconscious. So why is he checking if I'm alive? The back of my knees ache where he kicked them, and I want to punch him in his dumb face. But that wink holds me back.

That and the fact that Vega has a pulse gun, and mine is out of reach.

Sabik pulls his hand away. "You killed her!"

"She's dead?" Yuri sounds shocked. "Vega, what did you do?"

Sabik stands, leaving me staring at his boots. "The button is red!" he shouts. "I can see that from here!"

That's when it clicks into place. I was busy going for my weapon when I should have been ducking. Sabik kicked my legs away. Vega thinks I fell because she shot me.

There's warmth in my chest. Sabik saved me. Sabik is on my side. I stare at his laces. He missed a hole on the left boot when he did them up.

"I didn't mean to," Vega says, her words coming fast. "I forgot it wasn't on stun."

Yuri's breathing hard. "Oh Beta. What have you done? No one was meant to get hurt."

"I'm sorry!" she says. "I'm changing it now. I forgot. I should have switched it back."

I can't tell if she means that or not. She hates me. Does she hate me enough to kill me?

"I'm sorry. I am. But we have to go, Yuri," she says.

There's no response. I can't see Yuri from here. Don't know what he's doing.

"Yuri?" Vega asks.

"I … there was something. In the forest. I saw it on the way back." Yuri's voice wavers, like he doesn't quite believe his own words.

Silence for a moment. Then Vega speaks. "Someone was in the forest?"

"No. An animal. A big animal."

My eyes go wide.

"What?" Sabik says.

"You're imagining things," Vega says. "You're letting them get into your head. We know Ursa killed Orion and Cassius."

"Vega," Yuri says. "What if there really is a creature?"

"Don't be ridiculous," Vega says, but there's a tremble in her voice. "We have to go through with this. I've … I've killed Ursa. I'll be arrested. I'll face the Exit. And they found the weapons. They'll use this as an excuse to stop the flights."

"Vega, think for a moment."

But her voice is rising. "We have to go, Yuri! Before Leda and Sirius finish with the landing checks. Think of my brother. He'll be for the Exit too if they force us all back up —"

"Vega …"

"I'm not letting Perseus die! He's all I have!"

But then Sabik leaps, his boots disappearing from my frame of view.

There's a thump, the sound of a body falling, then a groan.

"Yuri!" Vega screams. She's pointing her pulse gun. My body tenses, ready to jump.

Then Yuri appears in my line of vision, on the ground between the chairs, struggling with Sabik. Sabik's on top of him, but Yuri has one of his wrists. Sabik grabs Yuri's thick black hair with his free hand.

Vega hasn't fired. Sabik and Yuri are tangled together. Yuri's bigger, but he's caught off guard, and his uncertainty is holding him back. Sabik uses his opportunity to swing Yuri's head into the corner of a metal bulkhead. Hard.

Yuri grunts and lets go of Sabik's wrist. He raises his hands to his head. Sabik rolls off him. Jumps up, runs at Vega. Like an idiot.

There's a zap, and Sabik collapses, falls right in front of me.

My breath stops. My heart stops. No. Not Sabik. I want to grab him, help him.

In the silence, I hear voices outside the main door. Sirius and Leda.

Try to breathe. Sabik. Oh, Sabik. Please let her have switched the pulse to stun.

I turn until I can see Vega. She's staring at the door, passing her gun from one hand to the other. I can't see what color the button is. Yuri has one hand on his head, still lying on his back, eyes screwed shut in pain, dark blood between his fingers. Vega runs back over to him, reaches in his pocket, and pulls out a white box.

"Stay there," she says. "I'll take care of this."

"No, Vega ..." Yuri manages.

She shoves whatever she's taken from Yuri into her own pocket and runs back to the door, gun in hand. Sabik doesn't move. Vega is focused on the door. I have to take the risk; I crawl to Sabik, quietly, and touch his familiar face. He's warm.

Of course he's warm. He was only just shot. He'd still be warm, even if ... I blink, fast. Reach for his pulse and find it, fluttering gently against my fingers. I close my eyes. Gulp down the panic. Thank Beta. He's alive. Sabik's alive. Vega did change her pulse. Perhaps it was an accident when she shot me. But now what?

There's an alarm button on the wall, right next to Vega. I have to get there.

Yuri groans, tries to roll over. His eyes open, focus on me. I freeze. The main airlock buzzes and begins to open.

"There you are!" A cheerful voice outside the shuttle. Leda.

Vega raises her gun.

"What are you —" Two zaps, cutting Sirius off. Two thumps: bodies hitting the floor.

Vega launches herself through the airlock. Footstep clang on the metal as she sprints across the loading bay. I push myself up. Stumble to the shuttle door. Peer out into the bay.

Leda and Sirius are sprawled on the floor. Vega's already heading through the doors to the main corridor, disappearing from sight. I slap my palm against the alarm. The blare of the klaxon echoes off the metal walls. That should throw a wrench in her plan.

Leda's eyes are closed. Sirius is lying face down. I dash to them and kneel beside Leda, check her neck. There. A pulse. Thank Beta. Just stunned too. I pull out my linkcom.

There's a huge bang, and the whole ship shakes. The linkcom clatters to the floor.

A different alarm starts sounding, adding to the cacophony. My mouth is dry. I'm holding my breath, waiting for another explosion. It doesn't come.

That white box must have been the remote detonator. I missed a bomb. But I checked the vents! Where was it? I should have stopped her. Should have moved faster. The blast may have killed people. Sucked them out into space like the crew of the *Venture 2*.

Oh Beta, Vega. What have you done?

I run back to the ship, scramble under the seat, and grab my pulse gun, then run to the wallcom and ping Astra. The ship creaks. The scream of metal under pressure. The *Venture* is hurt. Can she hold on?

Astra picks up right away. "It's me," I say. "Yuri is injured. Sabik, Sirius, and Leda are stunned. Vega got away. Detonated a bomb."

"Where is she?" Astra asks. I can barely hear her over the blood rushing through my ears.

"Just left the offload bay. Probably heading for the engine room."

"I'll shut down the elevators. Warn the engineer on duty."

I swallow. "She may try climbing the spoke. She has a pulse gun."

"I'll send backup."

"I think the bomb took out an air circulator. If Vega gets up there with that weapon, she can blow out the bypass route. Trigger the failsafe. I've got a gun. I'm going after her."

There's a gasp, then silence for a second. I think Astra is going to argue, but she exhales.

"Good luck. Take care, Ursa. I love you so much, Little Bear."

I'm running before I've broken the connection.

CHAPTER 18

I sprint out of the cargo bay, down the corridor to the nearest spoke. The light above the doors is off, so the elevator isn't there. There's no point in calling it. By the time it gets back down, it'll be too late. I use my override code to force the doors open. They swish apart, revealing the hollow tube of the spoke. I step down into the space where the elevator should be and look up.

The tube of the shaft stretches up above me, the skinny emergency ladder riveted to the far side. The dark metal column is half lit with emergency white panel lights running up either side of the tube.

There, high above. The dark cube of the elevator, cutting off the rest of the spoke, its gears holding it against the shaft, not moving. Vega got about a third of the way up before Astra got the elevators shut down.

I grab the narrow ladder. Start climbing. Hand over hand on the cold rungs. Footsteps echoing up the tube above me. Getting out of the elevator will delay Vega, but she's got a good head start and she's strong. There's less gravity at that height, too. She'll be able to climb faster than I will down here where the artificial gravity is at full strength.

I climb quickly. Two rungs at a time. My hands are dark gray in the pale lights on either side of me. I'm soon out of breath, but I keep going, listening for sounds from above.

I'm about a hundred meters up when I hear the clang of the hatch on the elevator roof opening. It sounds like she's struggling to lift herself out. Heavy breathing, grunts echoing in the space. Kicks against the cabin walls as she hauls herself up.

My hands are sore from gripping hard to compensate for the sweat on my palms and the push of the ship's rotation. My lungs ache. Sabik was right, I am unfit.

More clanging above. Boots on metal rungs. She's on the emergency ladder. I keep climbing, listening to the rhythm of Vega's climb. I try to move my legs at a faster, quieter tempo so she won't hear me. Soon I'm at the bottom of the elevator. I adjust my handhold and peer down.

My heart freezes and I'm dizzy, like I've already begun the fall. But I keep holding on and turn back to the ladder. I start climbing again, keeping my body close to the wall, not looking down. Then I pull myself into the gap between the elevator and the side of the shaft, squeezing past the teeth of the frozen gears, trying not to think about what would happen if the elevator restarted now. It's narrower here. It's lucky I'm small. Instead of a sheer drop behind me, the elevator is at my back.

Metal clangs, from above, getting closer fast. Something falling down the shaft, hitting the wall on the way down, then the elevator roof. Something small and heavy. What?

I reach the top of the elevator and pull myself, panting, onto the level surface. My arm muscles burn. My thighs are hot blocks of pain. I wipe my sweaty hands on my landsuit. I wish I had time to take it off. It's too warm on board for it.

The hatch Vega climbed out of is still open, a hole down into the comfort of the padded cabin below, a world away from my desperate climb. Next to the hatch lies a hammer.

Where did that come from?

I look up. There's Vega. She's still a good way ahead, but I'm closing the gap. Above her, the doors to the engine room are open. There's a face in front of the familiar curve of the wall and the blinking red alarm lights. Aldrin is leaning out over the elevator shaft. He must have thrown his hammer, hoping to hit Vega. That's what the noise was.

Smart thinking. Shame about the aim. But he has to throw it hard in the low gravity up there, and it's nearly impossible to compensate for the ship's rotation.

I keep climbing, quietly. I don't want to give away that I'm here. It's my only advantage. Maybe I'll be able to creep up on Vega. She's slowed down. I just need to get within my pulse gun's range.

But then what? If I shoot her, she'll fall. She'll die. Can I do that?

We used to be friends. Until I made her choose between me and having a family.

I see the soles of Vega's feet on the rungs above me as she glides her way up. She has less gravity, but she has to be ready for Aldrin's missiles. She's not close enough to the engine room to fire her gun. Yet.

Hand over hand. Ignore the stitch in my side. Ignore the ache in my fingers. Ignore the elevator growing smaller below me.

Bang! A screwdriver slams into the wall near my head, then bounces off and continues its chaotic fall down to the elevator. Ah. Yes. The missiles are a problem for me, too. I crane my neck up. If a tool hits me and I let go, the fall down the shaft will kill me.

I swing to the side as a blowtorch hits the wall, then whizzes past.

Sounds from the bottom of the shaft echo up. Protectors, climbing the ladder, finally. But they're too far away. Vega doesn't look down. She knows they'll never reach her before she gets to the engine room. If Aldrin or I can't stop her, it's all over. My breath is coming hard. My hands are slippery with sweat. I can't stop to wipe them.

I'm not going to catch up with Vega in time.

How many tools does Aldrin have? He'll have to run out soon, and then what?

As if in answer, a linkcom falls toward me, hitting the wall. I swing to one side of the ladder as it whistles by. Aldrin must be getting desperate if he's throwing his linkcom.

I keep climbing quietly, gliding up the ladder in the low gravity. Watching the scene above me. Down comes an empty gear bag. That would be useless even if it hit Vega. And she's getting closer to the engine room.

Aldrin is holding a wrench. He's not throwing it. He's waiting, aiming. It must be his last missile. But Vega isn't far now, almost in pulse gun range. Aldrin's tongue comes out, licks his lips. Vega might be close enough to hit now. She knows it. She's still climbing, but slowly. She's watching. If she dodges this one, it's all over.

Aldrin will close the elevator doors, of course. But once Vega reaches the top, she can shoot the control panel, short it out. Then the doors will open and she can glide in, stun Aldrin, zap out the air circulation backup, and the ship will fall to Beta. She's too far above me. Even if I could shoot her, she's out of range.

But we used to be friends. Maybe that still means something. Maybe I can talk to her. Yuri told her about the creature. Cassius spoke to her about me. Perhaps she'll listen.

It's worth a shot. And what else can I do?

"Vega!" I shout, loud as I can. "Please don't do this!"

"Ursa?" She sounds shocked. Which makes sense. She thinks I'm dead. She turns, looks down at me. "You're alive!"

There's relief in her voice. In her face. It lights up as she smiles, just like she used to, when we were friends. And for one moment,

I think it's going to be okay. We can talk through this. We can make it right.

But then Aldrin throws the wrench, hard. Vega looks back up.

"No!" I shout. Too late.

The wrench hits her in the face, making a dull, awful thump. Vega screams. Blood sprays from her nose, her mouth. She lets go. Topples back from the ladder, arms out to either side of her.

She falls down the shaft. Slowly at first. She slides down, fumbling for a grip on the smooth metal, grasping for the rungs of the ladder, but they're too far to her left. She's twisting, struggling, her face a mess. Slowly speeding up, falling faster down the bare wall of the shaft, toward me.

I hook an arm through the ladder, twist it around a rung so I can't slip. I reach my other hand out. She sees me. One eye bloody and shut, nose broken, lip bleeding. She stretches out a hand, and I strain with mine. I grab her arm as she passes and catch her falling weight. It jolts me downward hard. I keep my other arm hooked between the rungs and the wall, taking my weight and hers.

It's too much.

I scream, pain blinding me for a second. Something in my shoulder snaps.

When I open my eyes, I realize I've let go of Vega.

Her body slams into the wall again. She yells my name. She tries to grab the ladder, but she's too far, and the rotation pushes her away. She keeps scrabbling, clawing for a finger hold on the rivets of the sheer wall.

I'm still hooked onto the ladder, jammed in place above the drop that's claiming Vega. I'm breathless with pain, craning my neck to stare at the sheer drop below me.

Vega keeps falling, accelerating, eyes wide, arms flailing.

She smacks into the roof of the elevator with a decisive thud. It takes my breath. Her body splays on the dark square of the elevator cabin, unmoving. Eyes stare blankly up at me.

I swing my good arm back to the ladder and hold on tight. I lower my head onto a cold metal rung and sob.

CHAPTER 19

It's a little while before the pain and shock fade enough for me to wrench my arm out from the wall. I scream as it comes free, and almost slip. But I clutch tightly with my good hand. It's lucky I'm so high up. I doubt I could do this climb at full gravity. I lean my weight forward onto the ladder and use one hand as much as possible, sliding it up the side for stability as my feet push me up. I'm soon almost weightless, gliding up toward the engine room. Below me the protectors have reached the elevator. Have reached Vega's body.

When I get to the open elevator doors, Aldrin grabs my good left arm and I float into the *Venture*'s heart. Alarms blare around us. The displays scroll red and orange text. Aldrin guides me over to the control chair and sits me down. The movement jolts through my shoulder, and I close my eyes, hiss with the pain.

"Are you okay?"

I can't answer that right now. I pull out my linkcom and ping Mom.

"How's Sabik?" I ask, struggling to keep my voice steady.

"He's fine. Just waking up now," Mom says. I can hear the

rustle of her clothing as she moves. I can almost see her, linkcom pressed between her shoulder and her ear, as she keeps working on her patients.

"Leda? Sirius?" I speak through gritted teeth. "And the bomb?'

"No deaths reported. The protectors are will be fine, and Yuri is recovering too, although he has a bad concussion. But lots of minor injuries are coming in, including Celeste."

"Celeste?"

"Stomach pains," Mom says. "I'm checking them out now."

I swallow. "Okay. You go." I break the connection. Breathe.

Minor injuries. I guess that means the blast didn't kill anyone. Good. But what about Celeste? Is the baby okay?

I'll go to her as soon as I can. But I'm no medic, and right now there's work to do. My shoulder is bad, but it's bearable if I clench my teeth and I don't move it. Aldrin floats next to me, and I scan over the info feeds, the flashing lights, the warning messages. I put the information from the feeds together in my mind, build a map of the *Venture*, and see where the damage reports are centered. It's good to have a distraction from my shoulder.

Ecocarriage 3. Of course. Yuri knew the ecocarriages best. I should have checked more than just the vents. The bomb could have been anywhere among the purple plants.

There were no people in the carriage at the time of the blast, luckily. But as I read the feeds, I spot a much bigger problem. The main generators are next to ecocarriage 3, and the blast was a big one.

"The bomb went off near the air circulators at the rotationwise end of Ecocarriage 3," I say to Aldrin. "It blew out the hull and damaged the main generators. Three of the four cells have gone into shutdown. Ecocarriage 3 and the generator carriage have decompressed."

"Was anyone in them?" Aldrin has always been slower at reading the feeds, lacks the feel for them that I have.

"No, thank Beta. We've lost the crops, but the carriages have sealed and radioactive containment is one hundred percent. The air circulators have rerouted, so we're okay for now. We'll be limited on the power we can generate. We're lucky we still have one functioning cell."

Aldrin nods. "I'll suit up, get down there, and coordinate the repair team. You stay here. Antares will want a full damage report and repair estimates."

"I'll restart the elevators, man the feeds, and send all available engineers to you."

Aldrin heads for the nearest elevator as I activate the emergency protocols. I ping all the engineers and update them. Then I sit down to catalogue the faults on the info feed and figure out priority.

I try not to move my shoulder as I work through the data. Try not to think about letting go of Vega. Try not to think about her face when she realized I was alive. The relief, the smile.

Then her body on the elevator.

She lost her father and her husband. She feared for her brother's life. I should never have made her choose between me and Orion. If we'd stayed friends, none of this would have happened.

But I can't think about that right now.

I clench and release my fingers, noticing the blisters. My shoulder is bad, making it hard to think. I should get to the medcarriage soon. But there's so much to do here. The damage is serious, across multiple systems. But it's survivable. We were close. If Vega had gotten in here, one zap would have destroyed the air circulation bypass. The oxygen in the ecocarriages would have slowly increased to toxic, even explosive levels. The *Venture* would have set its failsafe in motion, broken apart, and fallen to Beta.

Jovan pings through to me. Checking I'm okay, praising my bravery. I smile. I'll reply as soon as I've catalogued the faults and got them to the engineers on site.

Astra arrives about five minutes later. She kicks off the wall by the elevator, closing the distance between us in a rush. Before I can update her, she grabs me and hugs me. I try not to cry out at the agony in my shoulder. Then she lets go. She looks pale, older than usual.

"How's Celeste?" I ask, trying not to let the pain show.

"I'm on my way to her now," Astra says. "I thought it would be quicker coming through the center. How are you?"

"Not good," I say. "Vega is dead because of me."

"You saved the *Venture*, Ursa. Your father would be so proud."

"I don't know, Astra. The damage is bad."

Astra takes a deep breath. "Tell me. I'll report to your mother."

I update her on the feeds and the reports coming in from Aldrin. The biggest problem is the cells in the generator. The damage might be minor, but they'll need to cool and be made safe before they can be repaired. And we'll need to fix the hull before we can get in there. It'll take months to do all that, restart the cells, and get them back up to full output. One of the four cells is undamaged, but that's not even close to enough energy output.

Astra looks grim. She knows as well as I do what that means. Ionizing the shuttle fuel into plasma is the main drain on our power. We can't keep up the flights to and from the surface and repair the ship at the same time. A decision will need to be made.

"I'll tell your mother. She'll need to call a ship's meeting," Astra says.

But that's when the ping comes through from Mom.

Celeste's in labor.

Mom's the medic attending the birth. Astra rushes to join them. I call another engineer to take over so I can get my shoulder seen to in the medcarriage. I've done all I can, and Astra's hug was the last straw. I have to get this sorted. And this way I'll be near Celeste.

It turns out it's a bad fracture. It's good to have a proper fix with a collagen and calcium injection and a PainFree patch. I'm in the open ward, in a treatment chair, its padding stained and fraying. There's the babble of many voices and the clang of medical instruments. Sabik, Leda, and Sirius are recovering in med beds opposite me. Medics bustle around them, moving with a reassuringly calm efficiency.

To my right, the carriage narrows into a corridor, on either side of which lie the isolation rooms, operating rooms, and birthing cabin. I wonder how Celeste is doing. Protector Adhara is standing in front of one of the other doors, so I know Yuri must be behind it.

A ping comes through to announce an all-crew meeting. It's scheduled for the early evening to allow time for the shuttle to go down to the surface to bring people back up.

Once my shoulder is sorted, I check in on Sabik. He's propped up in his bed, next to Leda and Sirius. He's still groggy, but when I sit in the chair next to him, he takes my hand.

"How are you?" he asks.

I stifle a laugh. "You're the one that got stunned."

"I didn't mean physically." He looks at me, and there's the old kindness in his eyes. "I heard about what happened to Vega. I know you weren't friends anymore, but ..."

I slump back in the seat. Glance over at Sirius and Leda. I don't want to talk about this in front of them. "I didn't want her to die," I say, quietly.

"Of course you didn't."

I don't tell him about catching her. About letting her go.

"Any news on Celeste?" he asks.

"Not yet. Her baby's early. Only by twenty days, but that's not good, is it?"

Sabik shrugs.

"They're letting the birth go ahead though, so the baby must be healthy. Right?"

"I really don't know, Ursa, I'm not a medic. But I hope so." He squeezes my hand.

Of course, my mother is too busy to ask. There's another ping from Jovan, thanking me again, wishing my sister well, and asking to see me. I must reply to him soon, once my head stops whirling and I can think straight.

"How's the ship?" Sabik asks.

"Not good. The bomb damaged the generator and half an ecocarriage."

He rubs his forehead. "There's so much to digest today. I'm sorry I got Yuri so wrong. I thought he was one of the good guys. I think he did too."

I exhale. "Everyone thinks they're one of the good guys."

"I heard you found a bomb in the vents. You think he planted it?"

I nod.

"So, he'll face the Exit."

The thought of more death makes my bile rise. "But he tried to stop Vega."

Sabik shrugged. "Planting bombs on the *Venture* is still treason."

I look at Protector Adhara standing in front of the medcabin door.

"I want to talk to him," I say.

Sabik tilts his head. "Is that a good idea?"

"Probably not." I find myself standing and walking toward the door.

As I approach, Protector Adhara turns and looks me up and down.

"Can I speak to Yuri?" I ask.

I try to read her expression, but I don't know her well enough. Is she angry at me for my part in her colleague's death? Her mouth is a line.

She shrugs. “I’m just here to stop him leaving. Don’t turn the lights up,” she says. “He has a concussion.” She opens the door, and I head inside.

It’s good that she warned me. The lights are dim, making the metal walls almost black, and my hand automatically moves for the illumination controls before I stop it. Yuri is lying down, a giant lump under the gray blankets. I pause in the doorway. It slides shut behind me, sealing us in together. I don’t move. There’s only a narrow gap between the bed and the wall.

I hear some shuffling and a grunt as Yuri turns over and props himself up in bed.

“You,” he says.

I can’t make out his eyes. Can hardly see his expression.

“I didn’t know your father was stealing food for you.” The words come out before I’ve thought them through.

There’s a pause. When he speaks, Yuri’s gruff voice sounds tired. “He was a medic. He knew the problems malnutrition could cause. He wanted to look after me.”

There’s silence for a moment. Then the rustle of bedclothes as Yuri puts a hand to his bandaged head. “I did see something in the woods. A creature. Something like a big wolf or a jaguar. I thought you were making it up.”

“Why would I make it up?”

He shuffles in the bed until he’s sitting properly now, his bulk too large for the tiny cabin. I can see why he’d feel cooped up on the *Venture*. “When we first arrived. It was clear in everyone’s faces.”

“What was?”

“Wonder. Or fear.”

I say nothing, waiting for him to elaborate.

“Most people were so excited to be on the planet. But some were scared. I knew it was only a matter of time before something happened.”

"Like what?"

He winces as he shifts. "Like war. Like the *Venture 2*. When things were stolen from the engineering shed, I knew it was beginning. I knew I had to act."

"Nothing was stolen. I checked myself."

Yuri leans forward. "Do you think Sabik's a liar?"

That makes me pause. It doesn't feel right. "He lied about the path in the forest."

"But that was for a good reason." His thick brow crumples, and he rubs at it with a slab-like hand. He's clearly not used to doubting himself. "And Jovan was taking mealpacks into the forest. Stockpiling food and weapons. We had to do the same if we were going to have a chance."

I tilt my head at that. Then I remember the conversation between Cassius and Yuri back in the hut on Beta.

"He was taking his lunches at Maia's grave. Even Cassius told you that was a picnic."

"The pattern was so clear. Your enemies were dying. People were frightened. They were returning to the ship, just like you wanted."

"Cassius wasn't my enemy. I didn't like Orion, but he wasn't my enemy, either."

"I know you didn't kill them, now."

I clench my jaw. "Am I meant to thank you for finally realizing I'm not a killer? After you accused me in front of the whole crew?"

Yuri shrugs, and I want to see him react, want him to drop this nonchalance. I want to see him acknowledge what he's done.

"Vega is dead," I say.

He exhales. "I know. But I didn't kill her. I tried to talk her out of it."

And I'm suddenly furious, suddenly want him to hurt like I hurt right now. "You planted the bombs. Sabik says you'll face the Exit for treason."

He straightens up. "I want my daughter to have freedom. I want her to grow up healthy and strong, just like my father wanted for me." He lifts his chin. "If the price for good parenting on this ship is death, so be it."

I want to slap him. The door behind me hums, then slides open. It's Iola, a senior medic. "I have to check on the patient," she says.

There's no room for the two of us in the small space next to the bed, and I'm glad for the excuse to get out of there. I don't look at Yuri as I duck past Iola and into the main medcarriage.

I ping Mom, ask how the birth is going. She replies immediately to say that it's going to be a while yet. That Celeste is resting, and I should too. I pace, unable to get Vega's face out of my head. Feeling angry and guilty. Feeling the exhaustion of the sleepless nights catching up with me.

Pounding grows in my head, in spite of the PainFree. I can't stay here. The medics have to squeeze past as they tend to their patients.

I head back around the rim to my cabin, return Astra's pulse gun to the safe, and lie on the bed, thoughts whirring.

A PING ON MY linkcom wakes me. The lights are different now. They were the light glow of early morning when I lay down, and now they're the bright glare of the day cycle. I try to remember what I'm doing. Where I am. I read the words that scroll across the linkcom, and clutch it tighter.

It's from Mom. The birth went well. Celeste's daughter is small but healthy. She's calling her Beta.

I swallow the lump in my throat and read the rest of the message.

Mom says Celeste wants me to see my new niece and have a talk after the all-crew meeting, which Celeste won't be going to. She needs to recover and take care of her newborn.

I check the time, and almost drop the linkcom. I've slept for hours and missed several messages from Jovan. I send him a quick ping to apologize. I barely have time to jump in the wash cubicle before I have to run to the all-crew meeting.

I hurry down the corridors to the council room, shuffling past people who are moving slowly. The room is full. Jovan waves from the other side. I wave back, but it's too crowded to get anywhere near him. I squeeze onto the nearest bench before Mom, Astra, and the other council members enter and the room falls silent.

Mom takes the podium, brow set in a frown. "For those of you who haven't already heard, Yuri has freely confessed that he planted the bomb Vega detonated. She died in the attempt. We're lucky we didn't lose anyone else."

Most of the agricologists look genuinely shocked. I guess it wasn't a wider conspiracy.

"You all know it's been a struggle to keep up the regular shuttle flights. But the explosion turned our problem into a crisis. We can't support habitation on board the *Venture* while running the shuttle to and from Beta. A decision must be made, and it must happen today." Mom clutches the podium tightly. "We must vote on whether to return to living on the *Venture* until the generator cells are fixed, or to break the ship up now and descend to Beta."

I see hands raised to mouths. Widened eyes. It's a hell of a choice.

"If we keep the ship, people are free to stay on the planet if they wish, but they're on their own." Mom doesn't try to hide the emotion in her voice. "We may be able to provide a shuttle down every few months, but we can't guarantee it. It'll take at least six months to fix the ship."

"If we don't keep working on the buildings, the half-finished ones will rot and collapse," Capella, the Head of Construction, says. "We'll miss the main sowing season. We won't have the buildings and harvest we need to survive the winter on the planet."

Mom nods. "If we return to the ship, we'd have to wait over a year for full settlement. I would recommend all crew return to the ship in the interim, but I won't force anyone."

"I'm staying on the ground," Capella says. "Someone has to look after the people there."

I swallow. What chance does she have there? The releases aren't finished. They haven't built the hydroelectric dam. There are hardly any solar generators set up, and without them, the huts will be freezing in the winter. Will there be enough food available from foraging?

And I can feel it. Our tiny crew, this crowded room, this small group. The flame that is our whole world, flickering. Weakening in the face of the wind.

Astra steps forward. "Fur and DNA that was found at the sites of Cassius's and Orion's deaths does not match anything in Alpha Earth's archives. And Yuri has testified on record that he too saw a creature in the forest. There is no longer any doubt that there is an unidentified beast on the planet, killing our crew."

Louder gasps this time.

A voice from the crowd. "Can't we clear the forest? Push it back from the village so whatever is in the woods can't get close?" It's Almach.

"That's what we're thinking," Mom says. "We'd need to finish mending the landclearers, though, which can't happen until regular shuttle flights are resumed."

"When do you see us settling permanently?" Capella asks.

Mom pauses, obviously thinking. "If we repair the ship and then use the *Venture* as our home base while completing the buildings, clearing back the forest, and setting up the hydroelectric dam and mines, we could have the planet fully safe for settlement in a decade."

Mutterings in the audience.

Astra raises her hands. "We all know it's not ideal, but we can do this. We lived up here for four hundred years safely. How many people have died since we landed?"

Capella shakes her head. "What about the women who got pregnant after the population limits were lifted? Will they be forced to abort?"

Mom exhales, and I can tell she's thought about this. "No, they will not. But we have one ecocarriage out of action, and our power is low. We'd need to reinstate the Exit, but would offer settlement on the planet as an alternative to euthanasia."

I shift in my seat, thinking about what Cassius said. About valuing people for more than just their obvious uses. About not throwing them away because they're old or injured. Is involuntary exile for the sick and old any better? But what else can we do?

"And what about Yuri?" Sabik asks.

"The investigation isn't done," Mom says. "Yuri admitted planting the bomb, but he tried to dissuade Vega from detonating it. There may be a more appropriate sentence than the Exit, using Yuri's skills under supervision on the planet, where he can't be a threat to the ship."

I close my eyes, grateful for Mom. She's always been a healer.

The debate continues around me. Questions asked by everyone and answered calmly by Mom, hands tight on the podium in front of her. She pauses before each answer. Her voice is smooth and measured. But nothing changes the facts. I tune it out. It's obvious we have to return to the ship. Why is it taking so long? I wish they'd get the vote over with. I want to see Celeste and her baby.

"Any other questions?" Mom asks, finally.

The council room is quieter than I've ever seen it. Either there's nothing more to ask or everyone is dumbstruck. The agricologists cluster together at the back, eyes wide. Rigel rests his head on his husband's shoulder. Sabik sits next to them.

"Okay. The vote has been now been sent to your linkcoms."

Shuffling. The sounds of people pulling out their devices. People vote quickly, then sit, fiddling with hair or clothes. No one thinks long before they make a decision.

"Has everyone had a chance to vote?" Mom asks after a while. There are murmurs, which she takes as a yes.

"Merope, Capella." Astra hands the Head of Genetics and the Head of Construction her display screen. "Can you check the results?"

Capella takes the screen, and they both peer at it.

"Sixty-eight percent in favor of returning to the *Venture*," Merope says, satisfaction in her voice. "A two-thirds majority."

Capella stares at her feet.

"It is decided, then," Mom says. "There will be one more shuttle trip to the surface tomorrow afternoon to drop off equipment and anyone who wishes to stay, and to pick up possessions and raw materials. Then no more flights for at least two months. We will focus on repairs."

There's one more vote, for the permanent Head of Protection. No one stands against Astra, and she's acclaimed. Mom adjourns the meeting, and people get to their feet slowly and shuffle out, voices muted. Sabik's still sitting on his bench near the exit. I wander over, sit next to him. The bandage has come off his right hand, but the flesh is still a little pink where he burned himself.

"I'm sorry," I say. "I know you loved it on the surface."

"I'm staying there, Ursa."

"What?"

"You heard me."

People squeeze past us. I turn sideways, tuck my legs up against the cold edge of the bench so they can get by.

"But ... it's too dangerous. You might not be alive when we come back."

"Humans managed without our tech for millennia."

"But they'd been born into that world. And they died all the time from preventable stuff."

"I'm good at growing food and foraging. If I'm there, people will have a better chance of surviving."

People file past, their clothes a blur of gray behind Sabik's messy hair.

"It'll be easier to survive up here," I say. "Things can go back to how they were."

"I don't want to go back to how things were. I love it on the planet. There's space and light. For many of us, the time on the ship was the bad old days."

That hurts. "But, Sabik, we —"

"You got what you wanted. You can stay on the ship." He pushes himself to his feet, shoulders slumped, and starts to walk away, following the last of the other crew members.

CHAPTER 20

Celeste raises a finger to her lips as I enter her medcabin. She's lying on the narrow bunk. In a metal bassinet mounted on the wall is a tiny bundle wrapped in gray, threadbare sheets. A shock of dark hair sticks straight on top of a tiny head.

I squeeze into the narrow space next to the bed, lean over the bassinet. Stare down at bow-shaped lips and a brow crinkled into a puzzled expression, even though her eyes are closed in sleep.

Her ancestors and Sabik's clearly have a lot in common. But I'll make sure her hair isn't always a mess, like his. Teach her the importance of brushing it, making it as silky as his can be, when he takes the time.

"She's beautiful, Celeste."

A wide, proud smile.

"I'll help with her," I say. "I know it's going to be tough now, without Orion. But I'll be the best auntie. I promise."

She shakes her head. "I'm going down to the surface, Ursa."

My blood turns cold.

"This planet is hers, it's her future," she says.

"I know that. But what's the hurry? Why can't you wait until we all go down?"

"When that will be? A decade? More?" She turns to her daughter. Runs a finger across her soft cheek. "Do you think you're the only one having to relearn everything? Yes, it's scary. It's a lot to get used to. The size of outdoors, the weather, all of it."

"Exactly! So why would you go down now?"

She looks up at me. "Have you seen how comfortable the children are on the planet? It's natural to them already, and that's what I want for Beta. I want the planet to feel like home. If she grows up on board, she'll have to relearn everything, just like us. I don't want to put her through that."

"But it's so dangerous."

"There's a false sense of safety here, Ursa. Children raised on the ship are shorter, weaker than they were on Alpha. We die younger. There's only so much supplements can do. They will have longer, healthier lives on the planet."

"But all the accidents ..."

"Once we're used to the surface, there won't be as many accidents. If we retreat to the ship, it's Beta's generation that'll have to get used to the planet. They'll be the ones that have accidents. I'm not doing that to her." She looks fierce as she peers down at her child. "It's my job to make life easier for her, not pass on problems we're too cowardly to face."

That one stings. "What about the creature?"

"We're safe in the village. And we have to face it sometime."

"But ... Astra is here."

"Not for long." Celeste rubs at her eyes. "I can't believe you're supporting her. She's committing suicide."

"What are you talking about? Astra's safe up here."

Celeste stares at me. "She'll face the Exit."

I'd forgotten about that. It didn't matter before, when we were colonizing the surface. "But … she's okay. She's got time."

"I don't think she has. On the night Orion died, she smelled …" Celeste squeezes her eyes shut. "I think she's having incontinence issues. And she's getting more stooped all the time."

My chest constricts. "Well … even if that's true, she can go down to Beta."

Celeste laughs. "She won't. She'd think she'd be a burden on us. You know Mom: she's so old-fashioned. And so attached to this ship. It's Dad to her, in many ways. She'll never leave."

I stare at the baby's chest, rising and falling as she sleeps. I swallow.

"I'll talk Astra out of it. And I'll be here. I'll help."

Beta stirs, and Celeste raises a finger to her lips. The baby makes an odd creaking noise, then her eyes open and a thin scream floods the tiny cabin. Beta turns pink-red. Her mouth is wide open as she wails, and I can see down her little throat.

"I have to try to feed her," Celeste says. "And you should talk to your own mother."

"What? Why?"

Celeste moves the child closer, starts adjusting her top.

"That's not for me to tell you. Talk to Nashira."

I HEAVE THE DOOR to our cabin open. Mom's sitting on my bunk. She stands when I come in.

"You met Beta?" she asks. "What did you think?"

"She's cute. But noisy." The conversation with Celeste has rattled me.

Mom laughs. "I know what you mean. I thought the same about you."

"You did?"

"You screamed all the time. I didn't know what to do. Beta has that in common with her aunt. Celeste will need a lot of support."

"But she's heading to the planet. She'll be all alone."

Mom drops her gaze to the floor. "Not all alone."

I wrap my arms around myself. "No. You're captain of this ship. You belong up here."

"I'm the captain of this whole colony. I'm responsible for everyone's survival. They need a hospital. I'll finish my work there and help Celeste through the first few months, then I'll come back on board."

She looks up then, eyes wide. "Having a child is hard, Ursa. No one is ever prepared for it. But if Celeste has support, if I teach her a little, give her confidence in herself, maybe things will turn out better for her and Beta than they did ..."

There's a long pause. But I know what she's saying.

"For us?"

Mom looks relieved. "I was far too young, barely older than you are now. I loved you fiercely. But I couldn't stop you crying. Astra could. It seemed selfish to keep holding you, keep you screaming when Astra could make you happy in seconds."

Her eyes are red. "I let Astra take over, because I couldn't bear to see you upset. It seemed like the best thing, although it broke my heart. I threw myself into work." She sits back down on the bunk. "And by the time I'd grown up, realized it was just my inexperience, it was too late. I found myself on the outside of my own family, and I didn't know how to get back in."

She looks small.

"Mom ..."

"You grew up great, thanks to Astra, and you don't need me. I'm not an engineer, so the ship doesn't need me, either. But Celeste does, and the colonists on the planet do. So, yes, I'm going with them."

I slump down next to her on the bunk.

She continues. "And there's Perseus. We don't have space in the medcarriage for a long-term patient. It'll be tough to keep him alive without the ship's tech. If I go down, I can help."

I close my eyes. Poor Vega. She ended up putting her brother in more danger.

"I'm glad you're looking after Perseus," I say, finally.

Mom takes my good hand.

"You're so independent, Ursa. And I'm proud of you for that. Just don't end up like me, okay? Let others get close to you."

The center of me is hollowing out. Mom squeezes my hand, and I stare at the metal wall in front of us.

I SPEND THE NEXT day working, like everyone else. Some of the construction workers will be retrained in basic engineering so we can make some headway on the maintenance logs. And the outside repairs are restarting, with all the dangers they entail.

There's so much to do, but the ship full of hurrying people feels right. Feels like home. I fix my blowtorch and get things ready for the last shuttle. The least I can do is go down to the surface to say goodbye. There are over a hundred people settling there, and the corridors of the ship are crowded with families making their way to the shuttle with their possessions or saying goodbye to their friends and loved ones. There's weeping, pleas for people to change their minds, parents begging children to stay on board, sisters begging brothers to come down to the planet.

As I prepare to board, I spot Jovan moving boxes into the cargo bay, ready for loading. He catches my eye and raises a hand in greeting. I head over.

"What are those?" I nod at the boxes.

"Artificial wombs and some genetic material," Jovan says. "I heard your sister and mother are heading down to the planet with the baby. If I set these up with prepared embryos, show them how to use them, they can make animals for the releases themselves."

My stomach fills with warmth. He's giving them a better chance of survival.

"Thank you," I whisper.

"I had to do something for Celeste, especially after she lost Orion. Something to keep them alive until the next shuttle. We owe them that." He runs a hand through his hair. "And I wanted to talk to you, thank you for all you did. I'm so sorry about Vega."

My gaze drops to the floor. I don't want to think about Vega.

"I … I was going to catch up with you after the meeting, but I saw you talking to Sabik. Are you two …?"

I look back up at his wide eyes. He runs his hand through his hair again. He's nervous.

"No," I say. "We're not back together, if that's what you're asking."

A smile flows over his face. "Good. I mean … well." He laughs. "Do you want to sit together? On the shuttle down?"

"Yeah. I mean sure, if you want."

He beams at me. I think about what Mom said, about keeping people at arm's length. She and I aren't that different, I guess. My closest companion for these last months has been my imaginary version of Maia. But maybe I can change that.

Jovan and I board the shuttle together. Celeste is already in the front row, next to Astra, both their faces blotchy red from crying. Celeste's baby is screaming in her arms. Mom's next to them, brow lined with worry. Sabik sits in silence at the back with the other agricologists.

Jovan guides me to a window seat, and I strap myself in. I watch the wheel of the *Venture* through the thick silica glass as we detach and head down to the surface. We'll be heading home to the *Venture* soon and staying until the planet is safe. I have what I wanted.

But this isn't how I thought it would be.

Jovan turns to me with a sympathetic look, as though he's reading my mind.

"Don't worry. They'll soon realize how tough it is down there. When we send the shuttle in two months, they'll be ready to come back. We'll all be together again."

Hopefully he's right. Hopefully they'll survive that long. But Beta is so small in Celeste's arms. A tiny flame of life. So vulnerable.

It's a smooth descent down to the surface, until we hit the lower atmosphere. Gray fog fills the windows as we judder through thick cloud, and we land with a bump. I step out of the shuttle to a gloomy world. It's as dark here as the corridors of the *Venture*. But at least it's not raining yet. The wind whips around me as I head down the metal stairs, and I hug myself. I won't miss this cold. This unpredictable weather. We all get onto landbike trailers, which bounce along the path through the wood. Everyone stares at the trees nervously, but there's nothing to see but branches and glowferns.

Once we reach the forest camp, Celeste needs help with her luggage, so Mom and I give her a hand as Jovan takes his genelab equipment to the half-finished hospital. It starts to spit rain as we lug Celeste's boxes to her hut. I pull up the hood on my landsuit. I can't get a word in over Beta's crying, and once we're inside, Celeste paces up and down, patting her baby's back and trying to shush her.

Astra, Mom, and I help Celeste unpack a little. I don't know what to do. What to say.

"Are you sure you won't come back with us?" I ask Mom and Celeste.

Celeste shakes her head.

"What about the creature?"

"We won't go near the forest at night. I'll take a pulse gun if I go during the day."

"But … the baby. She'll be safer on the *Venture*."

Celeste looks fierce. "I know what is best for my baby. I've had this fight with Astra already. I'm not going through it again."

I glance at Astra. She looks worn out, heartbroken.

"I didn't … I just mean, there isn't much food, and …"

"We have dried supplies, plus what we can get from foraging. And there will be fruit on the trees soon, early crops in the fields. Beta won't need to take probiotics and supplements to make up for the limited diet and lack of light. The water is cleaner. The air is fresher, better for her tiny lungs. She'll grow up strong and live longer."

I want to keep arguing with Celeste. Point out all the ways she's putting her child at risk. But I'm not going to change her mind, and I don't want to leave on a bad note. This might be the last time I see her. So I swallow my objections.

I can't stay here anymore.

"I should go."

Celeste's eyes glisten. "The planet would be better for you, too, Ursa. Make you healthier, fitter. I'd love to have you here. And I'm worried about the ship. It was never meant to last this long, and now it's been damaged."

Astra clutches her hands together, looking at me, obviously afraid I'll change my mind and stay with Celeste. But I shake my head.

"I'm sorry. There's too much to do on the ship. We need all the engineers to fix her."

Astra exhales. Celeste's gaze drops to her baby's head. "I'll miss you, little sis."

I step close and put my arms around her and her baby. It's awkward, as Beta keeps screaming. I wish I could be there for her and Celeste, to help them to survive until flights can start again. And I'm suddenly glad Mom will be.

I step back and wipe my eyes.

"I love you, Celeste."

"Love you too."

Mom comes over. Gives me a hug. "I'm so sorry, Ursa," she says. "For all the ways I let you down. I love you."

I want to tell her she's letting me down again by staying here. But I do understand, so I bury my head in her shoulder instead. Celeste and Beta need her more than I do. I have Astra.

"Love you too," I mumble into her landsuit, before pulling away.

"I'll see you back on the shuttle," I say to Astra.

I can't look back as I head out of the hut. Can't see Celeste, Beta, and Mom huddled in the primitive room. I head toward the landbikes alone. None of this feels real.

Jovan's leaving the hospital. I'm so glad to see him, I run across the mud to his side.

"Time to go?" I ask.

"We've still got thirty minutes. Don't you want to say goodbye to Sabik?" He points him out, over at the edge of the village, apparently unbothered by the rain. He's with a group of agricologists. They're pulling a tarp over a heap of wood. Looks like they're planning another bonfire tonight.

"I guess I should," I say, trying to sound normal in spite of the heaviness in my chest. I don't want to say goodbye to anyone else. It makes it all too real.

"I'll give you some space," Jovan says. "I'll be waiting for you on the shuttle."

I smile at him. He's so tactful and thoughtful. We're standing close to each other, and his eyes are on mine. Neither of us looks away, and the moment lengthens between us.

He leans down, just a little. I push myself up on tiptoes, and just like that, our lips touch. His are soft and a little wet from the rain. He slides a hand around me, pulls me into him, into his warmth. I try to relax into the kiss. But there's so much going through my head, I can't concentrate.

After a moment, I pull away. His eyes are still closed. I admire his high cheekbones, glistening with water. His full lips. But it's like I'm looking at him from a distance. Then he opens his eyes and smiles, wider than before.

"I'll catch up with you at the shuttle, then," he says. "Launch is at 1720."

I watch his back as he jogs away. Why didn't I feel anything when we kissed?

Perhaps I'm like my mother. Perhaps I can't get close to people.

No. It's just that things are changing so fast. There has been too much death. I used to feel something when I kissed Sabik. I need life to get back to normal, on the *Venture*.

I take a deep breath and jog over to Sabik. I don't think he saw the kiss. He was too deep in conversation. Not that it matters, of course. As I approach he glances up and waves. He finishes securing the tarp and walks over.

The rain changes as he approaches. I can see the downpour coming across the village just before it hits us, like a wall of darker sky swooping in from the forest. It flattens Sabik's messy hair, makes it look like black sap. It runs down over his eyebrows, making him blink. I pull my hood lower over my face, but it doesn't stop it getting in my eyes, too.

"Let's get inside," Sabik shouts as the hiss grows around us. There are puddles already, the rain hitting them like drops of molten solder. We slosh our way into Sabik's hut. It smells like wet wood. I try to shake off the water on my landsuit, in my hair.

"Planning a bonfire?" I ask. "In this weather?"

"It's going to clear up later."

I don't know what to say, so I listen to the drumming on the roof above us, the drip of my landsuit onto the floor.

"I'm worried about you," Sabik says. "Don't go back to the ship."

"You're worried about me? You're the one on the planet. How are you going to survive?"

"This place is designed for us," he says. "Some of the landclearers are fixed, and the fields are partly planted. The village is almost finished, and, thanks to Jovan, we can continue with the releases."

"There's something in the woods."

"No one has been hurt during the day. We'll take care. We avoid the woods at night anyway. You're less safe on the ship."

I tilt my head to one side. "How did you work that one out?"

"It won't just be Vega and Yuri. Sooner or later, there will be fighting over the ship. It's just been postponed."

"You don't think we'll ever be completely safe?"

"I don't think there's such a thing as complete safety."

I should argue, but I'm exhausted. The rain has chilled me, and I'm numb and tired. I want to curl up in my cabin and have this all go away. Have things go back to the way they used to be.

But that's never going to happen. I check my linkcom.

"I've got to go," I tell Sabik. "We're taking off in fifteen minutes."

"I'll take you back to the shuttle."

"You don't need to."

"I want to." He holds the door open, and we step out in the rushing downpour.

I'd warmed up a little in the shelter of the hut, but out here I'm shivering again.

Sabik nods toward the landbikes, and we tramp over to them. Sabik pushes his wet hair from his face and climbs on the nearest one. I get on the back. I almost put my arms around him, like

I used to. But I reach for the back handgrips instead. He waits until I'm settled, then guns the engine. I try to peer between the trees as we go, but rain is in my eyes and all I can see are the glowferns. By the time we're at the shuttle, there's mud splattered all over me. I try to wipe it off, but my hands are as filthy as my clothes. I can't wait to get dry and warm, back on the *Venture*. I can't wait to put this mess behind me.

I give Sabik one last hug before I step up on the boarding platform. "I'll miss you."

"I'll look out for your family. See how I can help."

"Thanks."

Tears mix with the rain on my cheeks. I take one final look at the surface. There's not much to see. A muddy mess and a dark forest. The horizon is gone, swallowed up by the downpour that's staining the whole world gray. My mother, Celeste, and her daughter are somewhere on the other side of the trees.

I wipe my wet face on my even wetter sleeve. I can't stand to be here anymore.

I wave to Sabik and step inside. The people on board are quiet, and many are as muddy as I am. Astra is near the back, head in her hands, back heaving. I scan the faces.

"Where's Jovan?" I ask. The few people who hear me shrug.

"Don't leave without us." I step outside again. Sabik's figure is disappearing through the rain, slouching toward the landbikes.

"Have you seen Jovan?" I shout, trying to keep a tremble from my voice. "He said he'd be waiting here for me."

Sabik turns and shakes his head, so I pull out my linkcom and ping Jovan.

No reply.

I peer down the forest path and scan the shuttle camp, blinking against the heavy rain splattering into the mud all around me. Jovan isn't here, and there are no landbikes coming. The chill of dread snakes through my insides as I peer through the rain. I try not to think of waiting for Maia at the shuttle that day. I check my linkcom again. It's 1720.

I ping the engine room. Aldrin is on duty. I ask him to find Jovan's linkcom and tell the shuttle to wait. We'll miss this overhead pass of the *Venture*. Jovan will be disciplined.

When my linkcom pings again, I check it, hoping it's Jovan explaining why he's late. But it's Aldrin, sending Jovan's linkcom's coordinates for the last five minutes. I switch to map view, and my breath stops in my throat.

Jovan's in the forest, near Maia's grave.

And he's not moving.

CHAPTER 21

I run in the direction shown on my linkcom and slip, falling face-first into the sludge. I push myself up. Spit out the rotten taste of mud, the clammy dirt on my tongue. An arm grabs me and pulls me to my feet.

"What's happening?" Sabik says.

"Jovan. I think he went to say goodbye to Maia, but he hasn't come back." I shove my linkcom into his hand.

He peers at the display, then looks up and into my eyes. "Come on. Let's find him."

We hurry toward the path to the graveyard. The sky lights with a flash. I'm glancing around trying to work out what it is, when there's a loud rumble from right above me. I drop to my knees and cover my head, instinctively.

Another bomb? The shuttle?

I peer through my arms, but the shuttle is still there. Everything is the same. Sabik kept running, but now he's stopped and is looking back at me.

"It's a thunderstorm," he says.

I straighten up, feeling stupid. Of course. They're louder than I imagined.

"I can look for Jovan," Sabik says. "You stay here."

I shake my head. I have to find Jovan.

We sprint off the runway and down the mud-soaked path together.

But the linkcom's directions soon lead us off the path and into the trees. There are mini-rivers running along the forest floor, puddles that are deeper than they look. I'm soon up to my ankles in mud, and water spills over into my boots. My feet are soaking. Another rumble from overhead. I keep walking, trying to ignore how much it sounds like a giant beast growling. The flash makes me flinch, makes me clutch a tree, although that's probably the worst thing to do. Didn't they say to avoid trees in a thunderstorm?

I keep going, wiping at my eyes and trying to follow Sabik. He reaches into his tool bag and brings out a machete. He hacks at the forest as we go, leaving a trail of oozing red sap. I stumble after him, tripping over roots and fallen branches, glowferns swishing around my ankles, but we're taking too long.

More lightning, with rumbles almost immediately after. Even louder than the rhythmic crash of blood in my ears is the mad hiss of rain on the trees. The noise of each thunderbolt shakes through my rib cage. The flashes make the forest painfully bright. I look up just in time to see a forking bolt of light slam down from the sky just ahead of us.

My hand is shaking as I check the linkcom again. We're almost there, where Jovan should be. I try to listen, but the wind in the trees and the hiss and patter of water block out any other sound.

Sabik stops, and I run into his back. "What's that?" he shouts over the rain.

I peer where he's pointing. There's a gap in the glowferns. A large hole in the ground, half full of water. The next flash of light illuminates solar panels and other tech from the ship, deep in the mud. What a waste. Then I spot a scrap of something red, right at the bottom.

Oh no.

I shove past Sabik, who grabs my shoulder as I pass, but I push on, slide down into the hole, splashing toward the red.

But it's too small to be Jovan.

The hole is a good meter deep and just as wide. I'm up to my knees in mud and water, the chill cutting through me. The red thing is mostly buried in the slurry at the bottom. Wires and tubes lead into it. It's soft, more like plastic than fabric. I wade through to it, pick it up, and stare for a long moment.

An artificial womb.

Now that I know what I'm looking at, I spot other genelab tech in the hole around me: the corner of an accelerated cell division unit sticking out of the growing puddle; empty food packs; discarded test tubes, a small centrifuge, and packages of medblood and nutrients floating in the mess. Enough for a mini genelab. They could splice and grow things with this. Someone dug a hole here and hid this stuff. But the artificial womb is falling apart and smells like rotting chemicals. It's been buried for a while, by the look of it. A shovel lies in the mud next to the hole.

Who was digging here? Were they trying to find something … or to hide something else in the same place? The used womb is still in my hands, the rain washing away the mud. It's stretched out larger than I've seen before. Too big for any of the releases we've had.

I swallow hard, as it all finally makes sense.

I glance up in time for the sharp stab of light in the sky to burn its way across my retinas, leaving me blinking, momentarily blind. Then there's a crack like the world opening above me.

I throw the womb back in the water.

"Someone made the creature here," I shout to Sabik as I clamber out of the hole, hands digging into the soft mud of the sides. The veins of lightning are visible on my eyelids when I blink. My throat is trying to close against the panic. "They were feeding it, too. It's probably near. Do you have a pulse gun?" I fumble in my gear bag. I'm getting mud on my kit. I don't care.

"No." Sabik holds out his machete. "But you can have this."

I shake my head, pull out my blowtorch, and turn the flame as high as it will go. I don't know how much use it'll be in the rain, but it's the best I can think of.

There's a howl, half muted by the rain, but clearly not the wind, not the thunder. It short-circuits me. Freezes me in place. I look over at Sabik. He's wide-eyed as he pulls out his linkcom, hits the alarm. "We should go back. They'll send protectors." He shouts over the cacophony of the storm.

"Jovan could be hurt." I pause to wipe the water from my face with my forearm. "The protectors will take time to get here."

Sabik nods, jaw set. I try to walk calmly, but I'm nauseous and scared my resolve is going to crumble. My foot hits something buried in the mud. There's a crack, and my leg slides out from under me. I fall on my back, breath knocked from me.

"Are you okay?" Sabik yells.

"Yeah." I get up onto my knees and my hand lands on the thing that tripped me. It's cold. Smooth. I pick it up. A broken jar. Some kind of clear liquid oozes out, running over my fingers and mixing with the rain. "What's this?"

Sabik takes it from me. "Don't know. Stinks, though."

It does. Like sweat or urine. I wipe my fingers off on my thigh, and Sabik throws the broken jar on the ground. "Come on, then," he says.

I check my linkcom again for Jovan's coordinates. A few more meters. It's hard to push myself on. Every atom in my body is screaming at me to stop. The hairs on my arms are standing on end.

There's another flash then. But it's not as bright, and when the rumble comes I flinch, but it's more distant. Perhaps the worst of the storm has passed. Perhaps things will be okay.

But then there's another flash, and I see him.

Jovan. Eyes open. Blood.

I turn away, but it's seared into my memory. He's torn open. Right across the chest, down to his waist. Glistening pink lumps of guts exposed to the air. Sabik reaches for me, but I push past him, grab a tree, and vomit.

There's no point in checking for a pulse. Not when he looks like that.

I retch again, onto the ground.

Jovan can't be dead. He's coming back with me to the ship. I'm going to let him into my life. I choke on the sick in my throat. My stomach spasms. I heave more and spit it out into the glowferns. The rain washes it into the mud. My hands shake as I clutch the tree. And the next flash is weaker. As soon as I can move again, I straighten up.

I can't even cry. My brain is stuck on the image of Jovan in the mud.

"The creature must be close," Sabik says. "I'm sorry, Ursa. But we have to go."

I don't move. Jovan and I are going back to the ship, together. That was the plan. I need to fix this, somehow. Fix Jovan. Put things back the way they are meant to be.

I know how stupid that is. But it's all I can think.

Sabik grabs my hand, pulls hard.

Then we're running. Twigs scrape across my face, and blood joins the rain and tears on my cheeks. Roots catch at my feet, but Sabik drags me along. I feel blind. Stripped of sense and meaning. All I know is we're fleeing toward the shuttle camp.

Sabik halts, and I keep stumbling on until he yanks on my arm, hard. Stopping me, nearly pulling me over. Then I hear it too.

Breathing. Not mine. Not Sabik's. Loud enough to hear over the rain. Even over my desperate breath.

It pulls me back into my body. My muscles lock me in place. Mind whirrs into action.

There it is. The shadow between the trees. Mottled black and brown fur. Teeth bared in a growl that exposes the bright pink of its mouth. The sound reaches into my spine. Primal fear freezes me where I stand.

It's huge. The size of a tiger. The shape of a wolf.

Beautiful, too. Muscles moving under wet fur, fluid as water. It paces in front of us. Ears pointed, listening. Yellow eyes fixed on me.

Breathing hard. Too hard. No wonder I could hear it that night in the forest, even over the rustle of the trees. Lung problems, because it's genelab made, accelerated growth. I should have realized.

I hold up my blowtorch. I don't stand a chance. I need a real weapon.

I see it then, on the creature's right foot. A red-raw patch of exposed skin. Fur gone, flesh blistered beneath. It's limping, favoring its left paw. I know what it is. I've seen electrical burns before.

Jovan. Oh, Jovan. You might still save us.

I swallow. We only have one chance. I have to be brave. We have to go back to his body.

"Come on," I say, my voice too quiet. I pull Sabik backward.

He resists for a second. But then he sees my expression, and he lets me lead him. I take one careful step at a time, watching the creature, backing through the trees, glancing over my shoulder when I dare. We don't run. I can't risk falling.

The creature follows. Stalking us. Long muzzle, teeth bared, exposing huge incisors. The teeth I saw the night Orion was killed. I hold the blowtorch tightly as we back up. My mind is racing now, putting things together. Making a shape out of the pattern.

Jovan knew the animal was here. Why else would he be deep in the forest, away from the route to Maia's grave? I want to believe he was running from the creature. That he stumbled here. But it's too far, too deep in the woods.

He was a geneticist. He made the monster. I want to be sick again.

Why did he come back? To kill the creature? To feed it? To hide evidence? Whatever the reason, he wasn't stupid. He didn't come unarmed. And he shot the creature, but only hit its paw.

Jovan's pulse gun must be here. Near where he fell.

We've backed up far enough. Out of the corner of my eye I see the body.

I can't think of it as Jovan. Can't turn to see the staring eyes and blood.

His hands are empty. I drop to my knees and fumble in the mud around him with my free hand, still watching the creature.

The gun must be here. He must have dropped it when the animal attacked.

A roar. The creature's back is arched, head low. Yellow eyes on Sabik, black pupils small. Muscles bunching up under skin.

It leaps. Sabik screams.

The creature is on him. White claws flashing. Teeth on Sabik's hand. Red blood. Sabik's flailing, screaming, falling back into the mud beside Jovan's body.

No. Not Sabik, too.

I'm on my feet, lighting the blowtorch. I run over and point the flame at the creature's flank.

It's a second before it reacts. Then it jumps back with a growl that sounds more angry than hurt. It releases Sabik, but he keeps screaming. He's on the ground, holding his hand. It's dangling from his wrist, barely connected.

The creature roars again, the fur singed on its shoulder.

The vowels in Sabik's scream form my name. He's trying to point with the blood-covered fingers of his good hand while clutching his semi-severed hand at the wrist. I look away, into the undergrowth where he's indicating. There are plants. Glowferns and different shades of green and brown. How am I meant to find the pulse gun in this mess?

Wait. There.

Brown mud hiding a brighter shade of green, revealed by the bioluminescence. What did Sabik say when we saw the landclearer? You don't find neon colors in the forest.

I shove the blowtorch in my back pocket and dive for the half-buried glimpse of bright green. The object is hard in my hands, a red light shining on the tube. Thank Beta.

I'm twisting, rolling over to face the monster. It jumps. Lands on my chest, sideways. A crushing weight on my lungs. Teeth in my thigh. I try to focus through the pain. Push the gun against fur. Find the button. Close my eyes. Squeeze.

There's a zap.

The weight on me doubles. Stops my breath. Fills my mouth with fur and water. I choke and fight for air.

I kick at the creature. Push, roll, and I'm free. It flops to one side.

I lie on my back, gasping, staring up at the needles on the branches above and the dark clouds beyond. A quiet rumble, now. The rain pours off the tree into my eyes, blinding me, into my open mouth, and I'm coughing again, gagging on the rain. I roll onto my side in the mud, push myself up, blink until I can see again. I check the creature.

There's a red welt right in the chest. Its mouth is open, drawn back from the teeth. The tongue is loose and the eyes closed. The head is tilted back in the mud.

It's dead.

"Sabik!" I turn to him.

He's pale. Lying on the ground. Still clutching his hand. His blood is black in the light from the glowferns. And it's coming fast.

I swear, then crawl over, ignoring the pain in my thigh.

"Stay with me!" I fumble the pulse gun into my back pocket with the blowtorch and unzip the jacket of my landsuit. The fabric is too thick to use, but my undershirt might work. I lift that over my head, then bite hard into the bottom hem. I yank my head to the side, and the old fabric rips. Good.

I kneel and bind the first piece tightly around his arm below the elbow, a quick tourniquet. The artery in his wrist is severed. I take the next piece of cloth and push it against the wound itself, pressing as hard as I can to stop the blood. He cries out, but holds still.

He doesn't have long. I close my eyes and pray help will come in time.

CHAPTER 22

Sabik is moaning quietly now. Is it hurting less, or is he too weak to scream? He's moving, almost convulsing under the pressure of my hands. I can barely make out his features in the soaking dark of the forest. His mouth is contorted with pain. I'm hurting him, pressing on his wound, but I have to keep up the direct pressure. Have to stop his life flowing out. Wet runs over my hands. I can't tell how much is rain and how much is blood. Is he going into shock?

Don't let him die. Please.

Noises. Not just the rain. Not just Sabik's moans. Footsteps. Swearing.

Thank Beta. I shout, voice raw. "We're here! Help us!"

The sounds speed up. Snapping branches and crunching twigs.

"Ursa!" It's Mom.

"Hurry!"

Then Mom's through the trees. She stops when she sees the creature and Jovan, and stares.

"Here!" I say. "Sabik's injured."

She snaps out of it and is on her knees at Sabik's side. I want to hug her, but I don't let go of the wound. Mom moves quickly, checking his breathing and pulse. His eyes are open and wide. For a moment I fear the worst, but he blinks.

"Are you hurt, Ursa?" Mom asks, glancing up at me.

My thigh burns, the slash in the flesh hot and deep. I peer down. I'm bleeding, but it's not flowing out. Just glistening on the landsuit, invisible against the wet red fabric.

"I'm okay."

Mom gently pulls Sabik's hand from my grasp. She puts pressure on his wound, where my hands were. They feel empty. I sit back on my haunches, helpless. Her hands fly over Sabik's injuries, removing my bandages, peering under them before swiftly replacing them.

Mom finishes checking Sabik over. "Can you hear me?"

There's a long pause, then a whispered, "Yes."

More footsteps behind us. Protector Adhara bursts out of the trees, lugging Mom's medic pack. Taking in the scene in one glance, Adhara steps back and puts a hand over her mouth.

"We have to get Sabik to the ship," Mom says. "Get the stretcher from my pack. Now."

Adhara takes a second to register this, then she opens Mom's pack and unfolds a narrow stretcher. She kneels beside Sabik's feet, and Mom moves to his shoulders.

"On three," Mom says. "One, two, three." Together they shift him. He screams.

The rain on my skin reminds me that my landsuit is unzipped and my undershirt is ripped. I do up the jacket, quickly.

"What's Mom doing here?" I ask Adhara.

"She heard about Jovan going missing and came to the shuttle. She got there when Sabik's alarm pinged through. When she realized you were in the forest, she started running, threw her kit at me, and told me to carry it."

I glance at Mom. She's not looking at me. "Give me the perfusion kit," she shouts at Adhara over the rain.

Adhara nods and pulls things from the bag.

"That's the one," Mom shouts, pointing. "Fix it on his wrist."

Adhara moves to Sabik's wrist with a red box. His injured one.

"Other side," Mom says. "Oh, I'll do it."

Adhara moves back. Mom gets into place and slides a needle into Sabik's wrist, then hits some buttons on the red pack. It starts pulsing, and she sets it on the stretcher next to his head. She takes off my ripped undershirt, now soaked red, and replaces it with clean bandages.

"Pressure pack," Mom says. Adhara stares in the bag. "That thing." Mom points. Adhara pulls out a black sphere with four straps on it. She passes it to Mom, who attaches it to Sabik's wrist. It shapes itself to fit, putting pressure on his wound. His hand is barely attached to his body. I swallow down the nausea.

"Ready to move," Mom says. "Here." She holds Sabik's machete out to me. I take it automatically in my bloody hands.

"Lead the way," she says. "As fast as you can."

I pull out my linkcom, check the display in map mode, and walk. It's slow going. I have to find wide gaps between the trees, big enough for the stretcher. I hack the branches in the way, or hold them back so Mom and Adhara can maneuver Sabik. They grunt behind me, and Sabik moans as he's bumped around.

At least that means he's still conscious.

My hands are slippery with rain and blood. It's hard to hold on to the machete, hard to hack at the wood. My lungs burn. I keep peering at the linkcom. I walk into branches until there's more blood on my face from the scratches. The slash on my thigh gapes with each step, but it's shallow, bearable, and I bite down the pain.

I start to sob when the trees thin ahead and we're back on the path from the graveyard to the shuttle. We run, my pace an awkward limping lumber. It's not long before there are bright lights ahead.

"Help!" I shout. "We're here!"

Then we're out of the trees, stumbling over the mud toward the runway. Colonists run over, shocked eyes wide. I wonder why they're looking at me like that, then remember the blood on my face, my lip swollen where a branch hit it.

"I'm fine, I'm fine! It's Sabik. Please, hurry."

They push past me, help Mom and Adhara.

Mom shouts above the gathering crowd. "He's had a thousand-cc perfusion. Get another kit ready on the shuttle and start the engines. We have to get him to the medcarriage now."

The boarding platform is floodlit, a bright island in the wet of the runway. The shuttle is roaring, engines prepped. Others are here now — agricologists and builders — running along, helping to carry the stretcher. My thigh makes keeping up tough, but I'm not holding up the shuttle. Rain washes the blood from my face and hands.

Many hands lift the stretcher up to the boarding platform, but they back off to give us room to get through the main doors. Mom and Adhara push Sabik onto the ship. I slip in after them, and the doors slam behind me, sealing us into the warm, familiar shuttle.

I stand there, panting. Mom glances up from setting up the second perfusion kit.

"Find a seat," she says. "Quickly."

I jump into a chair in the second row, leaving the front row open for Mom, Adhara, and the stretcher. I flinch as the movement stretches my wound and buckle myself in. Once Mom has hooked the safety lines up to Sabik, she dives for a seat herself, in front of me.

"Ready." Adhara speaks into her linkcom.

Acceleration presses me gently back in my seat as we speed down the runway. I grit my teeth. There's a scream from Sabik. I try to see how he is, but his face is hidden by the chair back in front of me. I thump it.

"How is he?" I ask, shouting over the roar of the engine.

"Ursa?" Sabik moans. I can see the side of Mom's face. Her expression is grim.

"Everything's going to be fine, Sabik," I say. I hope that's right.

The flight is agonizingly long. The shuttle launch was late, so the *Venture* had already passed overhead. I press the heel of my hand down on my wound. The blood flow has slowed, and the pain pulses with my heartbeat. I'll need it sealed on board. Mom fiddles with the tubes leading into Sabik's body. She asks how I am again, her voice wavering. I tell her I'm fine. Tell her to focus on Sabik.

I strain to see what's happening, but the damn chairs are in the way. Mom says they need more blood, and painkillers. Sabik stops his moaning halfway there.

I hope he's just doped up. I can't think about the alternative. I've already lost Jovan.

Then I remember what Jovan did. Why didn't I realize sooner? I saw his anger, his rage at the planet over Maia's death. I shared it. I just didn't realize how deep it went. Maybe it was visiting the graveyard so often that did it. Weeping at his sister's grave. Seeing the space around it just waiting to be filled. But in trying to fix things, he started to fill the graveyard himself.

He was the one who suggested using an empty landclearer to smuggle me down. He must have gotten the genelab tech down the same way. Sabik saw him smuggling *genelab* tech out of the engineering hut. That's why there was no missing engineering equipment. Why didn't I realize?

All this death. When will it end? What if Sabik's right? Will there always be war between those who want to keep the *Venture* in orbit and those who want to pull her to the ground? Will there be another Jovan, another Vega?

When we finally lock rotation with the *Venture* and gravity kicks in, I'm out of my chair faster than oxygen from an airlock, in spite of my wound. Sabik's eyes are closed. What does that mean? They unbuckle him as the airlock hisses open. Medics are waiting for us.

Then they're off. Out of the loading bay. Down the corridor to the medcarriage. I try to keep up, but they pull ahead of me. The airlock between the carriages is already open, revealing the white walls of the medcarriage.

As soon as we get in I'm pushed away and Sabik is wheeled into an operating bay. Soundproof doors close between us.

I peer through the small window. They're scurrying around Sabik, cutting off his landsuit, putting on wires and more tubes. Mom's shouting at someone, hand outstretched for a tool. But the chaos of the medcarriage is silenced by the thick glass. All I can hear is the breathing of the *Venture*. The hum of her fans and the purr of the boosters.

We're home, at least. The *Venture* is the best place for Sabik. She'll look after him.

I feel a hand on my shoulder, and I jump.

It's Astra. Her eyes are shining.

"I heard about Sabik," she says. "I'm so sorry."

I turn around and collapse into her arms. I'm shaking, my back heaving with sobs.

"Oh Beta. Let's get you to the engine room. There's nothing you can do here."

I barely notice the elevator ride. She's right, of course. I need to ground myself. I can get help for my leg later. I don't want to pull any medics away from Sabik. And I can't stand to stare in that window at him, helpless on the stretcher as medics buzz around him.

Astra pats my back and holds me as the weight of gravity eases from us. The elevator doors swish open, she pushes away from the wall, and we drift into the engine room, linked together.

"Can you give us some space?" Astra says to Aldrin.

He nods, unstraps from the controller's chair, and heads for the elevator without another word. No doubt he heard about what happened to Sabik.

As soon as he's gone, Astra helps me into the center to float in the weightlessness. I curl into the fetal position and hide my face in my hands. I listen to the beeping and soft humming of the monitors. The *Venture* cradles me in the space at her heart. I breathe deeply, taking in the scent of warm metal, the synthetic smell of our world, our home.

After a while, I open my eyes. I'm glad Astra is here, sitting in the controller's chair. I wouldn't be able to get back to the sides without her. I'd be stuck. And I need this weightlessness, this freedom, right now.

"Better?" Astra asks.

"A little."

"I'm glad. Now, what on Beta happened? Where's Jovan?"

She doesn't know. Of course she doesn't know. There hasn't been time for anyone to write a report.

I don't want to tell her. Don't want to remember his mangled body. The genelab he must have built. I pull myself up to a sitting position in the air facing her and force the words out.

"There was a genelab on the planet. The creature was made there. It killed Jovan, and we killed it."

Astra's eyes are wide. "Jovan's dead?"

I nod.

"I'm so sorry, Ursa."

I swallow hard. Try not to think about his body. About our kiss. "Was he visiting Maia's grave?"

Deep breath. "No. I think Jovan made the creature to scare people off the planet."

Astra shakes her head, mouth open. "I'm sorry, Ursa."

"It's dead now, at least. It can't hurt anyone else."

Astra nods. Considers for a moment. "Are you sure? Couldn't Jovan have made more?"

"I only saw one womb unit. It would take a couple of months to grow something like that, even with the cell division accelerators."

Astra is tapping her chin. "But we can't be sure, right?"

"No, I guess we can't."

"There may be enough to breed. We need to warn the colonists. We can stretch our resources to send the shuttle down for the people who change their minds."

I hug my knees. "Sabik is badly hurt. He might lose his hand."

"They can grow a new one for him, but it'll take a while. Your mother is the best with grafts and transplants, and she's already back on board. Do you think you can convince her to stay to help?"

"Not unless Celeste and the baby come back."

"I'll talk to Celeste. She'll want what's best for Sabik."

My stomach is warm, despite the horror of the afternoon. Sabik, Celeste, and Mom, all back on the *Venture*. Life will be normal again.

"How did you kill the creature?" Astra asks.

"Jovan had a pulse gun. I found it in the mud."

She's silent for a moment. "You still have it?"

"Um ... I ..." I fumble in my landsuit. It's in my back pocket, next to the blowtorch. "Yeah." I get it out, feeling the sharp edge of the chipped casing against my thumb.

Astra swings out from the wall and takes it from me, then

returns to her seat. "Good. It'll be evidence for the investigation."

The pain in my thigh is a dull throb. It's good to be back here. But I replay the events of the last few days in my head as I float, and I feel queasy.

"Yuri was right," I say. "Someone was killing the colonists in order to scare us all back on the ship. He just got it wrong when he thought it was me."

The alarms of the engine room are silent, but the displays still flash to one side of Astra, lighting her cheekbone blood red. "Yuri planted bombs on this ship," she says. "He put us all in danger. Jovan was misguided, but I'm sure he did it for his sister, to stop other people dying."

There's something not right. I stare at the feeds. All the numbers are wrong since the bomb went off, so there's no comfort there. Astra's not meeting my eyes. It's as if she's waiting for me to say something else. There's cold spreading through my stomach.

A sensory memory comes back to me. My thumb brushing over the chip on the pulse gun I just handed over. The one I found by Jovan's body.

It was chipped. I chipped it when I was adjusting the blowtorch casing.

It's Astra's gun.

How did Jovan get it? I put it back in Astra's safe. She's staring down into her lap. The world shifts around me. Things click into place, forming a new and horrible shape.

She told me she'd been spending time with Jovan. Talking to him. How could she not realize what he was up to? She's better at spotting a lie than anyone I know.

My mouth is dry. Astra. My Astra. She would have suspected, at the very least. But it was more than that.

After all, who loves this ship more than Astra? I've lived here for seventeen Alpha years. Astra's been here for over fifty. Her husband, my father, devoted his life to keeping her in the sky. Everything I feel for the *Venture* is magnified in Astra.

She looks up. Sees my wide eyes.

"You worked it out, didn't you?" she says. "How?"

I consider denying it. But I know the shock is written on my face.

"That's your pulse gun. You lent it to Jovan."

Astra looks almost relieved. "Oh, Ursa. You understand, don't you? We had to do something. People were dying. Maia and Seginus were only the start."

"Cassius and Orion are dead," I say. "Not because of the planet."

Astra lets her gaze drop to the pulse gun in her hands. "We were hoping Orion's death would be enough. But Cassius was talking about accelerating the colonization. I had to act."

I need to stop floating. "Get me to the side."

"Let's talk this out."

My jaw clenches. The thing is, I almost do understand. But Cassius and Orion didn't deserve to die. Especially not like that. I'm wishing she'd tell me it's a mistake. That I've misunderstood. All around me the lights of the wounded *Venture* flash.

Everything is wrong. Everything is broken.

"You ... you let me go into the forest on the night Orion was killed. It could have been me." It's hard to get the words out. They feel absurd in my mouth.

"I tried to stop you. But you were never in danger. The creature avoided humans."

"That's not what we saw."

"Jovan engineered a pheromone that drove the animal crazy. Everyone was safe as long as they weren't marked with it."

"I was safe? Sabik was safe? And Jovan?"

"Jovan went to kill the creature. It had done its job. He wanted to keep the village safe. Jovan was a good man."

I want to laugh at that. But then I remember him setting up the genelab in the hospital to give Celeste and Beta the best chance he could.

"Perhaps the storm spooked the creature," Astra says. "Or it attacked Jovan in self-defense. Or perhaps he got some of the pheromone on himself."

The jar I slipped on. The stinking oil in it. It was on Sabik's hand. I wiped it on my thigh. The smell of urine and sweat.

Oh no.

I remember Astra at the bonfire, putting a hand on Orion's shoulder as he headed into the forest. The smell of sweat as she wiped her hands. Astra, stinking of urine on the night Cassius died. I told her he was going into the forest. Perhaps she caught up with him and laid a concerned hand on his back.

She marked them both for death.

I look up at her face, soft skin folded into familiar wrinkles, and see the fear in her eyes: fear of the planet, fear of losing the ship, fear of losing what's left of Dad.

"It's done now," she says. "We can convince everyone to move back on board now."

I'm numb. The whole ship together again. It could be like it was. We'd be safe.

Wasn't that what I wanted?

"Please, Ursa. I need you to support me."

I cover my face with my hands. Breathe into their warm darkness. Lies and deceit have been tearing this colony apart, turning us on each other, fighting over the future of the ship.

Circles of death. Over and over.

I'm quiet for a long time, thinking over my options. She would never hurt me. And anyway, she can't. Not in the engine room. Aldrin saw us come here together. She couldn't cover that up.

"I'm sorry," I say. "You killed people. You have to face the consequences."

She stares for a long time, eyes wide. She looks like I've stabbed her.

"I am willing to face the consequences," she says. "Willing to face the Exit to save the ship. It's the death sentence I've passed on myself. Please, Ursa, keep this secret and I'll face justice in a few months."

"We can't keep the ship together by lying to people."

Tears gather in her eyes. "You've made up your mind?"

I nod.

Astra swallows. "I don't want to do this."

My breath stops. She grips the pulse gun in her lap.

"No," I say. "You wouldn't."

"I have to, Ursa. For your father. For the *Venture*. For my daughter and her baby. I have to keep them safe. I have to get them back on board."

"People will know you killed me!"

Astra shakes her head. "An electrical accident in the engine room while you were fixing damage from Yuri's bomb. I'm sorry." Her words come out in a sob. "I have to keep this ship together. If there were any other way ..."

I try to twist around, try to reach the side. It's no use. I'm stuck in the middle of the engine room. I'm a sitting duck.

"No, Astra, please!"

"I have to save the *Venture*. I can't be selfish."

I kick at the air, pointlessly. "Okay! Okay! I won't tell anyone. I'll keep it secret."

"You're lying. I know you, Ursa."

I can't reach the sides. I let my hand drift slowly toward my gear bag on my hip. Perhaps I could get my linkcom, hit the alarm. But Astra shakes her head.

"Hands behind your back, Ursa."

I do as she says. Then my fingers feel the bump in my back pocket, and I have a plan. I stop kicking and hang there.

"I thought you loved me," I say. I let tears well up.

"I do. I love you, Little Bear. So much."

Her hand wavers, but she still points the pulse gun at me.

CHAPTER 23

Astra has to think I've given up. I have to time my move just right.

I hang there, floating helplessly in the middle of the engine room while one hand works behind my back, positioning, preparing. I open my eyes as wide as I can, try for my best little-girl look. Let the tears show.

"I love you too," I say. "Please don't do this."

Her hand shakes. She raises her other one to join it, to hold the pulse gun steady, aimed at me, finger on the red button.

"Please, Astra."

She swallows. "I'm so sorry. I really am." She closes her eyes.

That's my cue.

I turn the blowtorch on. It's pointed toward the side wall: a mini rocket pushing me out of the center as Astra fires. Her gun's pulse shoots past, just wide of the mark. It burns through the edge of my landsuit, scorching a patch of skin on my hip. I gasp. The pulse zaps into the console behind me with a crackle, and I smell smoke.

Astra's eyes open. She bites her lip and aims the gun again. Before she can shoot, the deafening alarm blares, then a stream of fire-suppressant gas hits us both, hurling me across the engine room and into the wall near Astra's chair. I scream as my bad thigh hits a control panel. But I grab a display screen and hold on with one hand as the carbon dioxide buffets us.

A few seconds, then the air pressure normalizes. I'm dizzy from the gas and my hip and thigh are alight with pain, but I'm no longer stuck in the middle. No longer a sitting duck. I've got a tight hold of the wall. I shove the blowtorch in my pocket and start clawing my way toward Astra, hand over hand around the curve of the engine room, grabbing on to familiar screens and input boards.

Astra is gasping. She got more of the CO2 blast than I did. She's trying to raise the pulse gun. Her eyes are unfocused, but she's gulping in air. I have only seconds.

The alarm keeps blaring, the ship crying out in panic. The pulse hit the elevator controls. They won't run until they're fixed. Astra's lucky she didn't hit the air circulators.

Wait. The air circulators. My heart beats faster. No, there has to be another way.

Astra's aiming again. I reach into my gear bag, grab the first thing my fingers touch, and hurl it at her. My linkcom. She dodges it easily, but it buys me a few seconds.

I kick off from the wall hard, flying toward her. I grab her arms and wrestle them back against her. I get hold of her hands, seizing the cold metal of the pulse gun. But her fingers are tight around the slender cylinder. I can't get any purchase on it. She won't let go, and she's trying to push it toward me. She grunts as she strains against me, but I'm younger, stronger. I push it away, twisting her hands back little by little until I'm forcing her to point it at her own chest.

Our eyes meet. I stare at the woman who raised me. Who just tried to kill me.

But I can't kill her. Not Astra.

She won't let go of the gun. I can't get my fingers in there, can't pry it away from her without risking getting shot. What do I do?

There's one thing I can do. One thing that will end this cycle of violence, of death. One way to honor Cassius, Orion, and Vega. One way to keep the colony together.

I push the gun to the side, away from me, away from Astra. She doesn't fight me at first. Doesn't know what I'm doing. I keep pushing the pulse gun. Inch by inch toward the wall. Astra's eyes go wide as she realizes. She starts struggling and kicking, but the zero-G prevents her getting any force in the blows. Her face is red, her breath coming in gasps.

I press the pulse gun against the air circulation controls. Move my grip. Grab her fist.

"No!" she screams.

I close my eyes. Pray for forgiveness from the *Venture*.

My hand tightens, pushing Astra's finger down on the red button.

Another zap, and we're thrown apart by the new blast of fire suppressant. The gun floats off across the engine room. I lose my hold on Astra and swing against a nearby console. Pain explodes in my burned hip, and I cry out. The alarms rise in pitch. The *Ventur*e is screaming, too.

The central air circulators are offline. The bypass is down. Air can't circulate around the wheel of the ship because of Vega's bomb and the hull breech. Now it can't circulate through the center. Soon there will be too much oxygen in the ecocarriages. Not enough in the rest of the ship.

The sound of the air rotors is wrong. The *Venture* is wheezing, fighting against her death. But she can't find a bypass route. I blew it out.

Her voice comes over the intercom, too calm in the chaos.

"*Air circulation failure. Betafall failsafe activated. Evacuate central core. Air diversion to carriages imminent.*"

I grab hold of the back of Astra's chair. She unstraps herself, pulls herself over to the main display panel. "What have you done?" She scans the readings. "Our home! Your father's work!" Her voice trembles.

I reach for her shoulder. "We have to get out of here. Now."

She stays at the main display as the meters turn red and error messages fill the screens.

"Astra!" I pull at her, trying to drag her away, toward the elevator. But she clutches tight to the handholds, and her back shakes. I lean forward, so I can see her. She's weeping. Eyes scrunched shut, tears escaping from her lashes, forming droplets that drift away from her face.

"*Air circulation failure. Betafall failsafe activated. Diverting air to carriages. Carriage containment in thirty minutes.*" The *Venture* again, calmly counting down to her own death.

"Please, Astra. Or we'll die here!"

"I want to die here! I've earned that! Everything I've done, everything I've given to this ship! I should get to die where I belong!" She waves a hand at the window, at the dark reaches of space.

The planet moves into view as the ship rotates: the bulging curve of it. It's a mess down there. I'll be trying to adapt to it for my whole life. Life will be scary and difficult. But it's our only future.

"I don't want to die, Astra."

She turns to me then, and her gaze is full of sorrow.

"Then go, Little Bear. I won't stop you."

"I love you," I say. But she turns back to the monitors.

I kick off the wall toward the elevator as fast as I can. I hit the door release.

Nothing happens.

Oh no. The first pulse gun blast. It took out the elevator controls.

I grab the side and swing myself back over to the control panel next to Astra. But the Betafall protocols have taken over, overriding the maintenance system. I punch in my engineer's code. The system won't accept it.

"I can't fix the elevators. It won't let me in," I say.

Astra keeps staring at the monitors for a long moment. Then, finally, she straightens up, kicks off the wall, glides to the elevator we came up in, and punches in her protector override code. The doors slide open. "You still might have time to get down the service ladder. Give me your screwdriver."

I push off the wall, floating to her side as she glides into the elevator.

"There won't be enough air. They're diverting it away from the spokes."

"Give me your screwdriver, Ursa, for Beta's sake!"

I reach in my gear bag and hand her the screwdriver. I watch as she unscrews and pulls up the square in the center of the floor. She tosses it into the corner of the elevator, where it floats, bumping against the walls.

"Get down there," she says.

I don't know if I can trust Astra. But does it matter, since I'm going to die anyway? I peer down the hole, plunging through the spoke. A kilometer-deep drop to the medcarriage. Even if there's enough air, will I have time to get there before the separation? I swing myself through the hatch, push myself to the wall, and start gliding down, holding on to the rungs.

Astra's head appears, framed by the hole in the elevator floor. "I'll send you the air from the engine room."

I look up at her face. At the lines around her eyes. "But you'll suffocate."

"Look after my daughter and granddaughter. Tell them I love them."

My vision begins to blur, but there's not enough gravity for the tears to fall.

"And look after yourself. I hope you haven't doomed everyone."

I can't move. I clutch the ladder, blinking and staring at her. Her hand moves, and I think she's reaching for me. But she grabs the floating elevator hatch instead.

"I love you, Little Bear. So much. Now go!" She slams down the hatch, cutting out the light of the engine room and my view of her.

And I'm still. In the dark of the elevator tube. Just breathing. Too fast.

"*Air circulation failure. Carriage containment in twenty-five minutes.*"

That snaps me out of it. I push myself down the ladder. I don't need to bother with footholds at first. I'm floating backward, downward, using the rungs, hand under hand, gliding lower as fast as I can. Breathing is hard. I don't know if it's the exertion or the panic or the limited air. The fans near the bottom of the shaft spin, sucking the oxygen from the spoke.

Now I'm far enough away from the axis to feel the pull of the centrifugal force. It drags me toward the carriages, getting stronger the further I get. I'm too heavy to use just my hands. I slip my feet onto the rungs. The gash on my thigh aches, stretches into agony with each step. The tears fall now, running down my cheeks.

"*Air circulation failure. Carriage containment in twenty minutes.*"

A quick glance up at the black square where Astra is working to save my life. I can't let the betrayal or the grief touch me. There's no time. Keep going. Down. Hand under hand. Don't think about anything but the ladder. Focus on the soft sound of my hands on the rungs.

"*Air circulation failure. Carriage containment in eighteen minutes.*"

My lungs are straining. There's gray at the edges of my vision.

"*Air circulation failure. Carriage containment in sixteen minutes.*"

Panting. The spoke is growing dark around me. It's not the lights failing. My grip is weak. I'm so dizzy. I stop climbing. Just hold on. I'm going to pass out. I'm going to fall. Just like Vega.

That seems fair, somehow.

"*Air circulation failure. Carriage containment in fourteen minutes.*"

A click, and the fans go silent, stop sucking air away from me. A few more seconds, then a hiss from above me. Astra, giving me her air. I can hear something else too. A lilting voice, singing in the silence.

"Our ship, our home, our one true place ..."

My father's favorite. I can almost hear his baritone behind Astra's soft, uncertain soprano.

"Our scrap of safety in outer space ..."

The light comes back into my vision, slowly. I can see the spoke again. Still breathing fast. Still light-headed. There's not much air for Astra to send.

"Our cradle, our grave, our spinning wheel ..."

She won't be able to sing for long. Her voice is already slowing.

"Our ark, our dock, our even keel ..."

I can't listen. Can't bear to hear her breathe her last. I don't have time, anyway.

"*Air circulation failure. Carriage containment in twelve minutes.*"

Get moving, Ursa.

My whole body aches. Breath is coming hard. But I have to move. Hand under hand. I peer between my legs. Still so far to go. No time to be careful. Don't think about Vega. Don't think about Astra. Don't think about Cassius, Orion, or Jovan. Don't think about Maia.

Keep climbing down. I grit my teeth.

"*Air circulation failure. Carriage containment in ten minutes.*"

Step, step, step. My feet clanging against the rungs, drowning out Astra's faint singing. I'm slipping in my hurry.

Faster. Faster.

"*Air circulation failure. Carriage containment in eight minutes.*"

The *Venture*'s voice is distorting in my ears. I clutch the ladder tighter as I go. Hands hot. There will be blisters, soon. Down. Down. Down. There's nothing in my mind now. Just the ladder. Just the rhythm. My thigh aches. My hip aches. My lungs ache. Darkness creeping in again.

"*Air circulation failure. Carriage containment in six minutes.*"

The *Venture* sounds like Astra now. But I know that's wrong. It's the lack of oxygen. I'm light-headed. I have to climb. That's all there is. Grabbing the bars. Quickly. Faster. Hands sweaty. I can barely see the ladder now. I'm shaking, dangerously dizzy. But I'm nearly there.

"*Air circulation failure. Carriage containment in four minutes.*"

Vega's voice this time. I peer down. Bad move. My foot slips. Sudden weight on my bad thigh. The slash rips wider.

I cry out, let go.

I swing away from the ladder. Clutching on desperately with one hand. My back crashes hard against the metal wall. Something gives in my shoulder. A scream ripped out of me.

Sweaty fingers slipping on the rungs, one by one.

Then I'm falling.

A few seconds of air rushing by. My stomach lurching.

I land on my back. The impact slams through my body. Tools clanging in my gear bag. For a few seconds, I lie in silence, unable to move, unable to breathe.

The shaft is silent. There's no singing anymore.

"*Air circulation failure. Carriage containment in two minutes.*"

Then the agony explodes through me. I let myself scream, long and loud.

The door is just a few feet away. I try to roll onto my stomach, then scream again. My lungs straining in the thin air. Stabbing pain in my chest.

Stop. Breathe. It's hard.

Try again. Roll. Scream. But now I'm on my belly. Knives in my torso.

"*One minute to carriage containment.*"

I'm clawing at the bottom of the elevator shaft with my good hand, dragging myself along. A few more feet. There's the door. I pound on it. The elevator doors are thick alloy. Will anyone hear me?

"*Thirty seconds to carriage containment.*"

I bang again and again. The skin on my knuckles splits. I yell, incoherent. No words left now.

I'm going to die here.

"*Twenty seconds to carriage containment. Nineteen, eighteen ...*"

They can't hear. They're busy with Sabik. They'll have monitors, the buzz of conversation, the hum of machines. But I hammer on the door, ignoring the agony.

"*Seventeen, sixteen ...*"

I'm being stupid. My gear bag. I fumble in it. No time to cut through the door with the blowtorch, and I don't have the strength to pry it open. But my fingers find the cold metal of my wrench. I pull it out. Bang on the door with that.

"*Fifteen, fourteen ...*"

The sound echoes up the elevator shaft. Loud. Deep.

"*Thirteen, twelve ...*"

I bang again.

"*Eleven, ten ...*"

Nothing.

"*Nine, eight …*"

Then there's a crack of light where there wasn't before. A grunt. Fingers in the gap, pulling the elevator doors open. Someone shouting for help.

"*Seven, six …*"

Hands, reaching out, grabbing my arm. Dragging me through the narrow space. I scream again.

"*Five, four …*"

My gear bag catches on the door, but they don't let go. They keep pulling, then there's a snap of the catch, the clatter of my tools.

"*Three, two …*"

People falling backwards, bringing me with them, toppling on the floor in a heap of pain and bodies.

"*One. Carriage containment in progress.*"

The door slams behind me, and the hands let go. I lie on the floor, closing my eyes against the bright light. Panting. The elevator door hisses as it seals, and the airtight metal barrier whirrs down on the other side, shutting off the spoke forever.

CHAPTER 24

"*Betafall failsafe activated. Carriage containment in progress. Carriage separation in two minutes.*"

I'm still whimpering, eyes screwed shut. My lungs feel like I've inhaled splinters of metal. My thigh is wet with fresh blood. But I'm breathing. My head is clearing, and grief is crashing through me.

"Help me!" a familiar voice screams, high and hysterical. "We have to get her to a bed!"

I open my eyes. The blurred silhouette of my mother is hovering above me, dark against the bright lights. "We have to get you secure before the descent," she says. "Someone help me! For Beta's sake!"

"*Carriage containment complete. Power diversion in progress.*"

The lights flicker as the power reroutes away from the engine room.

A medic pulls a stretcher alongside me. "One, two, three."

Before I can brace myself, they're lifting me. I scream again as I'm swung onto the bed.

"Get some anesthetic!" Mom's eyes are glistening. "What's hurting, Ursa?"

"My chest," I gasp. "My thigh ... my hip."

"Bring the scanner. Now!" She turns back to me. "What happened to you? What happened to the ship?"

Each breath is excruciating. Still, I try. "Astra. She was behind everything. She ... tried to kill me. A pulse gun blast activated the failsafe. Astra's dead."

My vision is clearing. Mom's mouth drops open. Then she glances toward the elevator door, as though Astra's about to burst in through the metal shielding on the other side.

"Where is she?"

"Engine ... room."

Mom sways.

"*Power diversion complete. Checking systems. Prepare for carriage separation.*"

Guion is at my side, running a hand-held scanner over my chest and wrist. "Two broken ribs. Her shoulder fracture has reopened. Moderate burn on her right hip, laceration on the right thigh, but she's not losing significant blood."

Mom leans on the stretcher. "Get a ten-microgram PainFree patch. We'll have to wait to deal with the hip and thigh until we're on the ground. She'll need a new calcium and collagen injection in her shoulder. Get a chest guard for her ribs, we don't want a lung to puncture in the descent." She squeezes my hand. "That should see you through to Beta."

"Sabik?" I ask.

She smiles. "Recovering."

"*Systems functioning within set parameters. Separation in progress. Brace for Betafall in two minutes.*"

Then the noises start. The *Venture*, screaming. The wail of metal on metal. The shriek of separation. She's pulling herself apart, shattering into pieces. And it's my fault.

Guion sticks a pain patch on my neck, and warmth blooms

through my blood. Mom lifts me gently as she slides a casing under me. I breathe in hard, eyes squeezed shut, the pain red against my lids. Mom closes the casing over my chest.

"*Descent in one minute. All crew members to designated places.*"

"Get moving," Mom says to the medics. "Secure your patients. Strap yourselves in."

Calm spreads through me from the PainFree on my neck. As the panic recedes I open my eyes and stare at the patches on the white-gray ceiling. Hundreds of years of fixes and mends. Generations working to keep this ship in the sky. All my hard work. Dad's innovations and hacks. Four hundred years of engineers before us.

I just threw it all away.

Guion wheels me toward the wall. I hear the click of latches and straps. The pain is evaporating, like dry ice. The grief is still there. A weight presses down on my chest, making it hard to breathe. Jovan. Astra. The *Venture*. I can't fit it all in my head.

Through my tears, I notice a shape in the next bed. I turn, and there's Sabik.

He's smiling, with a doped-up expression that suggests he's had even more PainFree than I have. He's sitting up slightly, his bed at an angle. I try to peer at his injured hand, but it's on the other side. He obviously notices me straining, because he raises a blob of bandages. I can't make out the shapes of the fingers, but they must have been able to reconnect his hand or I'd be staring at a stump.

He reaches over with his good hand and takes mine. "I overheard. I'm sorry about Astra."

I swallow.

"*Ready to uncouple. Prepare for gravitational adjustment.*"

"Now, people!" Mom shouts.

Shoes squeak on the floor as everyone rushes to their seats. Buckles clatter as they are hastily closed. Typical of the medics to stay by their patients until the last moment. A jolt and a clang shake the carriage. There's a long, slow squeal, then a sickening lurch.

The *Venture*'s death throes. She's being wrenched from me. My childhood. My home.

One last, deafening bang.

"*Separation complete. Betafall in progress.*"

Loosed from the spokes, we're no longer rotating. Gravity drops from us. Only the straps keep me in my bed, tightening against my chest guard. I gasp, but the pain is already distant. Sabik keeps hold of my hand. He's floating too, hair drifting around his face. With the doped-up smile he looks a bit goofy, really. Around us things rise into the air. Beakers, surgical gloves, blankets. Bottles rattle in the cupboard. This isn't a controlled separation. There wasn't time to stow loose objects.

"*Prepare for deceleration burn and adjustment to correct orbital position.*"

A scalpel tumbles end over end in front of the porthole opposite. Silver against the black of space. There's a shining ball in the dark on the other side of the fused silica glass.

It's the engine room, the heart of the *Venture*, tossed away into the void of space. Small and so distant already. A part of me strains toward Astra, as though it's not too late to bring her back. Then there's a burst of light as the engine room's secondary boosters fire, starting their long journey to drive the radioactive payload away from the planet.

It must have been a calm death, when she gave me her air. As easy as falling asleep. Maybe more than she deserved, considering how Orion and Cassius died. But it still makes me ache to think of her in there.

Our carriage's boosters roar as they slow us from orbital speed to entry speed. Things clatter to the floor as we decelerate.

The engine room is gone. Past the boundary of my window. It has enough power to escape this solar system, and it won't stop there. Inertia will take Astra's frozen body to the end of the universe in the *Venture*'s heart.

I'm crying. Body lurching with silent sobs. Tears running down my cheeks.

The medics are strapped into their jump seats on the opposite wall. I catch my mom's eyes, wide and wet. Sabik's hand is warm in mine as we fall to Beta together.

It's slow and quiet at first, except for the occasional purr from the boosters, using the ship's inertia and the planet's rotation to bring us into the right position for the main descent. Then, as we go down, the view from the porthole gradually changes from the black of space to a light pink, then a pink-red. The gravitational forces grow as we decelerate.

Then there's the squealing of metal under pressure, building to a scream as we descend and the atmosphere gets thicker. It's warmer, the friction on the carriage exterior leaching into the room. Is that normal? Or should the insulation be protecting us? The spokes are designed to burn up on atmospheric entry. Will that happen to us, too? I don't know what normal parameters are. Even if I did, I can't stop the descent now.

It's red-orange through the porthole now. We're inside a fireball.

"*Boosters firing for main deceleration.*"

The engines roar again, slowing us, increasing the gravity way beyond normal. The extra weight takes my breath. Stabbing pain in my lungs, strong enough to overwhelm the painkiller.

I peer at Sabik. His eyes are screwed shut, his mouth drawn with pain. But we don't let go of each other's hands.

The carriages are using the last of the *Venture*'s primary fuel to brake. There were debates, calculations in Dad's time when all the stocks were low. They left the minimum for Betafall. Is it enough? Will we land in the cleared space for the carriages? Will we hit the forest?

I close my eyes.

This is nothing like the slow, smooth descent of the shuttle. This is nearly free fall, barely controlled by hard braking.

Swearing, from the medics. Screams and a whispered mantra. Someone vomiting. I'm glad we're not weightless anymore. I wouldn't want that floating around.

What will happen when we land? How will we survive? Astra betrayed us. Jovan betrayed us. I destroyed the ship. This is no way to start a new world. Perhaps we should have stayed in space. Perhaps our ancestors should have stayed on Alpha.

Then there's a bump. Hard. Two more, in quick succession. The parachutes. Metal dishes and surgical implements clatter around us. Thank Beta for the painkillers.

"*Landing imminent.*" The *Venture*'s voice. Still looking out for us.

Gravity normalizes, and I gulp down a few desperate breaths. We must be only a few thousand meters above the surface. Hitting pockets of warm air on the way down. The carriage is spinning, then compensating. The boosters automatically correct our course, steer us toward one of the cleared patches in the forest, steady us down to the medcarriage's final resting place.

We land with a thump.

I open my eyes. Stare at the ceiling. Listen to the deep breathing in the room. Then Guion laughs, breaking the spell. Seatbelts clatter as they are unbuckled. Mom is at my side.

"How are you?"

"Still here."

"*Betafall complete. Main hatch opening.*"

I push against my straps. "Can you unbuckle me?"

"Of course. You also might want to ... let go." She nods down at my hand. I'm still clutching Sabik, knuckles white.

I let go. There are red marks where my nails dug into his skin. "Oh! Sorry."

"It's okay." Sabik grins. "I'm on some pretty heavy painkillers."

We hear the clunk of the outside door opening and the hiss of the inside door unsealing. The cold air of Beta fills the carriage. Pine and earth. Mom unfastens the straps that hold me against the bed, then leans over and unbuckles Sabik. I push myself up to a sitting position. My chest aches, but the feeling is at a distance. Like it's happening to someone else.

"You should rest," Mom says.

But I swing my legs off the bed. I need to know if the other carriages made it. If not, it's my fault. I stand up, then grab on to the bed as the carriage suddenly lurches. It takes me a second to realize nothing has really moved. I'm just dizzy.

Mom reaches for my arm. "Steady there."

"I'm okay. I have to see."

"You've got a fair bit of PainFree in you. You have to be careful."

Sabik is out of his bed, too. His injured hand is across his body, and he holds his good one out to me.

"I'll help."

Mom sighs. "Just a quick look. I need to gather injury reports, anyway. Then back to bed. We all need rest and time to recover from this." Her voice trembles.

I hug her. She holds me gently, but there's an intensity in her grip. I know she'd be squeezing me tight if I weren't injured. Her face is wet against my shoulder.

"I almost lost you," she whispers. "I almost lost you."

The world spins when I close my eyes. Mom doesn't let go. I have to detach her arms as I step back, then take Sabik's hand, grateful for his steadying influence.

The door is open. The medics stumble down the stairs to the planet. Some are crying. Most are silent, clutching at one another. Sabik and I follow them into a cloudy Beta evening.

We keep walking, both unsteady, careful in the muddy puddles as we move away from the murmuring medics, staring out at our new home, at the patchy gray skies as the last of the light drains away. The spent parachutes flap in the breeze behind the medcarriage.

We're on a slight rise. Circled around the main camp are the other carriages, their open doors squares of brightness dotting the twilight at regular intervals. I count them, quickly. Twenty. All accounted for. No smoldering wreckage. The streaks in the sky must be the spokes.

There will be a lot to check tomorrow. The solar panels on the ecocarriages will be a priority. And I'll need to check the functioning of the remaining generator cell, although without the shuttle flights we should be able to get by with solar power for a bit, if we make a few adjustments.

Stop, Ursa.

Leave your job for one night. Tomorrow we can get on with the business of staying alive. For now, it's enough that we're here, and we're together.

Sabik heads toward the tree line, still holding my hand. I follow, not asking where we're going, just stepping carefully downhill between the trunks, feeling unsteady. There are lights making their way toward the carriages, through the woods. Linkcoms, no doubt. People trying to find out what happened. They must have seen us falling to Beta.

But Sabik steers us away from them. It's not far to the edge of the village, to the clearing. The log benches are set up around the bonfire. The tarp has been pulled off, but it's not lit yet.

Of course. There was going to be a bonfire tonight.

Well, now is as good a time as any. I stride toward the heap of lumber, reaching into my back pocket. I pull out my blowtorch, adjust the settings to make the flame as large as possible, and point it at the wood. I'm not trying for atmosphere. I'm just starting a fire. The logs are blazing in seconds. Sabik and I slump down onto a bench together.

There will be more accidents now, bodies in the graveyard.

No. I won't accept that. I'm an engineer. I can help. There are ways to make this planet safer. I'm going to find them. And I can adapt a landbike for Perseus, too.

We watch the flames in silence. There are patterns in there. Shapes jumping and dancing. Figures in blue, red, orange, and yellow.

"You know," I say, "if we hooked up a thermoelectric generator to the fire pit, we could use it to supplement the solar panels until we get the hydroelectric dam working."

"I'm glad you're down here, Ursa," Sabik says.

Sparks float out of the fire, twisting on the updrafts until they disappear. Unlike them, I'm permanently earthbound. But that's okay right now. We're together. We made it. Our little flame flickered its way through the dark of space. Now we're a small fire, with room to grow. One day our fire may light this whole planet. Perhaps send out sparks to other worlds.

Or maybe that's the painkillers talking.

Stars are coming out, pinpricks in the vastness of space. And I can kind of see it: why Alpha Earth and our ancestors sacrificed so much to get us here. They did it to do what I'm doing now.

They did it to know there was more to life than the only world they'd ever known. They did it to look at the sky and dream of the fire of humanity illuminating the dark. Blazing across the universe.

A few of the other colonists are joining us now. Clustering together on the other log benches. The murmur of conversation drifts across the clearing, the light dancing around us all.

"What exactly happened?" Sabik asks, quietly. "With Astra, and the pulse gun blast?"

I think for a moment. Try to find the words. But they won't

come. I've lost too much today. There's too much grief waiting to come crashing down. "Can ... can I explain it all later?"

Sabik nods. He understands. But I'll have a lot of questions to answer soon. I'll have to tell Celeste about Astra. And I'll be here for her and Beta. I'll keep my promise to her mother. I'll take care of them.

More people are coming now, from the village and the other carriages. Gathering in the light of the bonfire, a warm beacon on this dark planet. Then the singing starts. A simple, mournful lullaby. Phoebe leads it.

"For all we've lost, we'll sing and weep ...

We need our rest, comfort of sleep ..."

I've never heard the song before. It's just Phoebe's clear voice at first. Then more join in around the fire as the refrain is repeated. I find myself swaying in time.

Tomorrow we wake under foreign skies ...
Stretch our limbs, greet the new sunrise.

This planet killed Maia. But she loved it. I remember her face, snowflakes in her eyelashes. "I'll put Maia's memory panel on her grave."

"That's good," Sabik says. "We need new traditions."

The flames crackle, jump, and spark. Dancing, growing, alive. Warming us, chasing away the cold, the wet, the dark.

There's a small gasp from Sabik. "Look." He's staring at the ground.

I tilt forward to follow his gaze, my body kept straight by the chest guard.

It's a green plant, sticking out of the earth next to our log. An unlikely place for it to grow, but it makes sense. It's sheltered from our boots by the log, and warmed by the fire.

"I promised you flowers," Sabik says.

It's not a flower yet. It's a tiny white bud, no bigger than my smallest fingernail. Delicate, fragile, and closed. Sabik's hand is next to mine on the rough bark of the log. Fingers almost touching.

And right then, I know we're going to make it.

ACKNOWLEDGEMENTS

So many people helped me with this book. So many people to thank. I am sure I will forget people who deserve thanks, because I was bad at keeping notes. Sorry.

I had great advice on countless revisions of this book. Thanks to all at Kidcrit, especially Valerie, Helen, Don, James, Judy and Wendy for your consistent help in the early drafts, and Marsha for setting it all up. Thanks to all at Online Writers Workshop who gave me feedback, and to C.C. Finley for picking the first two chapters as an Editor's Choice. Also to The Literary Consultancy — Jane Adams for her report on this book and Aki Schilz for all her support. And of course thanks to Rebecca Swift, TLC's founder, a wonderful champion of authors who died earlier this year.

Thanks to all my amazing beta readers — Leah Bobet, Ian McIntyre, Pier Van Tijn, Lena Coakley, Anne Laurel Carter, Tanaz Bhathena, Tanis Rideout, Mel Mercer — without all of you and all the fantastic advice you gave me, this book would be a much weaker version of itself. Thanks to Maya Davis for your excellent advice, insight, and the useful resources you provided. I hope my changes allow people to see my characters a little better, and see themselves in them.

Thank you so much to Lydia Moëd, my lovely agent, who was so enthusiastic about this book right from the start, and really *got* it, and is a fab person to have in my corner. Thanks again to the wonderful team at DCB/Cormorant, particularly Barry Jowett, Bryan Jay Ibeas, Marc Côté, and Andrea Waters.

And thanks, as always, to those members of my family who had yet another book foisted upon them. Jo, Mum, Dad, Matt — thank you for your patience and all you do to help me have more time to write.

ABOUT THE AUTHOR

Kate Blair is a native of Hayling Island, UK, and is now a Canadian citizen living in Toronto. Her first novel, *Transferral*, was a finalist for the Manitoba Young Readers' Choice Award and the Saskatchewan Young Readers' Choice Snow Willow Award, was longlisted for the Sunburst Award, and was a Canadian Children's Book Centre *Best Books for Kids and Teens* Starred Selection. *Transferral* is currently being adapted for television.